TEA BY THE SEA

TEA BY THE SEA

a novel

Donna Hemans

 Red Hen Press | *Pasadena, CA*

Book design by Mark E. Cull

Library of Congress Cataloging-in-Publication Data

Names: Hemans, Donna, author.
Title: Tea by the sea / Donna Hemans.
Description: First edition. | Pasadena, CA : Red Hen Press, [2020]
Identifiers: LCCN 2019042532 (print) | LCCN 2019042533 (ebook) | ISBN
    9781597098458 (trade paperback) | ISBN 9781597098533 (ebook)
Subjects: LCSH: Domestic fiction.
Classification: LCC PS3608.E47 T43 2020 (print) | LCC PS3608.E47 (ebook)
    | DDC 813/.6dc—23
LC record available at https://lccn.loc.gov/2019042532
LC ebook record available at https://lccn.loc.gov/2019042533

The National Endowment for the Arts, the Los Angeles County Arts Commission, the Ahmanson Foundation, the Dwight Stuart Youth Fund, the Max Factor Family Foundation, the Pasadena Tournament of Roses Foundation, the Pasadena Arts & Culture Commission and the City of Pasadena Cultural Affairs Division, the City of Los Angeles Department of Cultural Affairs, the Audrey & Sydney Irmas Charitable Foundation, the Kinder Morgan Foundation, the Meta & George Rosenberg Foundation, the Allergan Foundation, the Riordan Foundation, Amazon Literary Partnership, and the Mara W. Breech Foundation partially support Red Hen Press.

First Edition
Published by Red Hen Press
www.redhen.org

ACKNOWLEDGMENTS

I am grateful to many for ongoing support.

Thanks to Kate Gale for welcoming *Tea by the Sea* into the Red Hen Press family, and to Tobi Harper, Monica Fernandez and Natasha McClellan for marketing and production support. Thanks also to Sha-Shana Crichton, who found this book a home, and Rachel Gul, who has done a tremendous amount to help this book thrive in the world.

My thanks also go to Stephanie Allen, Doreen Baingana and Karen Outen, who provided feedback on early versions of the book, and for the many brunches and literary outings that have sustained me over the years; and the Maryland State Arts Council for grants that helped me write and edit the book. A special thanks to the Jamaican Writers Society (JaWS) and the Jamaican Copyright Licensing Agency (JAMCOPY) for reviving the Lignum Vitae Writing Awards for Jamaican writers, and recognizing the manuscript with the 2015 Una Marson Award for Adult Literature.

As always thanks to my family and friends whose love, support, and stories sustain me.

For the descendants of Annie and Eustace

TEA BY THE SEA

PART 1

Unforgettable, and Forgettable

1

Lenworth was back on the main road to Anchovy proper, past Long Hill's deep ravines and its corners and its peak, and long past the canopy of trees that shaded the steep road snaking up from the coast. He was on foot this time, with the baby in the crook of one arm and an oversized bag that he pulled with the other hand. Having mistaken one house on a hill for the one he sought, he was lost and the driver who had taken him there had already left. On that stretch of road, without the towering trees the sun's heat was like a glove on his body, too close and too heavy, and the sweat dribbling along his spine and in every crevice more of an annoyance than a cooling mechanism.

He worried about the baby and the heat, whether she was too young to be so exposed to the elements. Still, he kept her covered under a thin blanket; thin socks covered her toes. The car ride had lulled her to sleep, and she slept as if she had already grown accustomed to the sounds around her—a cow mooing in the distance, a dog's disinterested bark followed by the growl of another, a couple of goat kids *maa*-ing nearby, and honks from a vehicle that navigated the hilly road's deep corners. Since she was quiet, Lenworth suspected she was comfortable, and he willed her to remain that way—at least until he got to the house, which he imagined couldn't be too far away.

The road had widened and flattened, and to his left were the abandoned railway tracks. That was his mistake; having sat for two hours already in the car, he had simply wanted to be at the house on the hill and had forgotten the written instructions to turn left at the junction where the tracks crossed the main road directly in front of the secondary school with the blue and white walls. Now he watched for the point where the tracks began curving toward the main road and an unpaved road to the left of the railroad crossing. He watched for the vehicles approaching from behind and passing on his right, turning to face the road each time a vehicle approached. He was careful not to brush up against the hip-high fever grass with its long, sharp blades or the patches of cowitch that would surely leave temporary welts on any exposed skin. Had it been another time, he would have pulled a handful of the stringy love bush and twirled the thin, yellow strands of the parasitic vine around his fingers. He loved the rubbery feel of it, how easily it snapped apart in his hands. Yet it was sturdy and resilient, able to regenerate itself from just a small piece.

The ground was hot—so heated the asphalt had softened and bubbled in places. The ordinariness of it all—the late summer afternoon's heat softening the asphalt, the sounds of natural life itself persevering—comforted him. He needed the comfort, for there was nothing ordinary or comforting about what led him to that road that day. But he wouldn't think about that—not then, not there.

At last, he saw the point at which the railroad tracks crossed the main road. He saw the school, children in uniform, the open field next to the school. Further up that unpaved road another fork, the Nurse's house with the scrolled iron gate, and finally the overgrown yard behind a cut-stone wall. At the gate were two letters, an "M" and an "O," the only remnants of the name someone had once given the property.

Up on the hill was the abandoned house, a small and compact building that looked like it grew out of the side of a cliff. There was nothing elegant about the house. Two concrete columns that were once painted white held up a small verandah and framed a door to a cellar. To the right of the columns, a set of concrete steps rose up to the red floor of the verandah and the aqua railing that hemmed it in. The back of the house jutted out of the hillside, or so it seemed. The kitchen and dining room backed up to a small cliff, with only a sliver of space between the walls and the cliff in which ferns and moss grew. The rooms—three, if he counted only the distinct ones, or four, if he counted the space in the middle with a curtain for a wall—were small, but the house would do. And despite the duck ants that formed black nests along the walls, the rotting floorboards he would have to replace, and the temperamental plumbing and electrical work, the house would be his refuge.

The line of children and grandchildren, who would have claim to the house and most of whom had migrated abroad, had no use for it—too small, too remote, too old, too generous with old-world charm (if it could even be called charming at all). Lenworth's own father, who had migrated to England and never returned, had no use for it either. Even if his father wanted it, he would have been further down the line of relatives with competing interests in the house. The house was now temporarily Lenworth's, so long as he paid the annual taxes and for any necessary upkeep.

Lenworth put the baby on one of the beds and stepped back outside for a long look down the hill, out across an old fowl coop, over the fruit trees that crowded one half of the hill, and down on two houses visible in the distance. He imagined his older relatives standing on the verandah as he was, as far back as the 1930s and 1940s, and looking out at what they had managed to acquire despite the myriad obstacles set up to ensure their failure. He shook his head. "It will do," he told himself. Then he stepped back inside in the semi-dark to set about boiling water on a makeshift stove and mixing the baby's formula.

Anchovy welcomed Lenworth. Some folks remembered his family name, Ramsey; his granduncle, Baba Orville; his great-grandmother, Adina; and that Adina had eight sons and one daughter—Lenworth's grandmother who married and left Anchovy for some other town. And there was Miss V—102 years old with the memory of an elephant—who knew his family tree and could recite almost perfectly who begat whom. Around Anchovy and in nearby Montpelier and Mount Carey, people introduced him as Sister Adina's great-grandson, cousin to the Ramseys, and relation of Baba Orville who used to own a rum shop in Anchovy and lived over on the road that ran behind the train tracks.

"Them dead long time now, and who lef' gone abroad. Him come to take over the house that lock up all these years."

"He come from good people."

Such was his welcome into Anchovy. He was subsumed, welcomed without question, and pitied for having so young a baby to raise on his own.

Anchovy in those days was quiet, a little slip of a town seven miles from Montego Bay on the main road from Reading on the north coast to Savanna-la-Mar on the south coast. Except for a bird sanctuary off the main road that led to Anchovy, rafting on the Lethe River, and an abandoned railway station, Anchovy and the small towns immediately surrounding it weren't known for much. Anchovy wasn't a market town—not like Brown's Town, which Lenworth had just left and which swelled on market day (Wednesdays, Fridays, and Saturdays) with vendors from nearby and faraway towns, who spread out beyond the covered market in makeshift stalls along the road or simply pushed their bunched or packaged goods at potential customers with a plea or a price. Even a Thursday afternoon in Brown's Town, when stores shut early to prepare for the Friday and Saturday afternoon swell of customers, felt more alive than Anchovy did. But the relative quiet of the town wasn't what mattered. What did? Plum wouldn't find him there. Really, no one would look in that particular location for Lenworth, since he had only an indirect connection to Anchovy through distant relatives. More important, it was not a connection his immediate family members or acquaintances would know.

Indeed, Plum looked for Lenworth. She returned to their small cottage on property that at one time had been a large pimento and cattle estate. The pimento and the cattle were long gone, the surrounding land subdivided and developed as residential plots. All that was left of the estate were the cottage and the larger house, which from the outside looked like it would crumble without much prompting from a single puff of wind, then decay. But it was only an illusion. Inside was an artist's dream. Every inch of wood on the floor and the ceiling had been replaced with hand-sanded and hand-carved mahogany. The plaster walls had been rebuilt with new concrete walls, which were painted a light cocoa, orange, and green, the paint brushed on to make the walls look as distressed as the outer perimeter of the house. Necessary, modern conveniences were interspersed with remnants from another time—enamel bowls, yabbas, and shutters that banged in the breeze.

On her return, Plum passed the main house with its front walkway flanked by two large monkey jars, flowering bougainvillea and hibiscus, and dwarfed by the flame of the forest trees behind it, both in full bloom. The flowering plants, with their red and pink and yellow blooms celebrating life, taunted and teased, made tears flood Plum's eyes again. She walked past the house to the cottage in the back and found the rooms had been stripped of Lenworth's things—his CDs and books and papers and clothes. He didn't have much, but everything belonging to him was gone. Plum's clothes hanging in the wardrobe were meager, forlorn, and childish, a reminder that she had only just begun her adult life.

Plum ran back out—tottered, really—and found her landlady, Mrs. Murray, the artist who had given new life to the decrepit and rundown historic house.

"Look at you," Mrs. Murray said. She held out her hands, palms upward and fingers splayed, surprise and joy in her voice.

"Have you seen him?" Plum asked.

"Lenworth? No."

"He's gone."

"What you mean, gone?" The levity in Mrs. Murray's voice was absent now. She looked over Plum with one sweeping glance, capturing Plum's heavy breasts and swollen belly and the distraught look on her face. She caught Plum before she fell, held her up, linked their arms, and walked her back to the cottage.

Inside the cottage, Plum lay on the floor and bawled, rocking and heaving on the ground like a Pentecostal possessed by the Holy Spirit, throwing off the landlady attempting to hold and calm her. When she had no tears or sobs left to pour out and no strength to stand up, she knelt and looked around at the borrowed furniture that came with the cottage, then stood and looked around again for something of Lenworth's, a handwritten explanation, a clue to where he had gone and why. But she found nothing, no sign that he had lived there at all.

Had it not been for her breasts, achingly full, it would have all felt like a miserable dream, a nightmare that Plum wasn't actually living, and from which she would wake at any minute.

Neither had words for what had happened. Lenworth was gone and so was her child, the daughter she had planned to name Marissa. They let the silence steep. For Plum, the quiet was less painful than the sounds of life—the twitter and buzz of birds and bees, the swish of leaves, the wind in the trees, a donkey braying in the distance. Mrs. Murray's lone parrot, which had escaped its cage again, cawed incessantly, taunting them from a guava tree.

"I hate that bird." Plum did the only thing she could in that moment. She stepped outside, picked up a small stone, and threw it at the parrot, forgetting that its wings had been clipped to prevent it from flying away.

The parrot flitted from one limb to another, cocked its head, and repeated what Lenworth had taught it. "One plus one equals two." It paused, then said, "Lenworth, leave the bird alone," repeating the two phrases exactly how it had heard them. Day after day, Lenworth had stood by the parrot's cage feeding it dried corn and repeating "one plus one equals two" with the expectation that the bird would fool an unsuspecting stranger into thinking it could count. And Plum, if she was nearby, always told Lenworth to leave the bird alone. But the joke was now an unwanted reminder of what had been. Plum reached for another, larger stone.

"Come, come." Mrs. Murray pulled Plum's hand back. "Don't mix my bird up in this business with you and him. Come lay down and rest. I going to make you some soup, and when you wake up we'll figure this out."

2

At another time, Lenworth would have been in a school help-ing students with chemistry experiments or tutoring a student in math, teaching Pythagoras's theorem and square root and cube root. Now, he was on the verandah of the abandoned house in An-chovy, again looking down the hill, across the overgrown plot of fruit trees on the land he had claimed as his refuge, and at a house with a rusting zinc roof. Algebra seemed abstract, and the symbols and rules to solve the equations like something that belonged to an-other era. Even the elements of the periodic table seemed like a use-less thing to teach. Nothing he had taught had any use for him here on the hill, and he imagined that his former students who didn't go on to a university would eventually say the same about advanced math or chemistry.

This—the detour from teaching high school math while saving toward an engineering degree—was temporary. He didn't know yet how he would get back on track to his ultimate goal—the engineer-ing degree—but he knew one thing: Picking up and starting over was far easier for him as a man than it would have been for Plum. Single fathers got pity; single or unwed mothers generally didn't, and more often than not, they suffered setback after setback that hardened their hears and blunted their future.

The sun dusted everything with a pale yellow. Dew glistened on the grass and to the left of the verandah, water dripped from a broken gutter onto the house's exposed concrete footing. Away from his property and in the flat land below, a woman hung clothes on a line. Lenworth stood for a long while looking on, trying to decipher the woman's age. He saw no children, no other person walking around the yard, and from that distance he thought the woman was older, a retiree perhaps.

Looking out like that on the acre of land, the houses in the valley, Lenworth imagined the pride a rich planter must have felt when he looked out from his verandah at the acres of sugar cane or tobacco or banana spread out before him—all his own. Not that Lenworth owned anything at all. Not the old house or the fruit trees. He was simply making do. Lenworth was used to it, this business of making do with what he had. After all, he had grown up with a mother who did just that, who made soups out of next to nothing; who stretched a tin of corned beef with canned beans or cabbage or tomatoes and ketchup; who planted coco and coffee and peas, selling a little here and there; who reaped pimento berries from the trees that grew on their own and the surrounding land, dried the berries and sold crocus bags full at the cooperative market. She simply made do. That first week, Lenworth repaired the dipping floorboards, sprayed insecticide to rid the house of duck ants, and shored up a leaning door frame. And now he had the germ of a plan to solve the problem of who would help him take care of the week-old baby girl.

Already, Lenworth was failing his daughter, whom he had named Opal for no other reason than she looked up at him with eyes that reminded Lenworth of a precious stone. She cried incessantly as newborns are wont to do, but it was hard for Lenworth to comfort her. In his arms, she squirmed, more agitated than com-

forted, shifting as if, even at that young age, she knew she should
have been somewhere else.

Lenworth, with Opal in his arms, headed downhill. At the gate,
he turned left, looking for the blue house with the rusting zinc roof,
a verandah with a white railing, and clothes on a line in the back.

When he came up to the blue house, he hesitated, waiting for
a dog's bark or the scuttle of paws on the grass, then called out,
"Hello."

The woman, the front of her dress wet from washing, came out
onto the verandah. She wiped her hands on the already wet dress,
stopping for a moment to push aside a cat that had sidled up beside
her. She was, as he suspected, older—perhaps in her seventies.

"Morning, ma'am," Lenworth said as he walked toward her.
"How you do?"

Closer to her, he said his name, "Lenworth," and held out a hand
to grasp hers. "I'm staying up there at the Ramsey place."

"Sister Ivy. Yes, I heard that family come back to take over the
place."

"Yes, me and my daughter." He looked down at Opal, who slept
with her head on his shoulder. "Don't want to bother you. I come
down here 'cause I'm looking for somebody to help with the baby
girl. Just during the daytime."

"Where her mother?"

"Died in childbirth." How easily Lenworth's story formed.

"Sorry to hear. Such a painful thing to have to grow up without
her mother." Sister Ivy also looked at Opal, at the wisps of hair visible under her hat and her tiny fist laying on Lenworth's shoulder.

Lenworth felt a pang of guilt, but he didn't let on. He simply
shifted his eyes away as if he were blinking away tears.

"What you feeding her?" Sister Ivy shifted the conversation so
easily it seemed like a practiced move.

"Formula."

"Arrowroot porridge good for young baby. Easy on the stomach."

Lenworth nodded as if he knew about feeding a baby arrowroot porridge or even how to make it.

"Let me see. Miss Daisy daughter looking work. Gwennie too. Let me ask them."

"Thank you."

"Come back tomorrow."

The morning was already half-over and the sun high in the sky, but here he was returning home, climbing the hill and looking again at the old fowl coop. Each time Lenworth climbed the hill, the old chicken coop, which was enclosed with chicken wire fencing and unfinished wood, bothered him. It was too close to a cherry tree, and where it stood, to the right of the house, it seemed out of place. Had he been the original builder, he would have put it behind the house, out of sight. But there was no room in the back; the house itself backed up to a cliff and the sliver of space between the cliff and the house was wide enough only for a small body to pass. Lenworth had two options: tear it down or put it to good use. He wouldn't be raising chickens. He was sure of that. Neither would he raise pigs or goats or even bother with a dog.

Lenworth sat on the verandah in an old rocking chair with Opal. That too, sitting on a verandah in the middle of the day, was something he would never have had time for in his past life. If not teaching, he would have been tutoring, and setting aside every extra dollar to work toward becoming an engineer. He wouldn't think about that past life, how he had come to be here in Anchovy alone with the baby girl, who at that moment was scrunching her face as if to cry. He moved her to his chest, stood up, and walked the length of the verandah. Lenworth put his past firmly behind him, patted down and buried his guilt, and went on with his thoughts on how to reestablish his life.

When Opal fell asleep again, he put her inside and went to the fowl coop. Inside, he looked around, up at the roof and down at the sagging wood frame. He imagined it as something else: a workshop where he could remake things. For the moment, he would shelve his long-held dream of being an engineer and instead return to an old habit of turning other people's garbage into something of value.

By evening, Lenworth had acquired and spread fresh sawdust on the ground, reinforced the sagging wood frame, built a work table out of an old door, and unearthed from the cellar and the crawl space beneath the house the first pieces of unwanted things he would convert into something useful.

Sister Ivy, halfway up the hill, called out hello. Lenworth jumped. He had fallen asleep on the verandah. Inside, Opal cried—the sound full-throated and loud. It had been years since he had worked like that—cutting overgrown grass with a machete and hauling old lumber from the crawl space beneath the house. Every muscle in his body ached.

"Come, come," he said to Sister Ivy. He rubbed his eyes and went to get Opal.

Back on the verandah, the crying baby cradled in his arms, he pointed to a matching rocking chair. "Sit down, please."

"Porridge for the baby." Sister Ivy held out a bag with a bowl inside. "It can't be easy for you. Alone with a baby so young."

That was the pity and concern Lenworth expected. Without question, he would not have earned Sister Ivy's empathy so easily had he been a woman. His sister hadn't earned it—not even their mother's—and his mother hadn't earned it from anyone else either.

Sister Ivy held out her hands for Opal, who still wasn't soothed. "Porridge still warm," she said. "Put some in a bottle."

By the time Lenworth returned to the verandah, Opal was calm, lying still and looking up with unfocused eyes at Sister Ivy. She drank the porridge easily, lying in the old lady's arms as if she belonged there.

"So far away from family," Sister Ivy said. "Why you come back here?"

"Where else to go?" He bent his finger back and listed his reasons. "Only child. Mother died. Father, gone abroad long time. No family to speak of." Only the third reason he listed was true. As he spoke, he knew he was invalidating and burying his brother, sister, and mother, who were all indeed alive and well in the southeastern part of the country.

"Went to school with Walter. He your father or uncle?"

"Uncle."

Sister Ivy nodded. "Good people them. Good people."

Lenworth let her believe his surname was also Ramsey, allowing the second untruth—that Walter was his uncle and not a cousin—to morph into the community's collective truth. He became Lenworth Ramsey in that moment. Up until then, he hadn't contemplated a whole new identity, but now he assumed it wholeheartedly and developed a new piece of his autobiography that explained why his legal surname was Barrett. His excuse would have made his mother weep, though, for he knew that if anyone ever asked, he would have said that his mother had given him the wrong man's surname to protect her own indiscretions.

"Life hard when you don't have anybody," Sister Ivy said. "Until you find somebody, I can watch her in the daytime."

"I don't want to take up your time."

"No, no, don't worry yourself. My children gone abroad and no grandchildren here for me to look after. So what to do with myself? I plant my garden. That's all. I used to run the basic school up the road there, so taking care of her is nothing at all."

He looked at Opal, asleep, content, pressed against Sister Ivy's bosom. For the second time that day, he felt guilt at what he had done, what he had taken away from Opal. But it was too late. Once he left the hospital with the baby and without Plum, there was no returning. He couldn't face Plum. Not ever.

3

Plum had nothing left in Brown's Town, and yet she stayed in the cottage, hopeful Lenworth would return, and dependent on the kindness of her landlady, Mrs. Murray. The landlady was indeed kind, an artist who never forgot her meager beginnings and who gave freely of her time, her money, and herself. She fed Plum and let her stay in the cottage in exchange for household help. Mrs. Murray became mother and father, too, for Plum refused to call her parents, declining to let back into her life the people she believed had already abandoned her twice, or the aunt with whom she had lived before setting up house with Lenworth.

Mrs. Murray inquired of the school on Plum's behalf for a forwarding address, a hint of where Lenworth had come from or where he could possibly have gone. She, too, came away with nothing. The school wouldn't or couldn't release any details, not to Mrs. Murray, and not to Plum, who returned to the school time after time to plead for a morsel of information about her Lenworth, their Mr. Barrett. Plum got nothing, save for an ill-timed lecture from the school's guidance counselor, a British expat who had no business guiding or counseling and whose sanity the students had long questioned.

In those days after Lenworth's disappearance, Plum looked for him so fiercely that she could have been mistaken for a mad woman, a schizophrenic, who'd refused medication in favor of the voices that came at will. She wandered the streets, peering into buses and cars, locking her eyes onto the faces within, looking for the goatee, the small eyes beneath the bushy eyebrows, the hairline already receding even on one so young. But the folks who stared back at her could offer nothing.

For two months, Plum walked.

She visited a bush doctor, who prescribed bush baths to beat away the curse. After all, what but a curse on a mother could have made a father take off with their child?

She went to Wednesday night revival at the neighborhood Pentecostal Church. She answered the call to the altar, rose, and waved and wobbled and dipped in spirit, writhing on the floor and, surprisingly, babbling in tongues. She prayed morning and night, prostrating herself in the morning sun and in the moonlight, asking for a small window of hope. She succumbed to a riverside baptism, even. And still nothing.

She rode to Lluidas Vale, a place she thought he had mentioned living in once. She rode on through the town, which was no more remarkable than any other small Jamaican town, and looked out the window of the minivan at the sugar cane lining the roads of the expansive valley, hopping out on the very outskirts of town, just as the little shops built at random began popping up. The shops were like any other she had seen—the proprietor and her goods behind a partition built with chicken wire and wood and a small opening through which the shoppers poked their heads and spoke. The local postmistress, purveyor of secrets, had never heard his name, couldn't recall a young fellow of that name receiving mail there.

"What his mother name?"

"Don't know."

"You know his father first name?"

"No."

The postmistress's gaze shifted too, away from Plum's face, down to her still-swollen belly. "The baby father?"

"Yes."

Plum didn't want her pity. She set it aside as if it were something physical, a weight she could remove by hand from her body and cover under a rock.

And on to Greenwood in Trelawny, another place where Lenworth said he had lived. Except for the great house for which Greenwood was known, it, too, was unremarkable. A strip of a town split in two by the main road to Montego Bay and larger, more well-known towns a short distance away on the western and eastern sides. Again nothing. No one Plum asked knew of him.

All that and still she came away with no trace of where he had lived or where he could have gone.

Plum lay down to die. She chose the midday sun as her weapon, heatstroke and dehydration as the ultimate causes of her death. She lay on a narrow concrete wall, a remnant from the pimento estate, with her arms at her side, her back flat against the concrete and toes pointed skyward.

But her timing wasn't perfect. The gardener came to deliver yam and sweet potato he'd pulled from the ground in a nearby field the landlady leased. He did what he thought best: sprinkled Plum with water to lower her body's temperature and carried her onto the verandah, away from direct sunlight. And he called the postmistress and Nova Scotia Bank, the secretary in the office at St. Mark's Anglican Church, and the mechanic who serviced Mrs. Murray's car. He called the dry goods store. One by one the message circulated and not thirty minutes later, Mrs. Murray returned to find a groggy Plum, sitting up but listless, muttering gibberish.

Overnight, Mrs. Murray nursed Plum, and in the morning, with the sun still behind the flame of the forest, the hibiscus blooms uncurling and opening up again as if to greet the day, she pulled Plum back to reality, dismissed the coddling and pity. "You can't stay here forever. You have to go on with your life."

"What life?"

"You think you're the only woman who ever lost a child? Maybe not the same way. But it hurt just the same if you lose a baby at birth. Five times I went through labor. Only two children I raise. So I know it's hard. But you can't just give up on your life so. Not because of a man."

"The baby . . ."

"No. Listen. Some people will tell you that everything happens for a reason and that God has a plan for you. But I won't tell you that. I can't imagine that the merciful God the church preaches about would plan anything like this. But the one thing I know for sure, this is the one life you have and you have to make it work.

"So two things I'm going to do for you. The first one is to get you back home to your parents. It's not my business but you're too young to be wasting your life like this. You hearing me?"

Plum nodded.

"Tomorrow I'm going to buy a ticket for you to fly back home to Brooklyn. That's where you belong, with your parents. And the second thing is that I'm going to hire a private investigator—my son—to look for Lenworth and the child. My son just retired from the police force. Only one thing I ask from you. Go on to university. Get a degree and go on with your life. You hear me?"

"Yes, ma'am."

"The money, it's a loan. If you finish university you don't owe me a thing. If you don't get a degree, you pay me back for the plane ticket and the private investigator. You understand me?"

"Yes."

4

Three months on from the greatest loss of her seventeen-year life, Plum stood at the Donald Sangster International Airport in Montego Bay thinking of herself as a failed hunter who set her traps and caught nothing. She contemplated two things: the early Christmas travelers surrounded by their island carvings, straw baskets, and rum; and her own empty hands. In truth, Jamaica was Plum's trap, sort of, a trap she fell into when her parents reengineered her life without her knowing it and sent her away as if she hadn't mattered at all. In one simple act, her parents nipped their teenage daughter's behavior before it got out of hand, before she morphed into an uncontrollable teen headed for juvenile prison or an otherwise derailed youth. They acted swiftly, decisively, and without warning. Like training a bonsai plant, containing it before it followed its willful nature. Like clipping the wings of a bird to prevent it from escaping its cage and flying away.

Plum flew to Jamaica, her parents' island home with which they had a complicated relationship. Her parents loved the island but refused to live on it. Instead, they adopted Brooklyn but talked constantly of going back home to live out the last of their days, extolling the ease of island living, yet visiting and, while there, talking incessantly of the ease of things in Brooklyn—customer service and banking and shopping and dealing with government bureaucracies. They visited and talked of getting away from the family and friends who acted as though living in America meant her parents could bankroll their lives. And it was the place they held up for wayward children, as in: "You children born in America have life too easy. You don't appreciate what you have. You think when I was your age I could waste food like that. Sometimes all we had to eat was dumpling and butter, what we call slip and slide. And you here throwing away the chicken because you want a hotdog." And it was indeed the place where misbehaving children were sometimes sent as a last resort by parents frustrated with the negative influences in and around Brooklyn schools, and fearful that a disrespectful child would report abuse if punished.

That was Plum's fate. What contributed to her ouster from Brooklyn was the actions of Sandy, her close confidante and con-stant companion, who happened to be at a basement party raid-ed by police for suspicion of drugs. Plum's guilt was purely that of association, but her parents feared what could have been and act-ed upon the long-established threat they held up to their wayward child. Except they kept the plan secret from Plum.

Plum packed just the ordinary things: the obligatory gifts—soap, deodorant, perfume, plastic sandals, cheap plastic watches—along with the packaged breakfast foods that she sometimes preferred over Jamaican breakfasts of boiled ground provisions and ackee and salt fish, and callaloo and salt fish. All of that came before that flight out, before her parents clipped her wings, or in the midst of it, when Plum didn't yet know the details of her parents' plan, when Plum hadn't yet begun to hate her parents for shipping her away without warning. And she left the precious things to which she soon expected to return: a locked diary beneath her pillow; a gold neck-lace with her name; a set of Cabbage Patch dolls she had outgrown but which remained on her dresser and shelves, a reminder of child-hood years not very far behind.

Beneath the plane, the sea shimmered, the water black, then blue-black, then blue, the dots of life on the island finally emerging as houses and hotels and vehicles and the sprawling airport. Her aunt and cousins met them there and they loaded the suitcases—four—into the back of a pickup truck. Plum and the cousins climbed in too, Plum looking up and eying the clouds, her aunt reassuring her that the sky had been overcast all day and no rain had yet come.

"Before you know it, we reach home."

From the back of the van, Plum saw the towns in reverse, Rose-hall, Greenwood, Falmouth, Duncans, Rio Bueno and on to Discovery Bay. Her aunt's home was a four-bedroom house in Lakeside Park with a wrap-around verandah and a winding staircase that led up to the flat roof with a view of the sea and boats at a distance. The beach itself was just a five-minute walk. But in the week her mother was there, she never once felt the water. Instead, they went to other places, an old school on a hill, for one, which in summer months looked like an abandoned campus best suited as the setting for the kind of movie where the dead come back to life. Her aunt and mother disappeared inside an office, and from the verandah that wrapped around the building, Plum looked down on the mix of old and new buildings, a school unlike any she had ever seen. And then they were off to a dressmaker for Plum to be fitted for new clothes. "Just in case," her mother said, "you grow out of what you brought." In six weeks? Yet Plum had not been paying attention. When Plum thought back on it, it was too late. Her mother was back in Brooklyn, back in the brownstone near Prospect Park, calling with the unexpected news. She pictured her mother at the dining table, facing the kitchen, ready to run in to turn over frying meat or stir a boiling pot. "You enjoying yourself?"

"Yes, Mom."

"Well, listen, your father and I have arranged for you to stay and finish high school there."

"What?"

"Yes. That school upon the hill we went to? Remember it? That's your new school."

"But you said it was just for the summer."

"You can come home for Christmas. If you behave."

"You lied. You tricked me and you lied."

"It's for the best, Plum. Too many things here to distract you. And the last thing your father and I want to see is you in juvenile prison." A single phone call and her mother had removed any chance of her flying away, getting into the kinds of trouble teenagers always found.

And yet, tucked away in a strict boarding school for girls, she met him, her distraction—first as a tutor arranged by her aunt, and second as a chemistry lab assistant filling in for another teacher on leave—and regenerated wings. Her *Mr. Barrett* in school. Her *Lenworth* in private.

From the air, Plum looked down on a long, narrow strip of sand between the ocean and a mixture of squat and tall buildings. With modern civilization pushed so close up against the sand, Florida's seaside towns had little room to spread when hurricane-force winds pushed the waves high and strong up against the shore. It wasn't much different from Jamaica's seaside resort towns, where rambling villas were giving way to more and more high-rise hotels and resort communities butted up against the sea. The hills outside Montego Bay sprouted ever-larger houses, and along the coast so much space seemed to be set aside for visitors rather than those who inhabited the island. But the teenage Plum had paid little attention to all of that, reveling in her moments on the sand and in the azure waters, grateful for her little bit of freedom.

Plum changed planes in Miami and then she was airborne again, looking down on red roofs, white buildings, flamingo-pink houses, deep blue pools and murky canals. The houses were like perfectly spaced Lego blocks with little to distinguish them from a distance. The differences between Miami's planned housing and the island she had just left were stark. In Jamaica, buildings sprouted at random, and especially in the center of towns where old and new and incomplete-but-occupied buildings commingled alongside narrow congested streets, the lack of a cohesive town plan was stark. The orderliness of Miami's houses didn't matter much to Plum, except for the fact that the differences underscored how much her life would change now that she was returning to her childhood home.

And on to Brooklyn, also a world apart from island life, familiar to the child still inside her, and unfamiliar to the woman she had become. Back to parents who opened their arms and drew her in as if they hadn't exiled her from their lives and then abandoned her when she found unexpected trouble. Plum stepped into their embrace, her response tentative, theirs full and inviting. For the moment, their embrace, this timid welcome, was all Plum had. Realizing the extent of her isolation, Plum cried, letting her head fall onto her mother's shoulder as she had done as a child. There was desperation in Plum's embrace, a need to belong.

"Glad you came back home," her father said, as if the choice to stay had been hers. "Don't ever think you can't come back home."

"Yes." Plum wiped away the teardrops glistening on her lashes, and let the moment be what it was: an inevitable reunion.

Plum had forgotten how bright America was, how the fluorescent lighting in the airport allowed no shadows or dark corners. Outside the terminal, even with the winter's cold burning her fingers and toes and grabbing hold of her breath, Plum slowed her steps and looked up to catch a glimpse of a star. She had forgotten that too, that the city's lights muted the starlight, that nightfall didn't mute life. Two years away and Plum had grown accustomed to the quiet the nights brought, the chirps of nocturnal life rather than the incessant honking and beeping from vehicles on the road, her aunt saying, "I don't want night to catch me on the road" as if the dark was the devil himself.

Back to the suspended life she had grown away from and moved past. The Cabbage Patch dolls and stuffed animals, all rainbow colored, were in her room awaiting her return. There was her locked diary with its key dangling from the cover, full of petty concerns; a pink-and-white radio with a cassette tape of poorly-recorded songs and a radio announcer's voice cutting in and out of the music; a pair of black ballet shoes; and another pair of hot pink plastic sandals.

That first week back, Plum walked up and down the blocks, looking for familiar faces and places, recalling scents and sounds of her interrupted Brooklyn childhood. She cried when she found that what she had moved past—the smelly Utica Avenue stores with dusty and cheap plastic wares, peddling a plastic Christmas and unbearable holiday cheer; the men still hanging on street corners and looking out on a world that seemed to be passing them by—weren't the things that mattered. The friends Plum had left behind—Dionne, Roxanne, and Walter, who were now two shiny, bubbly young women, and one confident and swaggering young man—had gone on to colleges in Pennsylvania and Buffalo and Atlanta. And Plum, the one who had been sent away to bypass the undesirable temptations of Brooklyn, had returned empty-handed to a city she no longer loved, a child's bedroom with dusty Cabbage Patch dolls and old music on cassette tapes. She had moved past nothing that mattered.

5

Sister Ivy reordered Lenworth's life, coaxed and coached him into a manhood he never imagined, but did it so subtly he thought he had done it himself. He was the son she never had, and she the mother he wished his own could have been—educated and independent and assured. Exactly what he wished for Plum. So when Sister Ivy said, "Every baby must be blessed," Lenworth's only reply was, "Yes, of course."

They were on the verandah, Sister Ivy still in her Sunday best. The brim of her hat quivered with each movement of her head and each coo directed at Opal, who lay with her head cradled by Sister Ivy's knees. The afternoon was quiet, almost mournful and funereal. The radio played in the background, but the music—a mixture of gospel and slow songs about lost love—and the announcer's drawl fed the mournfulness. Even the clouds, thin and wispy, drifted listlessly across the sky.

"Not a christening or a baptism. Just a blessing. She'll get baptized when she's older, when she can make that decision for herself and choose to be baptized."

Lenworth nodded again.

"But you going to have to come to church with me between now and then. Show them you are a Christian."

"Of course." Lenworth nodded again.

"She must favor her mother. She don't have a thing for you."

Lenworth heard the unspoken question, "You sure the baby is yours?" But he brushed that aside, for he was sure that Opal was his. Opal had his chin—round where Plum's was a bit more elongated—and toes—long and thin and the second toe longer than the first—or so he thought, but he didn't say that.

Sister Ivy looked up at him and back at Opal. "Dead stamp of her mother, no true?"

He didn't want to, but he found himself describing Plum. Unforgettable: flawless skin, like whipped chocolate batter; almond-shaped eyes that turned down at the outer edges and irises a shade lighter than her dark skin would suggest. Lips softened with a dab of natural cocoa butter. She had a way of making him think ordinary, everyday things were extraordinary. Not that he didn't already know that many things tossed aside had secondary uses. Plum made him look even more keenly at things he wouldn't have given a second thought: orange peel that he normally tossed on a heap made a great tea; thick and hardy coconut shell, when polished and smoothed, made a unique bowl.

He chose his words carefully, tiptoeing around what he knew to be true: Plum made him forget he was an adult and she a graduating student. Made him forget to hold himself back. He fell with head, heart, and soul, taking her with him, mixing up love and desire and loneliness with the fear of being exposed and the fear—both hers and his—of being abandoned again. And in the end, the adults would believe he led her, but the truth was that they tumbled equally into their illicit love.

Unforgettable. The girl in the pale peach dress, sitting in the back of the school auditorium giggling at something an adult onstage said, covering her mouth and her eyes, hiding the laughter. The girl in uniform sitting in the middle of a hired bus among girls in identical uniforms, yet somewhat different, eagerly looking out the window at the passing countryside, drinking in the hillside villages, the roadside vendors holding up bags of peeled fruit, peppered crayfish in bags, oranges tied to a stick, drinking it all in and questioning the need for the red mud lake, the logic of putting manufacturing residue that peels the skin so close to villages, the toxicity of such dangerous chemical residue so close to human life.

"Effluent," he said. "That's what it's called."

"Effluent." She twirled the word around her mouth, weighing it, tasting it, and returned to the practical. "Will it ever dry up?"

"Eventually."

"Then what will become of it?"

"Don't know."

"What an awful way to die. To fall into an acidic lake and watch your skin peel away."

"It doesn't happen often. Everybody knows how dangerous it is. Plus it's not that easy to get to it."

"Still . . ."

He remembered her as the girl in the red dress on the shop piazza, waving at him, her face scrunching up into a ready smile, her fingers reaching out to grasp at his then pulling back. The girl on the beach, hiding her bathing suit and her body beneath an over-sized T-shirt, holding her head in her hands and sobbing, comparing herself to a discarded bag of old clothes her parents found and shipped abroad. She hadn't been allowed to return to Brooklyn, to the brownstone on President Street, to the friends she hadn't bid goodbye, to summertime hopscotch and jumping rope. A single summer vacation had turned into one long, unexpected expulsion from the only life she'd known. Expelled. Excommunicated. Exiled. Each day she had another word for what her parents had done, for how they had re-engineered her life without her knowing it, for how they had sent her away as if she hadn't mattered at all. Unforgettable.

And forgettable: he walked out of the hospital with the baby girl and left Plum there, asleep and expecting to wake and nurse her child. Abandoned. Left again like a bag of old clothes. Liberated, was what he preferred to think. Without a baby holding her back, she would be free to pursue a fuller life—an education and a career—all the things that he had taken from her by making her a mother too early, all the possibilities his own sister, who had left home for the police academy and returned with a baby boy, hadn't had. He could list more than a handful of girls he knew with stilted and stifled ambitions. He didn't wish that for Plum.

Of course, he didn't say the latter parts, not how they met and not the truth about how he came to be Opal's only parent.

Monday mornings, Lenworth found himself collecting coconut shells from his neighbors. He could have gone on any day, but he knew with certainty that the red beans and rice that was a staple of most every Jamaican household's Sunday dinner would have been made with fresh coconut milk. And so he walked from house to house with a crocus bag collecting the hard pieces of shell that his neighbors would have otherwise thrown away.

Back in the workshop—the converted fowl coop—and Opal in the house with Sister Ivy, Lenworth broke the shells even further and polished the pieces before mixing them with resin and shaping bowls and platters and kitchen utensils and tabletops. He liked the solitude of the workshop, the smell of cedar and varnish, he liked Sister Ivy's smile when she passed in the evening and saw the shimmer of stained wood or polished coconut shell, or the simple, clean lines of a large serving platter he had completed.

Sister Ivy took charge of finding the wholesaler who bought most of Lenworth's pieces in bulk. It was she who sent him the women who sold goods in various craft markets and stalls in Montego Bay, and who bought small quantities of the smaller items they knew tourists would buy.

At another time, he would have thanked Plum for letting him see the value of discarded coconut shells, for reminding him that ordinary things were sometimes extraordinary.

Sister Ivy took charge of every detail of Opal's blessing as if Opal were her own grandchild. She set the date and time with the minister at the Mt. Carey Baptist Church, and saw to it that Lenworth went to service in the weeks leading up to Opal's blessing. And now on the morning of—a cool, cloudy January morning—Sister Ivy dressed Opal in white, a dress covered with frills and lace and a large bow on the front of the bodice, socks that were also fringed with lace, and patent leather shoes—all gifts from Sister Ivy's daughter who lived abroad. She led them down the hill away from Lenworth's house, Opal propped on her shoulder, and Lenworth walking behind them like a dutiful son, carrying two Bibles and hymnals and Sister Ivy's vast patent leather purse.

An anemic sun peeped through the clouds as if it welcomed a reprieve from its job. The road through the community was a mixture of marl and stone, pockmarked with depressions where puddles from the previous night's rain had formed. The vegetation to the right was thick and green and lush, and he suspected there was water underground that fed the vegetation in that particular area. It reminded him of home, the town where he grew up. As quickly as the thought came, he shoved it aside, for he didn't want to think of his mother in Clarendon waiting for news of the newborn grandchild or for him to come home with his new family.

Plum. He couldn't think of her either. This moment, Opal's blessing, should have been hers and his, not his and Sister Ivy's. But he wouldn't allow himself any regrets, not this particular morning.

The road emptied out on the main road toward Montpelier and the south coast. A few more turns and they were there, walking uphill to the old church, which had been destroyed by fire and slave revolts on more than one occasion, and rebuilt time after time. Without the sun lighting it, the building's gray stone and concrete walls were dull.

Lenworth had no particular affinity for the Mt. Carey Baptist Church, or for any church, and he wanted only to get through the morning's service, to escape the energy that infected the congregants in sudden bursts of "Amen" and "Hallelujah" and "Praise the Lord," and fits of uncontrollable quaking and rolling. He was never one for those kinds of histrionics and if he had to attend any church he preferred the more staid Anglican Church with its subdued form of worship.

For a brief moment he held Opal. It was just long enough for the minister to impart his blessing, but she squirmed and cried a full-throated howl, only settling back into a whimper and then quiet once she was back in Sister Ivy's arms. Lenworth knew then what the pattern of his life with Opal would be like. But again, he allowed himself no regrets. Everything he had done since that September morning when he walked away from Plum had been for Opal. Everything he did on that September morning had been for Plum—his gift to her.

6

January 16. Four months to the day. Plum pictured the baby girl, who would be lifting her head by now, grabbing at things, cooing and smiling. Instead of caring for her baby girl and Lenworth—her little family of three—Plum was in her mother's kitchen chopping vegetables and transforming leftover roasted chicken into soup for another threesome.

Little scent bubbles of thyme, onions, scallion, and roasted chicken hung in the air. She peeled and chopped pumpkin, peeled and sliced yellow yam and sweet potato, and kneaded flour for dumplings. Elsewhere in the house all was quiet, except for the cricks and creaks of the house settling, the radiator hissing steam, and the machines rumbling as they worked. This was her time, free of the sad love songs her mother played, free of the television newscasters and commentators to whom her father directed his ire, free really of the human instinct to socialize.

The soup finished, Plum left the house, timing her exit to avoid her mother and father's return, and their instinct to cajole, like a cuckoo pushing another species of baby bird from its nest. The sun was already going down, the leafless trees on the block and the brick buildings ablaze with the late-evening sunlight. The sounds—car horns and sirens and car stereos—that she'd ignored while inside the house, pressed in on her now. Plum tucked her chin into her scarf, and held her head down as if all that mattered were the steps she made on the concrete underfoot. She had no specific destination. In those early days back, Plum's routine was simple: she cooked and she walked through the neighborhood, up and down Utica Avenue, along Flatbush Avenue, Church Avenue, through Prospect Park in the middle of the day. Each day, she took a different route. She looked in store windows at the things she couldn't afford. She looked at babies in strollers, at the mothers caring for the babbling babies and calming the agitated ones, at toddlers in the midst of an ill-timed tantrum, at intact families walking in groups of threes and fours and fives, and at women rushing home from work, presumably to a waiting family. And she dreamt of what should have been hers. So as not to cry among strangers, she shoved the thoughts aside, and walked as if she wore blinders that were intended only to block out families.

Plum walked this time down Prospect Park West toward the public library, around Grand Army Plaza and back to the library. Its concave front entrance and beige walls were dull in the evening sun, and inside, where teenagers and serious researchers commingled, the delicate hush broke in random bursts—a laugh someone failed to stifle, a deliberate and annoyed shush, a whispered question, a book slapping onto wood.

Plum roamed, looked on at a mother and a toddler on the floor paging through a picture book. The child turned the pages quickly, stopping briefly at random pages and pointing, and the mother, unable to read the actual words, made up a story to match the pictures. Plum soaked up the child's quick and easy smile, her dimples, the dark ringlets brushing her forehead, how quick she was to reach for another book, how she commanded her mother to read, how easily she laughed when her mother quacked like a duck and mooed like a cow. And on to another book, which the child read by pointing to the pictures and telling the story she had heard before. Plum soaked up the child's voice, the way she mispronounced wolf as "woof," how her eyes lit up when she said "huff and puff."

"Your turn," the child said, and flipped to the front of the book, her eyes moving from the pages to her mother's face. In that moment, no one but her mother mattered.

Tears welled up in Plum's eyes, threatening to spill over at any moment. That moment should have been in her future. Instead of her, it would be Lenworth or perhaps another woman he got to take her place, who would matter, who the baby girl would look at with adoration. It was unbearable. She blinked away the tears and left that room and the building entirely without looking for career and self-development books as she should have. And walked again, up Eastern Parkway this time, past the museum and the Botanic Garden, aware of little except for the emptiness inside, and the ever-present, unbearable thought: Your daughter is gone.

✍

Back at home, her body chilled, Plum sat in the window seat with her toes curled in socks and hands wrapped around a mug of hot chocolate. She sniffed at the steam, the scent of cinnamon and nutmeg and cocoa tickling her nose, and tried to ignore her mother and father, looking on at her, the troubled daughter they did not understand and could not reach. Neither stepped forward to hug or to hold, as if afraid their touch could break her. At the moment, that was all Plum wanted: warmth, not pitying looks, and arms around to contain and keep her from falling apart, keep her from feeling that she had abandoned her baby girl. Instead of leaving, she should have stayed in Jamaica and continued to search. She shouldn't have accepted Mrs. Murray's offer so quickly, shouldn't have left the island entirely, shouldn't be in Brooklyn attempting to rebuild her suspended life without her daughter, who was by then a cooing, babbling being, holding her head up, grasping at things—his goatee, his bushy brows, his fingers—and smiling.

"Tell me," her mother said. "What did we do wrong?" She pointed to a chair, and Plum's father brought it forward from the dining room.

"Nothing," Plum said.

"We want to help you. You know that, right?"

Plum nodded, but kept her eyes down on the small bubbles and froth swirling in the mug, seeing the conversation for what it was—a planned intervention.

"You can't go on so. You should try and get into Brooklyn College or Kingsborough next semester. You have to do something, get your mind off things."

So simple, Plum thought. Just do something and she would forget. But she said yes.

"Everything passes," Plum's mother said. "No matter how unbearable it seems, you will move past it. You will."

That was also Lenworth's line. *"Everything passes."* Including, his love and his promise and Plum.

And it angered her, even then, how easily he had left her behind. Plum conflated the two defining events of her life—her being sent away as a teenager and Lenworth walking away with their child. They were one and the same: she had been abandoned, twice by her parents at the first sign of trouble and once by her lover. At that moment, her mother's attempt to intervene felt hollow, a little bit too late.

"I have some books," her mother was saying. "Jobs in healthcare, nursing."

"I don't want to be like you. Don't want to be a nurse."

"Maybe not nursing. Accounting. Banking." She put the books down, one at a time, a shallow thump rising up as she lowered each book. "You used to like to draw. No money in art. But if that's what you want to do . . ."

"I haven't drawn since I was probably ten years old."

Undaunted and looking away from Plum's sneer, her mother continued. "Anyway, you need to find a job. Do something with your life."

"You can't fix this, Mom. Working like you night and day, day and night, won't make me forget. Working, always working. Two shifts, and a second job. No. Not for me." Plum's voice was harsher than she wanted, dismissive.

"So that's what you have against us? We were working to feed you and keep this house. You think it's easy for an immigrant coming to this country?"

"What I remember is this: You on the couch sleeping, Dad at work, and me in the corner playing by myself or watching TV. Or it was the other way around, Dad upstairs sleeping, you at work. Either way, it was work and sleep. You know how many birthday parties I missed because you were too tired to take me?"

Plum remembered her childhood more by her mother's absence than her presence, the weekend dance and sports programs she hadn't participated in because her mother and father were too tired—one parent sleeping in the daytime and the other at night—and Plum, it seemed, parenting herself. Even then, she felt like she didn't matter, like her parents' world would not have fallen off its axis without her in it. Indeed, their life had gone on without her in it. They had sent her away and left her there when she found trouble.

"Birthday parties? That's what you upset about missing?"

"You know what else I remember? My pink leotards and tights that I never got to wear to a dance class. Not even one class because you could never fit it in. I found the leotards. They're still upstairs in my drawer."

"You know how hard we had to work to give you a good life? Never mind that you threw it away."

"You don't understand. All that time you had with me and you weren't there. And me? I have nothing. No time with my child at all."

"I can't change what he did to you. And you can't change it either. But you can do something about you."

"Who says I want to?"

"You have to."

Indeed, she did. Plum had a deal with Mrs. Murray: college or repayment of a loan. Plum swung her legs down and faced her mother.

"I'm not that girl you sent away. I'm not even the girl whose graduation you didn't bother coming to. I'm not that girl anymore. This is who I am, sad and angry and bitter. This is me, not a robot working every waking hour to hide from my life."

"Robot, hmmm. Hear this." She turned from Plum to her husband sitting at the dining table with his back to it. "All the work to put this girl through school and she calling me a robot."

"Give her time," he said, his voice a whisper.

"This is what I have to put up with in my own house?"

Plum got up and didn't look back. Upstairs, she stood by her bedroom door, her back pressed into it and the mug of hot chocolate that didn't soothe still in her hand. Up there, away from her parents, it occurred to her that what bothered her more was the weight her parents—and even Lenworth—placed on ambition over personhood, attaining wealth or power or status no matter the cost to themselves or others. It was ingrained in the immigrant dream. Work three jobs if you have to. Double your shifts. Send money home. If necessary, create the illusion of success, especially for family back home. Work, and work some more, whether you love the job or not. That was Plum's perception of the immigrant dream.

Perhaps it was also a woman's lot in life—get up and carry on, no matter what. Plum had suffered, was still suffering. Yet, her mother's only focus was that Plum make something of herself, be someone who mattered.

Indeed, in that room, there were still remnants of the assured teen, the girl who felt she could step out on a limb, balance herself, turn a cartwheel or two without slipping or breaking the branch. There were remnants of the girl who had a dream and a goal and a belief that she mattered. Plum stood there with her back against the door, looking for that girl who found her own way when her parents were too tired and too busy to take her to weekend dance classes. That girl joined her school's drama club and art club. She found a way to be seen and to matter.

She understood now that sometimes that desire to be seen as successful, to matter, was all a person had or could control. That really was all Plum had. So she shifted, found a target and homed in on it as if with a laser. She focused on mattering, on not being a person so easily discarded and left behind.

✑

Outside, clouds thickened and filled the sky like sprayed foam. Plum stood for a moment on the red brick steps and sucked in the cold air. As she breathed out, she watched the vapor trail from her mouth. No, she hadn't missed winter at all, not the bundling up in layers of wool or flannel or down, not the cold that bit into her skin as she walked, not the way winter weather and the wind transformed the street into a tunnel with cold air rushing in. She didn't miss the dry skin and cracked lips, the tiny cracks on the back of her hands, the way the cold numbed her toes and fingers, the way the wool scarf simultaneously scratched and warmed her skin.

Plum walked with purpose this time, past the now-quiet brownstones behind the leafless trees. Back to the library, and again a purposeful walk toward the reference desk and a librarian. And another purposeful walk to the careers section. Plum pulled random books on allied health and database management, unsure of what she wanted to do.

There was a time when she was sure of the trajectory of her life after she finished up with the boarding school to which she had been exiled. Back to Brooklyn for sure and college in Manhattan or Boston or Washington, DC, a major city instead of a sleepy college town. Once, on a beach, Lenworth had pointed in the direction of a three-hundred-year-old fort and talked about the engineer he wanted to become. And Plum had pointed west, in the general direction of an old plantation house that had been kept up to show off its glory, the wood floors and furniture polished to a shine, the expansive verandah with its view of the sea, the spacious bedrooms with massive four-poster beds and large windows that seemed to capture and release the breeze. "One out of two things," Plum said then. "I want to be the historian or the archaeologist finding out about other people's lives. Or I want to restore old houses so they look like that. Houses tell stories, you know? All those things that people collect say something about them. Where they've been. Who they love. You can walk into a room and find out so much about a person's life."

So grand, Plum thought now. Not even a full year had passed since that day on the beach. But that dream, that goal was a lifetime away. She didn't care anymore about other people's stories or past lives. She had her own stories, past and present, and now she had a firm conviction that despite her parents' claim, the fairytale endings—the scripted Hollywood kind—weren't really available to her. Hollywood's movies had told her that fairytale endings weren't available to a dark-skinned girl, or an immigrant at that. Plum believed it now, wholeheartedly. She tamped her dreams of glory down, and settled for a simple, ordinary dream, her immigrant parents' dream—a job that paid for food and shelter. There was no need to love the work; she simply had to be efficient at it.

Plum thumbed through the books piled on the table. She had no interest in her mother's career, nursing, or her father's, accounting. Any career in finance or business was out. Dealing with customers and their myriad problems and attitudes wasn't something she imagined doing.

She picked up another on careers in allied health, closed her eyes, cracked the book open, fanned the pages, then looked down at where her thumb had stopped. Laboratory technologist. Typing blood and testing body fluids in a lab. There were no complete stories there. Perhaps an indication from a virus or a parasite of where a person had been, whether a farm or forest or remote tropical village. Perhaps an indication of a diet of sugary foods or fatty meats or undercooked seafood or pork. But the samples offered no nuances of love or loss, no expectations or hope, just normal or abnormal ranges, normal or abnormal tissue and cell samples—the cold hard facts of sickness or good health.

7

A year on, September 16: the baby girl's first birthday. Plum pictured her daughter like this: hair parted in four distinct sections, each section a mini afro puff; pudgy cheeks; a smile that opened up dimples; skin as richly pigmented as hers; pudgy arms and legs in a frilly yellow dress. Except the baby wasn't hers. Just a stranger on the train, a baby who smiled openly at anyone who caught her eye. The child's mother, soothed by the monotonous clacking of metal against metal and the rhythm of the rumbling train, drifted off to sleep, her head drooping forward.

In a second the baby girl could be gone, snatched from her stroller, Plum thought. Any one of these strangers on the train could take the baby girl who smiled so easily at people, slip through the closing doors onto a crowded platform and away, disappearing into the darkened tunnel or up the stairs and into the throng outside. Improbable, but not impossible. Plum had lived it.

Plum wanted to wake the mother. And yet, how could she without alarming her? Who among the misfits and career types and students and tourists would snatch a child from a crowded train? She took stock of the passengers. Beside her, a man snored and another read a newspaper, his arms brushing up against Plum each time he turned the page and flattened the creases of the paper. Another man standing near the door looked continuously at his watch as if that alone would speed the slow train. Two girls sitting next to the door whispered and giggled. A woman—white, older—hid behind a book and played peek-a-boo with the baby girl. There was nothing extraordinary about a woman playing peek-a-boo with a child she didn't know, but Plum, already on edge, took note of everything as if capturing all the details that would matter in the end. Everyone was caught up in something.

The passengers' preoccupation eased Plum's anxiety, and she turned away from the child and her sleeping mother, tucked her head down and opened a textbook, flipping to a chapter on critical thinking. The words lost their shape and the sentences lost their structure. Everything—the anniversary of Plum's greatest loss, the smiling baby girl with her afro puffs, an exhausted and sleeping mother, that feeling of isolation even in a crowded train—led Plum back to that single night in St. Ann's Bay Hospital, waking with an awareness that something had changed.

The commotion around her had ceased and in its place was a quiet like death. Except, of course, she wasn't dead but achingly awake, the pain in her pelvis brightening with each passing second. She looked for Lenworth, and around for a bassinet or crib, some sign of the baby girl she planned to name Marissa, Spanish for "of the sea." Plum liked the promise of the sea, the flat unending body of water with its own will. It could take her anywhere or even no-where, which was exactly what she wanted for her baby—promise and freedom.

Again, Plum looked around at the beige walls and curtains, listened for the sounds of life, footsteps on tile, voices behind the adjoining curtains, a newborn's robust cry.

The nurse, when she came, was cheerful. "My baby," Plum said.

"Sleeping," the nurse answered. "Careful now."

The nurse—an older woman, gentle—stood by Plum as she maneuvered her legs to the floor.

"Dizzy," Plum said, and stood still for a minute while the feeling passed.

They shuffled down the hallway, Plum slow, the nurse patient, until at last they stood by the nursery looking through the glass for the Barrett baby girl. But there was no girl, just a name tag and sheets.

"The Barrett baby?" Plum's nurse asked.

"With her father," another nurse said, smiling as she spoke. "He had her. Proud man."

"Where is he?"

"He took the baby back to the ward."

"No."

The nurses looked at each other, each struggling to hold their emotions together, to move without indicating panic.

"He here somewhere," Plum's nurse said, turning to her again and taking her hand. "We'll find him, tell him you awake and ready to nurse."

Plum didn't panic immediately. As instructed, she waited in the ward, her legs dangling from the side of the bed. Five minutes, then ten, then thirty. The hospital buzzed with adrenaline and panic, and the nurses, once friendly and talkative, wouldn't catch her eye. Before she knew it with absolute certainty, before she heard officially that Lenworth had taken the baby girl and left, Plum cried. Her body slumped forward from the side of the bed, pain shooting through her pelvis, and her heart pattering so strongly in her chest that she brought her hand up as if it could slow the beats.

Plum imagined alternate possibilities: the nurse confused or unaware of written discharge orders; her baby in another part of the hospital undergoing tests or treatment; Lenworth at home preparing the cottage for her return; her child mistakenly given to a stranger. Nothing in Plum and Lenworth's history suggested he would have taken their child. They had planned for a life together, at least for the months immediately after the baby came home. He was making plans to find a new job teaching, at least for another year or two before heading to university in Kingston. "Town will suit you," he said to Plum, an indication that he planned for her to be with him. Even then, Plum didn't pare back her dream to study history or anthropology or archaeology. And neither did Lenworth. "Me, the engineer, making these big buildings, and you digging up the dirt. We make a good pair." Plum had smiled and tapped his arm, softly, playfully, gently.

We make a good pair, was Plum's last thought before Plum's nurse, the head nurse, a doctor, and security guards had come to say definitively that neither Lenworth nor the baby could be found.

Remembering that moment and the immediacy of her loss, led to this: Plum stood, gathered her things and walked toward the baby and her mother. She jostled the stroller hard enough to push the handle back into the child's mother and wake her.

"What's wrong with you?" the mother, her face red and puffy, screamed at Plum. "Look where you're going! Can't you see?"

"Sorry," Plum said. "Sorry." But jostling the stroller worked as intended. The child's mother leaned toward the baby.

Plum stood in front of the train door, willing it to open, unable in that moment to see through the blur of tears, to make out the names of the local stops printed on white tile. The express train rattled on. The passengers behind Plum, who initially looked on at the commotion Plum caused, had already looked away and wrapped themselves back into their lives. They had already moved on.

Plum couldn't go on, couldn't even go into the building that day and face the other undergraduates with their petty concerns—manufactured slights; Alan's wistful looks at her; Allison scheduling study sessions around a work schedule; Melonie giggling about a crush on Sean and prolonging cafeteria breaks to coincide with his break; the group hashing out the details of yet another party in a stuffy, dim basement. Most of all, it was Alan's plaintive looks—how she simultaneously pulled him to her and pushed him away—that she didn't want to face. Like a cat toying with a mouse, giving him hope and pulling it away just as quickly. She hated herself for that. But she wasn't ready, couldn't yet imagine having a boyfriend or building another relationship.

Above, students and staff moved through the pedestrian bridge, their concerns at the moment so remote from Plum's. Plum turned away from the building and went back the way she had come, back to the subway, the dank underground smell. Even among the strangers on a relatively crowded train she was alone. Plum shut her eyes and willed her mind to think about something other than the baby girl's birthday. The train rattled out of Manhattan and back into Brooklyn, screeching and clanging.

Plum didn't go home, but rode the train like a bum, looking out on the stations the train rattled past—Prospect Park, Church Avenue, Newkirk Avenue, Kings Highway—below ground at first then above ground. The brownstones and apartment buildings—red brick, beige or grey stucco—rolled by in a blur. Sheepshead Bay. Brighton Beach. Coney Island. From the train and in the sunlight, the lights on the amusement park rides were dim, almost useless. And nearly empty. Past its peak summer days, it looked like something trying to relive a glorified past. But it drew Plum anyway and she walked toward it, past the open-mouthed clown heads set up for patrons to squirt water into the clowns' mouths, bypassing the opportunity to win a stuffed animal.

Plum rode the Cyclone over and over, before switching to the boat that swung back and forth, higher and higher each time, screaming to keep from crying. But she did cry uncontrollably on a boardwalk bench, her back to the park's neon lights and the rides that seemed to go on forever, her eyes to the dark sea. She remained there all night, slept, but not for long, waking after only a few minutes and crying again when she remembered the significance of the day, her baby girl who was probably pulling herself up and taking her first steps. Bawling when she thought of all the milestones she had missed: the first voluntary smile, the first tooth, the first sound that resembled a word, the first step with help, the first step without help, the simple word "Mama."

Coney Island wasn't safe. Not then. It was overrun with drug addicts and dealers, prostitutes and pimps, the homeless and the insane who made their home beneath the boardwalk. But Plum survived the night and the elements, got up in the morning and walked away, hungry and grimy and cold, walked back across the deserted park, across Surf Avenue, and up the steps to the subway and a ride back toward Prospect Park. By then her emotions had flatlined and she sat like a discarded shell unaware of the other passengers, the conductor calling the names of the stops, the train screeching and shrieking through the borough.

Plum's feet, programmed to walk home, took her up Prospect Park West and on to President Street and the brownstone where her parents, more frantic than they had been when they discovered her bed empty, pulled her to them, then quickly pushed her away when they felt the particles of dust and sand and smelled her unwashed body.

"My God, child, you want to give us heart attack. Where you been all night?"

Later, Plum would think how ironic it was that the very parents who, upon hearing of her pregnancy, hadn't wanted her to return to their house and who took her in only because she was returned to them by her former landlady in Jamaica, those same parents worried about her not returning home one single night. But at that moment, confronted at the door by an angry and concerned mother and equally angry and concerned father, she wept again, fell to her knees, and cupped her head in her palms. "Today's her first birthday. I should be celebrating her birthday."

Until then, Plum hadn't spoken directly to her parents about Lenworth or the baby, hadn't given them the details of how he disappeared with their child. They knew, of course, because Mrs. Murray had told them. When they asked, Plum had skirted the issue, too pained to talk about the greatest loss of her life, how the memory of what she had lost sometimes overwhelmed and blossomed like algae in a stagnant pond, spreading out and taking over her whole being.

"Hush, hush." Her mother stooped, pulled her prostrate child up and into her arms. "Hush. Everything has its time, child. Everything has its time."

That, of course, was not what Plum wanted to hear. No matter what transpired, Plum couldn't reclaim the lost year, couldn't recreate the firsts that she missed—babbling and footsteps and smiles. Plum couldn't see beyond the immediate loss to that time her mother hinted would come. She pulled herself up, whispered, "I need a shower," and walked away from her mother who was saying, "I'm going to make you some cornmeal porridge." A hot meal was her mother's, and perhaps every Jamaican woman's, way of giving comfort and showing love.

Without looking back, Plum nodded. "Yes, thanks." She didn't say what she thought: that porridge was baby's food and her mother had long given up the role of babying her. That food could do little to erase the ever-present thought: your daughter is gone. That she feared she would live the remainder of her life with the gnawing hunger for the answer to the simple question: why?

PART 2

How to Hold Back Grief

1

From the beginning, it was nearly impossible for Lenworth to calm Opal. She cried as if she already knew that what surrounded her was inadequate. She cried as if she knew precisely what and who was missing. When she first learned to focus her gaze, she looked at his eyes and then away at the space near his ear as if looking for something next to him, as if she knew that another face should occupy the space that immediately surrounded him.

So it was no surprise to Lenworth when Opal, at one year old, looked at Sister Ivy and called her Mama, and at four, when she started attending the Anchovy Basic School, asked, "How come I don't have a mother? How come I only have a grandmother and no mother?"

They were in Lenworth's workshop, the converted fowl coop, Opal playing with a doll in the sawdust and feeding the doll bits of the curled ribbons of shaved wood that lined the floor like carpet, and Lenworth fiddling with an old tricycle with rusting steel, a red-and-white checkered seat, and green tassels hanging from the handles. Even at four years old, Opal was a wisp of a girl easily mistaken for a two-year-old, a wisp of a girl who was always a step behind the growth and development charts. He wanted to think she would grow up to be as lithe and thin as his mother rather than into the stocky frame he had inherited from his father.

Lenworth, with his back turned to Opal, pretended not to hear. He had known this question would eventually come. Yet he hadn't exactly prepared for it. All the other stories he had told about Plum had come without prompting. He always suspected that when Opal asked he would know instinctively what to say. He waited for the moment to pass, for Opal to move on to something else.

But, as if she knew he wanted her to let it go, she dug in, holding on to the topic like she would the end of a rope in a tug-of-war. She moved closer to him, grabbed hold of the green tassel and shook it. "What happened to Mommy?"

Lenworth looked down at Opal, away, and down again, then he stooped so they were eye to eye and gave her a fairytale. "Once upon a time, a man fell in love with a bird woman and he kept her like a parrot in a cage so she wouldn't fly away. Every day when he went off to work, she cried. He didn't understand why she was so sad all the time. He tried everything he could think of to make her happy. He bought her new toys. He painted her birdcage. But nothing made her happy. One day he found her crying and she told him she wanted so very much to see the world. She said flying again would make her happy. And he wanted her to be happy. So he opened the cage. He wanted to test whether she loved him enough to stay if he set her free from the cage. As soon as he opened the door to the cage, she flew away. And when she flew away, she left you behind so that I wouldn't be alone after she was gone. Your mother flew away, Opal, and she left you behind." He turned back to the tricycle with the bent wheel spokes.

Opal turned away too, lifting her dress as she moved, looking beneath to confirm what she already knew: she didn't have wings or feathers.

Getting up and stepping away from Opal, what struck Lenworth was how much his daughter looked like her mother. He already knew it, but the resemblance was even more striking now. Opal had lost the pudginess around her face and eyes. The distinctly almond shape of her eyes was more prominent now and her irises were more like topaz against her dark skin. Plum's eyes. Plum's smile. He hadn't missed the features as he wanted to believe. He had simply buried his guilt so deeply that he forgot that he hadn't created his child alone.

He imagined Plum now, a university student in the midst of her studies in anthropology or archaeology, or going on to a career studying the past and reconciling it with the present. Not in Brooklyn, though. He didn't imagine she would have returned there, or, if she had, she wouldn't have stayed with the parents she believed had abandoned her. He pictured her instead in Washington, DC, at Howard University perhaps, even though he knew nothing about the city except for what he learned from grainy images on the news. But a university as iconic as Howard, rich with history and culture, would have suited her well. He pictured her as he had last seen her, her head thrown back, eyes closed, a finger against her lips. Except she was in a library surrounded by books, moving on as he hadn't been able to.

✍

Sister Ivy came upon Lenworth quietly. Now, she came in the mornings to get Opal ready, picked up Opal from school and stayed for a part of the afternoon to watch Opal as he finished up in the workshop.

"Mobay High needs a carpenter," Sister Ivy said. "Fixing desks and such."

Lenworth, who had been sweeping sawdust into a corner of his workshop, stopped. He hadn't told Sister Ivy of his history with the girl's school and he didn't want to bring it up. This work, carpentering and making useful objects out of discarded scraps, was far removed from the adult life he had imagined for himself, an engineer building inspired projects and branding the world with his creations.

In four years, he hadn't been near a high school, had stopped thinking about equations and formulas. He measured the depth and length and height of wood and cut necessary angles, but he didn't think about theorems and calculations, algebra or geometry, just the bare shape and size of things. What Sister Ivy dangled before him would bring him much too close to the type of place where he had lost everything—the job and the dream and ultimately Plum. Not that he thought what had happened between him and Plum would repeat itself; there was no other like Plum, no one who could have taken her place.

"I can't," he said, and pointed to his workshop. "What about this?"

"More stable for you and Opal," she said. "And you have weekends and evenings to do your little tinkering."

He hated that she called his work tinkering.

"Let me think about it."

"Don't take too long. I told the principal you wouldn't miss such an opportunity and he's expecting you to come this week for an interview."

Lenworth couldn't think of a way out that didn't involve a revelation of his secrets. All evening he waited for his mind to settle on an excuse that he could give, but nothing he thought of was good enough.

Up on the verandah, Opal played with a one-footed doll. She held the doll on the railing and made it do cartwheels. Sooner or later the doll would tumble ten feet or so to the ground, and Opal would retrieve it and start again. Sometimes he thought she dropped the doll purposefully, part of an ongoing experiment to figure out the purpose of such inanimate things. He watched her now, the cloistered girl with only a doll, an old lady, and him as companions. He did his best with Opal. He was sure he could have done even more. But there was no certainty that a full-time job at a school would open up large possibilities for his family of two.

In the morning when he woke, he grated a ball of cocoa and set chocolate tea on to boil with coconut milk. Sister Ivy drank it most mornings and he left it on the stove for her and Opal, then went into the planted fields in the flat below the house, telling himself that he wasn't hiding from Sister Ivy, but simply pruning parasitic vines from the fruit trees and reaping bananas and plantains and cocoa to supplement the day's meals.

In the damp and overgrown plot of land, he waited out his time. But Sister Ivy, always punctual, didn't come.

Lenworth dressed Opal himself, brushed the plaits Sister Ivy made the previous morning, scrambled an egg and buttered toast, and walked her up to the basic school, where already the children romped on every empty space outside the school, and their squeals and laughter lit up the morning.

And on to Sister Ivy's house. Even before he knocked and got no answer, circled Sister Ivy's barking dog and held it back with a crooked stick, he knew that everything was not all right. There were lights on in the house that she would have turned out before going to bed. The curtains fluttered. She would have closed the shutters to keep out the bugs and mosquitoes and the drafty night air. Before he went in and found her stiff body, he knew one thing: the axis and balance of his life had once again shifted.

2

As if mothers were dolls one could pick up in a store, not long after Sister Ivy's death and Opal's question about her absent mother, Lenworth came back with one: a mother without wings, a new mother for a motherless, wingless child.

He'd met her—Pauline—at a bus stop as she waited for a bus going past Anchovy and on to Black River on the south coast. They sat together on the crowded bus, his legs pressed against hers, and her tangy sweet breath near his ear.

"Not even sardine pack up so," Pauline muttered, referring to the number of passengers already jammed in the bus. "Pack us up like sardine, and 'cause sardine don't cry, they think we won't cry too."

"How you know so much 'bout how sardine feel?"

Pauline smiled and shook her head. "You take serious thing make joke. All joke aside, there should be a limit on how many people the driver and conductor can pack up in a bus. It no right to pay you money and can't get no comfort."

"True."

"All the way to Black River pack up so. That no right."

The bus pulled away from the stop, the passengers lurching forward and back, and the tires screeching.

"See it there now. We not even lef' Mobay, and he want kill we already. He going kill we today. And me not even live my life yet."

"Yet?" Lenworth asked. "What you waiting on? Young girl like you."

"Young? Thirty-three," Pauline said. "Seven girls my parents have and I am the only one who not married and don't have any children yet."

"Seven girls?"

"Seven girls. My father wanted to try again for the boy and my mother say no, take what God give you and give thanks. By the time she was thirty-three, my mother had had her last child. So by that standard, I am old."

"You aren't old," Lenworth said, and he let his gaze drop to her bosom, her ample breasts straining against her shirt.

She smiled. "You too rude." She tapped at his arm, playfully.

A week later, they met again, Pauline timing her trip and her departure from Montego Bay to coincide with Lenworth leaving Montego Bay High School, where he had indeed taken the job as carpenter and general handyman. She knew he left at 4:30 and she waited till he arrived, smiled, and said, "So we meet again." And so began their courtship on the bus ride between Montego Bay and Anchovy, Pauline finding reasons to journey from one coast to the other, Lenworth looking out day after day for a glimpse of her, until at last Lenworth said, "We have to stop meeting like this. Make it more permanent."

"But I barely even know you," Pauline said.

"That's not a hard problem to fix."

"How you plan to fix it?" She looked at him with her brows raised. A half-smile stretched her lips.

"Give me a chance to show you."

"I'm not living with no man who isn't my husband," Pauline said.

"So we'll get married." Lenworth spoke as if marriage was a simple thing.

"I'm not marrying a man who my family don't know."

"Saturday then. I'll come meet your father. If you promise he won't chase me off with a stick or set his dogs on me."

But Pauline turned shy again, and by then the bus was in Anchovy, slowing at the railway crossing, and Lenworth was scrambling to extricate himself from the middle of the bus, away from Pauline and his newfound dream.

Two weeks passed without Lenworth seeing Pauline, without their impromptu meetings at the bus stop. As quickly as the courtship began, he gave up the dream.

※

"Tell me again about my mother." Opal was looking up at Lenworth, her face like a flower opening.

"What you want to know?"

"Where is her birdcage?"

"I don't have that anymore."

"Was she little like a parrot, or big like an ostrich?"

"Like an ostrich."

"Ostriches can't fly," Opal said it so matter-of-factly, Lenworth thought she was testing the veracity of his story.

But she was much too young to connect the fantastical elements of his story about a bird woman with the reality of flightless birds.

"Where you learn 'bout ostriches?"

"Mrs. Wilson has a big book with lots of birds it. She said ostriches are too big to fly."

"What else you learned at school today?"

"Nothing."

Lenworth turned back to the pan of white shirts he had left in the sun to bleach the stains. Soap suds spread on his arms like a sprinkling of powder.

"If my mother was big like an ostrich, how did she fly away?"

Rather than answer, Lenworth took the clothes outside. "Go get a book and come and read it to me," he said, as he was walking out. But inside his heart beat furiously. Sooner or later, he thought Opal would catch him in a lie and figure out for herself how unrealistic his story was.

❧

A month passed before he saw Pauline again, not at the bus stop this time, but at Montego Bay High on the verandah outside the principal's office.

He had been summoned, as he often was, to fix a broken chair or table, and he walked up to the administrative building with a tool bag. He whistled as he walked, forgetting for a minute that his voice carried, and the students, easily distracted, would look through the windows at him. Pauline stood on the verandah, breaking into a smile as he walked toward her.

"What you doing here?"

"Come to look for you."

"You disappeared on me."

"Just didn't come out this way for a while. And since I never had any way to find you, I come up here to look for you."

"Glad to see you."

"Sometimes you have to take a chance," Pauline said.

Lenworth knew without asking that she meant taking a chance with him.

"All right," he said, and with that word it was settled.

❧

Three days later, under a cloud-filled sky, Lenworth and Opal went by bus to Black River. Opal sat on Lenworth's lap, her face to the window, her eyes glued to the shifting shades of green in the hillsides and the valleys, and her finger pointing out women walking to or from a market or farm with a full basket balanced perfectly on their heads. A cotta, a circular pad of banana leaves, the only thing between the baskets and their heads. She pointed to a donkey pulling a cart, a rarity in those days even for Lenworth. Through town after town, there was something else that held her gaze.

How little he had exposed her, Lenworth thought, and he realized that most of what Opal had learned outside of school had come from Sister Ivy.

"We soon reach?" Opal looked up at him, her eyes so brown, so like her mother's that he looked away immediately.

"Soon."

Pauline was there in front of the bakery as she had said. She led them to a taxi, which took them away from the sea and the river, up a road filled with potholes to a small community clinging to life. Chickens roamed the yard, pecking at the dirt, and from further away he heard the distinct squeals of a pig.

"Everybody waiting," Pauline said.

Indeed, her parents were on the verandah, her mother standing with her back bent slightly as she leaned forward to hold up a tottering child. And her father, in an undershirt and stained pants, looked up at Lenworth with a probing gaze. Only then did he think he should have brought something, whether a bunch of bananas or plantains, or pears or breadfruits or a set of bowls he had made. Almost immediately he dismissed the thought, for he didn't want her family to think he was buying their approval.

"Good afternoon, sir." Lenworth held out his hand, pulled Opal forward. But she wouldn't budge, simply stood behind him and peeped around his legs at the three strangers and baby.

One by one Pauline's sisters came, and they too looked at him as if he were an unusual specimen or such a rarity for a sister to take a man home to meet the family.

"So, the little girl, what happen to her mother?" Pauline's mother stopped cooing at the child long enough to ask about Plum.

"Died in childbirth," he mouthed, and nodded thanks for the belated condolences. He had also come to expect the look of pity directed at Opal.

"Anchovy, eh? Long time I don't go that way." Pauline's father spoke. "Used to go that way all the time. You know a fellow name Thomas White?"

"No."

"He used to own an auto parts shop."

"No. Can't say I know him." Lenworth's heart quickened. He expected more questions like this, more indirect probing of his life and story. It wouldn't take much, he knew, for his story to fall apart.

"He probably gone long time now."

"Anchovy where your people from?"

How skillfully he got around the details. "Had a granduncle named Orville Ramsey, who had property out there from the '30s or early '40s. His house I living in now. Old house with problems, but when you starting out . . ."

On he went, sifting the truth, establishing himself as motherless and without siblings, a hard-working carpenter and general handyman. "Next time, I'll bring you one of the bowls I make. Coconut shell," he said. "So pretty when you polish it."

But that would be Lenworth's only trip to Black River. He left with Pauline, who packed her life into two bags and glided away from her parent's house and her plump and satisfied sisters.

Pauline was nothing like Plum, an inadequate replacement really. Lenworth realized early on that the woman he had married was a version of his sister and mother. She had no independent goals; her identity now was simply wife. She had waited her whole life for this, not him necessarily, but a man to give her the role she thought she was groomed to play. At that moment, Lenworth was content to let her play that role, if only to give Opal the mother he thought she deserved, and hold at bay Opal's questions about the bird woman who disappeared.

And even Opal seemed instinctively to know Pauline's inadequacies. She would not smile at Pauline. Instead, like she did as a baby, she looked at the spaces around Pauline as if she still expected to see someone else there—a bird woman with wings, perhaps.

3

Plum lived her life in limbo, like a planet in orbit outside its solar system, waiting light years to fall back into its rightful place. Living and not living, waiting to be summoned back to Jamaica, dropping everything and going when called, coming back to Brooklyn empty-handed one, two, three times. Each time, she picked up little shards of Lenworth's life, some pieces too small to matter, some large and useful, leaving her breathless.

On her third trip, one she took on her own without the summons of the private investigator, she stayed for four days in a cottage in Reading, a small town on the outskirts of Montego Bay and just off the main road to Negril. Three of the four days, she drove to towns along the coast—Falmouth, Ocho Rios, Port Maria—and into the hills, up to Brown's Town where she and Lenworth had briefly lived, and on to Lluidas Vale and Linstead.

Eight years later, Mrs. Murray's yard was much the same, like a garden painted by an artist, the blooms exaggeratedly bright. The flame of the forest trees that dwarfed the house were in full bloom. Where Mrs. Murray had had a hedge of roses, she now had ixora boasting small bunches of red and peach flowers. Spread around the yard were flowering bougainvillea and hibiscus, with red and pink and yellow blooms, and on the verandah were anthuriums, six of them, each with a rare purple flower.

"Look at you." Mrs. Murray held Plum at arms' length, then pulled her closer in a crushing embrace. "I so glad to see you."

"Glad to see you too."

"You hear anything?"

"Nothing yet."

"Don't give up hope, me chile. As they say, every dog have him day and every puss him four o'clock. His time soon come."

Plum held out a small package. "A thank you. It's not much, but it reminded me of you."

"Thanks, me dear. I just glad to see that you didn't just wither up and do nothing. That alone is a gift."

Like a child, Mrs. Murray shook the box, undid the tiny bow. Inside, on a bed of crinkled tissue, was a corrugated copper cuff bracelet. "Oh. You know me too well."

"Glad you like it."

"Come inside. No use standing out here in the heat. I want to hear everything. Medical technologist, right? Sound so important."

Immediately inside the doorway was a large painting of a woman sitting on a low wall with her head hanging low. Near the woman were two large monkey jars, a heavy wooden front door painted a shade of jade just like the one to the cottage where Plum had lived. The woman in the painting had no face, but the slump of her body told of despair. Plum stepped closer, tracing her fingers on the curve of the woman's back. "That's me, isn't it?"

"Yes. I painted it the day after you left."

"No face?"

"Sometimes the body says it all. And it's the emotion I wanted to convey."

"I see."

"I painted one him, but it was the devil with two horns. Stereotypical."

Plum laughed. "That he wouldn't be able to tolerate."

"Hope you don't mind the painting. Everything in my life inspires me, the good, the bad, and the ugly."

"Not at all. I like it. Puts my life in perspective, you know."

"Good. Well, you know I like my tea. So let me make some and then we can chat. Mint or black tea?"

"Mint."

They passed the afternoon like old friends, Plum reminding herself time after time how far she had come since Mrs. Murray *returned* her to her suspended Brooklyn life. Plum kept coming back to one thing: though she had indeed gone on and lived her life, a part of her life was still suspended, temporarily prevented from moving forward.

Except for the fact that Falmouth and Port Maria had well-known high schools where Lenworth could have sought work and the towns were close enough to Brown's Town, Plum had no specific reason to think that he would have gone to either place. Nonetheless, Plum, in a sundress and ballet flats, walked along narrow sidewalks and shop piazzas with worn and shiny concrete steps, looking through supermarkets and shops, the outdoor markets with their picked-over discount goods, searching among the myriad faces with varying shades of brown skin for a man with eyebrows so thick they came close to meeting in the center of his face, and a goatee. She pictured him with a shaved head or hair cut low to minimize the balding dome.

Each supermarket was mostly the same—poorly-lit with shelves of Milo and Ovaltine and sweet spiced buns; flour, sugar, and cornmeal in clear plastic bags; soup mixes and sugared drink mixes; boxes of sweet potato and plantain (both ripe and green), the smell of thyme so strong she thought someone must have accidentally crushed a bunch under foot.

He always liked a bargain, loved the business of haggling down a price, loved to haggle just for the sake of it. But not Plum; she wanted a price, a fair one, and saw no reason she, or any customer for that matter, should expect to negotiate just for the sake of it. So she went to the outdoor markets where haggling was common and searched the faces of the shoppers, hopeful for a glimpse of him. It was a desperate act, really, and she knew the futility of such a search. But she felt compelled to do something, to look at random faces in random towns, hopeful for something that would end her years-long search.

And at the end of each evening, before beginning the long drive back along the coast to the cottage outside Montego Bay, she sat in the car with eyes closed concentrating on breathing deeply, counting each inhalation and exhalation as if breathing were a lesson one needed to be taught. One, two. One, two. She learned this in high school, how to hold back grief, how to not let disappointment overwhelm, but promptly forgot that lesson immediately after Lenworth disappeared. Immediately after Lenworth left, and even now, she let the grief rip her apart, let the tears and the screams come rather than bottling them inside. But now she breathed and trapped her grief, one, two. One, two. One, two.

Composed at last, eyes and cheeks dry. She looked in the rear-view mirror and smiled, a slight reminder that everything would be all right. Then Plum was on her way back on the winding hillside roads—looking from the hilltop for the azure waters and white sands emerging as if they'd been hidden behind a curtain—cruising along coastal roads that bifurcated swamps, with the air conditioner off and the breeze whipping around the car; flying past the road to her aunt's house in Lakeside Park, thinking that she should stop and visit, thinking too of her aunt's direct and indirect reminders of Plum's youthful missteps, but continuing past the road to the anonymity of the cottage in Reading.

◆

Driving around like that reminded Plum of day trips she took with Alan in his parents' car to towns outside of Brooklyn—along the coast of Long Island, the New Jersey shoreline, upstate New York, and south to Delaware and Baltimore and Maryland's eastern shore. Alan wanted to see how others lived outside the confines of a concrete city, and Plum went along, partly to escape her parents. Plum and her parents lived two separate lives. Fully an adult, she lived in their house as if she was still waiting to belong to them again, waiting for them to welcome her fully back in their lives. They had. But Plum, still feeling like the girl abandoned on the island, still feeling like the girl abandoned in the hospital, kept her life distinctly separate from theirs.

Whenever Alan presented an escape, Plum accepted, knowing all the time that his motivations differed from hers. Alan was persistent, but not pushy. He never called them dates, just drives. They would sit in the bridge walkway that connected two buildings on campus, with a map between them, and pick a town within a four-hour drive. Plum packed sandwiches and drinks, and they'd leave early on a Saturday morning, just when the city was beginning to wake. Between them, they had just enough money for gas and tolls, nothing for emergencies, nothing for extra activities.

They talked about everything and nothing, Plum more careful than carefree in what she revealed about herself, cryptic even.

Once, Alan asked, "Why do you hate men?"

"Why do you think I hate men?"

"Well, maybe not men. Why do you hate me?"

"I don't hate you. I wouldn't be here with you in a town where I don't know anybody if I hated you." She paused. "Only one person I can say with absolute certainty that I hate."

"Why? What did he do to you?"

"You assume it's a man."

Alan laughed. "Yes, I know it's a man. What did he do?"

"Too long a story to tell."

"Two more hours before we reach. You have plenty time."

Plum turned to the window, her gaze on the vehicles whizzing past in the opposite direction, working through how to tell Alan about Lenworth and her lost child. But she didn't know where to begin, how to say without crying exactly what the mystery man had done and why, what specifically she was carrying with her and would carry with her forever. *It's simple,* she wanted to say. *He took my daughter.* But there was nothing simple about it, not the actual taking of the child, not the way he left her, not the heartache, the fruitless searches. She wiped away a tear and turned her head back to the passenger window.

"You don't have to talk about it if you don't want to."

She didn't. The moment lengthened, the silence becoming increasingly uncomfortable.

"You'll tell me one day for sure."

"How you so sure 'bout that?"

"Because one day, you're going to marry me. And when I'm your husband, you will tell me everything."

"You so sure of yourself."

"At least I made you smile."

Plum did indeed smile, but even then she knew that underlying Alan's lighthearted shift of the conversation were his deep feelings for her.

On another of those day trips, three years after they'd first met in a biology class, Alan had asked, "Why don't you just marry me?"

They were on Chincoteague Island, along the Virginia shoreline watching for the famous wild ponies. Plum didn't care for the po-nies, the swarms of wild birds, or the flat, brackish land. When she thought of an island, she pictured palm and coconut trees, a yard with an almond tree, white sand beaches, cliffs rising up from the ocean, a blue rather than black sea spread out before her.

Plum waited a moment, reached for Alan's hand. "Ask me again in a year," she simply said, prolonging the cat and mouse game, dangling herself but not committing to anything at all.

Plum's reason was simple: She wasn't ready to open herself up to the possibility of another heartbreak. She had rightly concluded from Alan's persistence that he would wait. He did indeed ask a year later after they had graduated, and another year later, and each time Plum moved the goalposts another year out. "Give me another year. I want to know for sure because there is no leaving after." That Plum was certain about, she didn't want to be left again. And there was no room in her heart or her soul just yet to love another the way she had loved Lenworth.

𝒟

Plum spent her last day in the cottage at Reading—a lazy Sunday—on the beach sifting through the sand for intact shells she planned to stack in bottles with sand. That evening, her hair damp and skin tin-gling from overexposure to the sun, Plum sat on the verandah with a small transistor radio by her side. A man's deep baritone came across. She preferred music to the talk shows, a preference honed during her teen years in Jamaica. In a sense, it was defiance. Plum hated what her aunt liked, and her aunt liked to listen to the nu-merous calls and complaints—whether about potholes, a fire station without a fire truck, firefighters who couldn't or wouldn't come to a burning house because they lacked water, the day's political scandal. The complaints all sounded the same. Years later, Plum knew she would come to the same conclusion she had as a teen: no matter the political party in power, the government had failed its people.

Plum reached for the knob on the radio.

"Sunday Contact." The radio host's voice was a rich baritone, one that made her think of sultry love songs on late night radio. "Find family and friends at home and abroad."

Plum paused, her body turned to the radio, her heart dancing to its own two-step. One-two. One-two. This wasn't one of the typical daytime-call-in radio shows, where callers listed their litany of complaints against the government and public servants and underfunded public works departments, or gave their own version of governing that they were sure would solve the country's ills.

Plum counted each breath, stood up, paced the small verandah, and switched from counting breaths to counting steps. Counting, as simple as it was, calmed her. She waited. A female caller gave simple details. *We called him Trevor. He used to work at an auto mechanic shop near the Duncans police station. His brother in England trying to reach him for five years now. Can't get a hold of him.* And another. *My mother took me to Jamaica when I was a baby. She thought I would be handicapped and she brought me and left me down here. Just left me in the hospital. Children's home I grow up in. I have my birth papers, born in Bronx, New York. Want to know my people.* And another. *I called last week from Hanover looking for my brother, my father's son. Tuesday he call me, tell me a friend hear the name and thought it was him. I just want to thank you.* And another. *My name is Rohan Bailey. But she wouldn't know me by that name. Growing up everybody call me Everton Bailey. Is not till I ready to take CXC that I find out my real name was Rohan. I come to understand that she have a youth for me, and I want to know my flesh and blood.* One after another, the callers gave details of the individuals they wanted to find, sometimes giving full names, sometimes aliases, sometimes just a tenuous connection to a place or a rumor of where the person could have gone. Again and again, the host asked for a number listeners should call.

Plum wrote down everything she knew about Lenworth, at least all the details she thought to be true: name, last known where-abouts, occupation, places he may have lived, that he would likely have an eight-year-old girl. In writing, she made note as well of all she didn't know: the teachers' college he attended, where exactly he was born and raised and where exactly he had lived before coming to Brown's Town. She dialed the number and listened too long to the busy signal. She dialed, again and again and again. Each time it was the same. One more time, she told herself. She had stopped counting the number of times she dialed the number, stopped worrying about the cost of the telephone calls. Until at last the baritone voice spoke back to her. Through tears, a nervous Plum told what she knew.

"Ah, so sad, eh."

The host sounded like he was next to Plum, leaning in to hear the rest of the story. Though she knew the image in her mind was wrong, Plum pictured him the way her doctor sat, elbows on his knees, eyes on her, her story the only thing that mattered in that moment.

"Eight years without knowing," the host said. "That's a long time to go on without knowing."

"Yes." Plum was close to tears.

"Lenworth Barrett, last known address was Brown's Town in St. Ann." The host repeated the details Plum had given. "May have lived in Greenwood and has an eight-year-old girl. The girl's moth-er, Plum Valentine, wants to find her daughter." He paused for a second as if he, too, needed to catch his breath. "Give us a number where callers can reach you."

Plum gave her own Brooklyn number and waited.

4

A month later, a breathless Plum hurried through the long corridor toward customs and immigration like a surgeon on a life-saving mission, zipping around wheeled bags, slow walkers, and businessmen in suits coming to the island for meetings. Her sandals slapped the tile and her heels, each thwack seeming loud and obnoxious in the cavernous hall. But Plum didn't slow her pace. Instead, she relocated the duffel bag she carried slung on her shoulder and pressed up under her arm, pushing her arms through the straps so the bag sat on her back like a knapsack. The bag itself was light, for she had packed hurriedly with two days' notice, rolling up five T-shirts, two pairs of jeans and two summer dresses, and wrapping a pair of sandals in plastic. She didn't need much—not even a bathing suit or beach wrap or her preferred box of tea.

Like puzzle pieces, the details came together after Plum's call to *Sunday Contact*. Some bits were useful, some not, but the most promising had come on a Tuesday morning before Plum left for her afternoon shift, from a woman who said she went to school in Greenwood with a Lenworth Barrett. "Sound like the same person you describe. Light complexion. Brows thick. Average height but he probably didn't finish growing. We were teenagers, you know."

"When I knew him, he was already a man," Plum said. "Thin build. Probably five-foot-ten. Had a scar across his forehead."

"Don't remember a scar. But could be him same one. Same habit of disappearing. All these years I couldn't figure out what happened to him. He sat right beside me in class. Middle of the school year and he just never came back. Desk sat there in the middle of the classroom empty for the rest of the year. We imagined all sorts of things about what happened to him."

Plum, nervous and breathless, asked, "What school you say that was?"

"William Knibb in Falmouth."

With that single detail, Plum called the private investigator who in turn called Plum back with something else: the name of the family that had registered Lenworth in school. Not his parents, but the couple with whom he had been living then. Two days later, the detective's telephone message was simple, "I have some good news. Come as quickly as you can."

Packing and going to Jamaica with so little notice also meant her parents had little time to object. Plum didn't mind at all. Having more time would have meant a prolonged argument, her spilling the excuse she gave at work for the sudden trip: her mother badly injured in a serious car accident and her condition grave. Plum had taken a week of vacation she hadn't yet earned, leaving open the possibility that her stay may be prolonged if her mother's condition didn't improve. She didn't want to tell her parents any of that, but when they asked how she would pay for it, she allowed them one secret: she had saved $50 from every paycheck she'd earned since her return to Brooklyn for this very scenario. And nothing they said would prevent her going to Jamaica to follow on a lead, even if she didn't have the full details.

Outside, Kingston greeted Plum with a whiff of hot air and sunshine so intense she shaded her eyes with a flat palm. She allowed herself a brief moment to suck in the air and wait for a breeze to come in off the nearby sea. But Plum felt nothing like the breeze she remembered coming off the coast in Discovery Bay. Here the air was still, stifling; in Discovery Bay the breeze was a balm even on hot summer days.

Ahead, the rental car agent's ponytail bobbed—the length of hair that dipped up and down her back unnaturally shiny and unnaturally long for a dark complected woman. Plum quickened her strides and caught up with the agent, matching the woman's efficiency. They looked around the car, Plum shadowing the agent, double checking for visible scratches and dents.

"Enjoy your stay," the agent said, with a little wave of her hand.

With a toot of the horn, Plum was off, heading to an office in New Kingston where the private investigator waited. What exactly he had to say, she didn't know. She had missed his calls and he hers. Three missed calls later—two of which Plum made to the detective—Plum simply left a message that she would come to hear the details of the life Lenworth had gone on to build without her.

Kingston wasn't familiar to Plum. She had spent her time on the north coast, weekdays at a boarding school for girls and every third weekend and longer holidays at her aunt's home in Discovery Bay. The city across the harbor was a dull blur, a place she was interested in only for the information it would yield. Later, she wouldn't remember much of Kingston, with its mix of high-rise buildings and tenements and mansions threatening to topple from the hillsides and ringing the flat city. But she would congratulate herself for following the directions she had written out with diligence and care, making her way through a crowded foreign city and finding the office in New Kingston.

David Murray wasn't what Plum had expected. He was thin, wiry, unlike his mother's squat frame, with eyes that bored into her as if he could read her thoughts.

"Pleasure to meet you after all this time," he said.

His hand was rough in Plum's and stronger than Plum imagined for a man so thin.

"I'm so grateful for all that you're doing. You don't know how much it means."

"Trust me, I understand. I can't imagine how much this hurt, but I understand. All right, down to business."

He alternated between perfect English and patois in a way that Plum couldn't. In her head, she sometimes spoke in patois, but when she opened her mouth and tried, she mostly sounded exactly like she didn't want to sound—like a foreigner trying on a foreign language or dialect, and failing.

David laid out a photo. "His mother." He tapped the picture. "This is where he grew up."

He pushed a second photo across the table. Plum leaned forward for a closer look, then lifted the pictures, her hands sweaty with nervous energy, her body still feeling the movement of the car. It was just a house set back in a yard with scattered tufts of grass and a gravel walkway, a small verandah with what looked like red tile on the floor. A single chicken pecking at the dirt was the only living thing in sight.

"Where?" Plum asked.

"Woodhall," David said, then added the parish, "Clarendon. A constable out there took these photos."

"Clarendon?" Plum closed her eyes, muttered "Clarendon" again. "No sah." She too sprinkled in the patois. "He never mentioned Woodhall at all. Not even one time. He talked about Lluidas Vale and Greenwood. But never Woodhall."

"I'm betting his mother knows where he is."

Plum allowed herself a smile. She nodded. "She must know, yes." The way she said it, angling her head with her brow knitted, Plum sounded and felt like her mother. Each nod of her head punctuated what she thought: Finding his mother and the family home meant finding Lenworth and her daughter.

"We can leave early in the morning, about six," he said.

"No, no. I want to go now."

He clucked his teeth. "Have a client I have to meet this afternoon. So not before tomorrow morning."

Plum looked up from the photo at him, the bemused look on his face, the giddy satisfaction of unearthing a clue and putting a puzzle together. "No, I want to go alone."

"Plum, you don't know these country roads. Nothing like the smooth highways you used to in the States. You not going to find street signs and house numbers. I mean, out in the deep country what we call a road you might think is just a donkey path. So better you wait till morning when we have all day."

"I know," she said, thinking of her teenage years traversing the countryside with an aunt who thought it her duty to remind Plum that her life was fortunate compared to others. "I have to go alone. It's . . . I want to talk to her mother to mother. Just me and her."

"Then let me call up to Chapelton, get a constable friend to escort you to the house."

"No police. No uniforms. I don't want to threaten her. Just want an easy conversation with just me and her."

"All right then."

He wrote directions, his hand moving across the sheet slowly, rounding letters and perfecting slants. "When you get off the main road you going to have to ask for directions. And leave before nightfall. I wouldn't want you trying to find your way in the dark on roads you don't know."

Plum wasted no time heading out of Kingston, following turn after turn, until she was on the highway to Spanish Town, driving past acres of cane plants, the thin green leaves waving in the breeze, the rich red dirt vibrantly colorful in the tropical sun. How she missed the island, the countryside especially, the stillness of an afternoon, the sea breeze lapping at her face through an open car window, winding down a hillside road, looking out and still being surprised at what she knew was there: the deep blue sea in the distance with its limitless possibilities, a perfect view. How she missed her aunt's house, the expansive almond tree whose branches had grown out instead of up, spreading so wide the tree resembled an oversized mushroom sheltering the lawn between the gate and the verandah. At fifteen years old, it was where she sat afternoon into evening, pining for Brooklyn, the city from which she had been expelled and to which she had reluctantly returned. But now, nothing of her life in Brooklyn measured up to her memories of wasted afternoons under the almond tree.

That afternoon, the windows down, warm air swirling around the car, familiar scents wafting in and out, Plum felt hopeful, as vibrant and alive as the bougainvillea and hibiscus blooms in the sun, as colorful as the croton plants in just about every yard. She wanted fruit but didn't stop for the roadside vendors, just drove on as if maneuvering around the ruts on the road and the deep corners was part of her everyday life.

Plum was lucky to find the house from the hand-drawn map and question after question to passing strangers. Plum looked down at the photo and up at the house, at the yellow paint on the outer walls, the blue on the verandah, and the red floor. A woman was on the verandah, Lenworth's mother—finally a connection to him.

The old lady stood up, set aside a sieve on which she rubbed dried pimento berries to remove the stems. "Good afternoon. You look like you lost. You looking for somebody?"

"Good afternoon, ma'am. Yes, it's you I'm looking for."

"Me?"

"Well, really your son."

"Which one?"

"Lenworth."

"Who looking for him?"

"My name is Plum Valentine. I knew him a long time ago."

The old lady looked her up and down, leaned around to look at the late-model car, a compact Toyota, and back again at Plum, her hair, her face, her clothes. "Years now I don't set eyes on him. Don't know where him gone. If he dead or alive, I couldn't tell you."

Defeated, deflated, Plum covered her face in her hands, and pressed her fingers into her eyes to stanch the tears. "No, no, no." Plum hadn't imagined this outcome at all, wouldn't have conceived of Lenworth abandoning his mother as he had abandoned Plum.

"Come, come." His mother grasped her arm. "Come out of the sun. You look like you 'bout to fall down and me too ol' to lift you up."

Plum moved, her legs like anchors, her body limp. In the yard behind the house, a child chased a chicken with a stick. The chicken, squawking, tried to fly.

"Boy, leave the fowl alone and find something to do." Turning to Plum, she said, "Them children setting to give me pressure."

Out of the sun, Plum looked the old lady over, picking out the features that Lenworth had got from her—the nose for sure, and the eyebrows. Not the body frame. Where he was squat, his mother was tall and thin, like an aged ballerina, Plum thought.

"Eight years now I looking for him," Plum said.

"'Bout that time since I last see or hear from him. Last time I see him he come and tell me he 'bout to give me grandbaby. Never did meet the mother or the grandbaby."

"Granddaughter," Plum said. "We had a girl."

"Oh, you the mother?"

"Yes."

His mother looked at her as if she expected more, perhaps bad news or Plum turning around to call the girl from the car.

"It's the only grandpickney I don't know. You have a picture?"

"No, no picture."

"Who she favor? You or him?"

Plum hesitated, looked his mother over. Tears welled up again, floating on the rim of her lids. "I don't know." Then Plum told her exactly how Lenworth had left her in the hospital and taken her daughter with him, a story no mother wanted to hear about her son.

"What you telling me? Lenworth do that? My Lenworth?" She shook her head, pressed her elbows on her knees and looked intently at the floor. She was as surprised as Plum at how he had left and taken the baby girl. "I would never imagine he would do such a thing. And he never say nutten?"

"Not a word. All these years, I've been looking for him. This is the closest I've come to finding him."

"Me can't believe it. All this time I thinking he turn big man and just shame o' his family, shame o' where him come from. But you telling me something different. He just shame o' what he do. Never think I would raise a son as worthless as that. He turn criminal."

"If ever you hear from him, I beg you, let me know."

"Mi dear, you nuh have to ask." His mother leaned forward a little and patted Plum's knee, the pungent scent of pimento wafting toward Plum's nose. "But if I see him, I'd probably beat him first. No, no. Don't laugh."

Plum looked up at the thick, grey clouds moving swiftly into place and out where pockets of pitch suggested that the road had once been asphalted and smooth. She wrote her telephone number and address on scrap paper, hoping as she did that his mother would soon have some good news. Plum said a quick goodbye and returned to the rented car and the maps and the long drive back on roads that looked like river beds, over cavernous potholes, and up across the Dry Harbor Mountains to the north coast. Coming away again empty-handed, no closer to finding Lenworth or her daughter. Tears blurred her vision as much as the raindrops on the windshield.

5

L enworth should not have been hers. Plum didn't tell his mother
that detail, nor did she tell how she and Lenworth met. Plum
saved for herself the little details: she and Lenworth on the verandah
of her aunt's house in Discovery Bay, Plum stealing glances at her
tutor's generous eyebrows, his milky-brown complexion, heavy eyelids, eyes more round than oval and the goatee framing his chin. He
was twenty-three, she sixteen, and by her calculation appropriate-
ly-aged—barely an adult but still worlds away from the boys her age.

Plum kept to herself how she first lost Lenworth during the Easter break, not long after they met. A complete misunderstanding
of the adults. That Easter afternoon, boys across the neighborhood
flew homemade kites, which whooped and buzzed as they dipped
and rose, sometimes as delicately as a bird and sometimes with exaggerated swoops. Plum sat in the front yard, beneath the expansive
almond tree.

Lenworth tried to project a serious voice, to distract her from
the kites' buzzing and whooping. But Plum, sixteen years old, had a
teen's apathy toward algebra and trigonometry and chemistry. And
she had even greater apathy toward the adults inside—her aunt Dolores, or Didi for short, and her parents, who recently flew to Jamai-

ca from Brooklyn to check on her progress and see for themselves whether she deserved the reward they dangled: spending the entire summer vacation in New York.

Inside, Plum's aunt distilled the stories her parents had heard in lesser detail by phone and letter. Plum had no voice in the storytelling, and was too distracted by the kites' coordinated dips and swoops to think too much about what her aunt would be saying and her parents comprehending.

Lenworth, realizing the futility of continuing, put the book aside. "What is it?"

"What?"

"No use in wasting their money or my time."

Plum stood, shook the cramps out of her legs, and pressed her toes into the soft grass. "They already expect the worst of me anyway," she said.

"All right then. Get it off your chest so we can continue." Lenworth put the books down and listened to Plum tell of being sent away like a bag of old clothes, unwanted and useless.

"Agency," Lenworth had said. He leaned back on the grass, his palms cupping his head, his toes pointed upward. "You and me both. We learn early what it means to have no agency and the exact opposite of it."

"Agency?" Plum pondered the word.

"Yes. Control over your life."

Perhaps it was the dizzying movement of the kites, the afternoon breeze coming off the nearby sea, the ease with which they spoke, but neither heard the adults stepping outside onto the tiled verandah or padding barefoot across the grass.

"Really!" Dolores's voice was high. "This what I paying you for, to loll about on the grass like tourist on holiday?"

"I was just explaining," Lenworth began.

"Explaining what? That's how you do math? I know she don't want to do the work but you should know better. I not paying you to be her friend. I paying you to teach the girl, to help her pass the exams." She turned around, not easing her voice, and repeated it all, as if Plum's parents hadn't also witnessed him lying about looking out from under the tree canopy at the kites, the dizzying movement of color against the blue sky.

"It's just . . ." is all he could say, for her aunt didn't let up, didn't pull back her harsh criticism of lazy loafers who want to get by without doing the work.

"Don't even think I paying you for today. Don't even think it."

"It's just . . ." he said again.

"You still here. Pack up your things and leave. Go."

And so Lenworth went out of her life as quickly as he had come.

Plum didn't think about his absence until a September afternoon, five months later, when he reappeared under the jacaranda tree at her school, sipping and spitting up a milky tea. By then, she was seventeen, in her last year of high school and imaging herself a woman living a life somewhere other than Discovery Bay, and he, a temporary assistant in the chemistry lab, working there to save toward his engineering degree. They picked up where they left off that Easter afternoon, bonding over tea and building a friendship that hadn't fully taken off during their first meetings, resurrecting it and letting it mature in secret.

He had taken to eating his lunch under the jacaranda tree and sipping hot tea in the afternoon sun. Though inexplicable to Plum, the hot drink in the hot afternoon cooled him. The afternoon they met again, the kitchen staff had got his tea wrong; it was sweetened with condensed milk. She caught him with spit dribbling on his chin, and without a tissue or a handkerchief to wipe it away. She smiled and handed him a tissue.

"Too bitter?" she asked.

"Condensed milk. I hate the taste of it."

"It's too hot for tea anyway."

"The hot drink cools your body down."

"No way."

"I teach science, remember?" He smiled as he spoke. "I read it in a magazine. If you drink a hot drink, it lowers the amount of heat stored inside your body. And it causes you to sweat more. You know this part. Sweat cools your body."

Plum raised her eyebrows. "Really."

"It's simple. A hot drink makes you sweat and sweat cools the body."

Plum sat on the empty corner of the bench, stretching her legs out before her as if settling in for a long afternoon's rest. "Fruit teas are better," she said. "Orange, sorrel. And ginger root. I can't have it here, of course. But it's the one thing that would make my life at this school a little bit better."

So day after day he brought her tea in a thermos, and the two oblivious to or unconcerned about gossip from students, sipped fruit or ginger tea together under the jacaranda tree. The bench where they sat looked down on the town sprawled below, the rusting zinc sheets atop the buildings, the minibuses picking up and dropping off passengers, higglers at the market haggling over produce and fruit and discount wares. Like a prisoner teased with freedom, Plum looked down on a whole life outside the gates of the school that she, as a boarder, sampled only on the third weekend when the boarders left the school for home. She longed to be back in Brooklyn, free to wander after school, free to stop in a shop for a candy bar or soda or pizza.

The ease with which they talked. Of her school. Of her parents. Of her wish to be back in Brooklyn, if only for an Easter or Christmas dinner, in a house overrun with family and friends, cousins fighting over toys that weren't theirs, her father's and uncles' boisterous laughter booming over the din of the television. Of his dream to build a bridge to replace the island's infamous Flat Bridge, which could accommodate a single line of traffic at a time and which flooded several times a year when heavy rain and debris swelled the river that flowed beneath. He imagined a replacement bridge with a higher clearance above the water or a crossing at another point in the gorge.

He liked the way she spoke, the hint of a foreign accent, her matter-of-fact manner. She didn't say "mister" or "sir" as the other students did, but spoke to him as if they were equals, not teacher and student, not liberated adult and young adult. Yet, they weren't *equal*. She was a student, not directly his student, but a student nonetheless, and a child he had once tutored at her aunt's request.

What shouldn't have begun, began as an afternoon kiss on the beach on one of Plum's weekends home with her aunt in Discovery Bay. A simple kiss near a sea grape tree on a beach used mostly by fishermen. Plum, never shy, turned shy, then bold again. He, never much of a romantic, driven mostly by an urge to build objects from useless things, became a different man, one emboldened, capable now of feeling love. Plum was everything he hadn't known.

Plum had only one tangible memory of that outing, a photo of Lenworth standing with his back to the water, his hands akimbo. She kept the photo in a tin with one other piece of paper that connected her to her early life with him. In reality, she had mimicked his pose, laughing as she did. But Plum didn't have that corresponding photo of her, her eyes nearly closed, her head thrown back and the length of her neck exposed. Beach outings on Plum's free weekends home became their thing. Plum liked the quiet mornings on the beach. It was the one outing to which her aunt didn't object because she understood the confines of boarding school life and the freedom of looking at and moving in the open sea. Besides, her aunt knew the woman who managed the beach, and she trusted that there Plum would be safe. And Lenworth made it his thing too, sometimes bringing sugar buns or plantain tarts for their early beachside breakfasts. If there were adults around, like the woman who managed the beach, he pretended that he had come for the water aerobics class.

The ease with which they played, romping on the sand like care-free children or lovers, she stopping where the waves brushed up against the sand, too afraid of the tangle of moss on the sea bed to wade into the water after him, he swimming out and waving from a distance, beckoning for her to join him. Sometimes if they were on the side of the beach where the moss wasn't a thick bed on the floor, she did.

Another Easter weekend, they had gone to Puerto Seco Beach, which on an Easter day was overrun with children and adults who had waited all year for the Easter Monday beach outing. So they had walked away from that public beach, around the broken fence to the free beach, past the lone fisherman mending a boat and the others who had come to the free beach rather than pay to swim and play at the moss-free, rock-free beach, and on to the edge of the community of villas perched on rocks above the coastline.

Her T-shirt, wet then, flattened against her stomach, and he saw for the first time the outline of her swelling belly.

The ease with which they fought. Because she hadn't told him. Because she had waited too long (three months along, she thought). Because her life, and his, would be utterly and completely altered.

But they made a plan. He went back with Plum to her aunt's house, the very house from which he had once been expelled and forced out of her life. Plum changed from a sundress to a T-shirt and shorts. Her belly was pressed delicately against a white T-shirt, the baby announcing itself to the world.

"Lawd, Jesus." Plum's Aunt Didi threw up her hands. "Look what trouble you bring here now. This is what you come to tell me?" She didn't wait for Lenworth to answer. "Child, how far along are you? Four, five months?" Plum's answer wasn't what she wanted. "You talk to your parents? They need to know before they come down here for your graduation and come to see this. Lawd."

She turned to Lenworth. "You better have something good to say, because this is not what I hired you for. You know what, you better leave. Just leave. Go. You can deal with her father when he comes."

Plum kept quiet. Her aunt didn't know, and Plum didn't reveal, that she and Lenworth had reconnected because of his work at her school. She preferred to let her aunt and her parents believe that she had defied their wishes and continued to see Lenworth in private. Her parents punished Plum's defiance. They didn't come at all for her graduation, simply cancelled their tickets and Plum's return ticket, leaving her to make her way with him, and leaving him without a platform from which to speak his intentions. Not that his intentions mattered in the end.

6

Had Plum found Lenworth and come to Anchovy then, she would have found a tomboyish girl with dimples like Plum's, almond-shaped eyes that were too brown to belong to someone with such dark skin. Had Plum come then, she would have found a not-yet-sophisticated Pauline worrying about the plumbing in the old house, the tank nearly empty of water, the duck ants again making nests along the wall, the springy floor boards in the tiny living room, termites that were slowly eating away the wood in the house. And she would have found the little girl who would not smile at Pauline, the tomboy of a girl who wandered off with the neighborhood boys as if there was something out beyond the house waiting to be found by her.

And she would have found Lenworth embroiled in another scandal, the circumstances somewhat similar to hers: a school employee and a student caught up in a friendship that seemed too close, a school staff rooting around for the truth, a girl clamming up and protecting him to the very end, and Pauline aware of the sketchy details of the school's inquiry, boiling with anger.

The house in Anchovy was too close, too small really to contain both Pauline's explosive anger and Lenworth's fear of exposure, without the two competing emotions surging and spiraling into a cataclysmic encounter.

Pauline, heavily pregnant and rocking her first-born, Craig, yelled through an open window, alternating between cooing and whispering to the frightened two-year-old and pressing her enormous belly against the window frame as if to catapult her words through the louvers. Pauline and Lenworth had forgotten Opal, who was too young to understand the nature of the quarrel, the possible loss of his carpentering job and too scared to move. So she stood still, a shadow in the shadows, a mute within the muted rooms, tears dripping down her face, her fingers laced together, her feet as stiff as a statue's. She wanted to go to him, the quiet one, but couldn't get her feet to move from within the shadows and propel her body through the lit dining room within reach of Pauline's voice and out to the verandah where her father sat. Opal stayed in the dark, uncomforted, neither savior nor saved.

In truth, Lenworth's situation with the student was not at all the same as his relationship with Plum. The facts that he should have told Pauline: The girl had taken to stopping by his campus workshop on a daily basis. He didn't turn her away. The girl's mother had found a letter to him and she refused to believe that nothing untoward had happened between her daughter and him. Lenworth thought it best to keep quiet lest someone dig deep and find out about him and Plum, the circumstances under which he had left his previous teaching job, and how he had left Brown's Town with the baby girl, how he had abandoned the baby's mother in the hospital.

Instead of fighting and risking exposure, he had walked away from the job and the school and into a verbal brawl with Pauline.

Lenworth stayed outside, still in the shadows, watered by the night's dew, weighing the mistakes of his young life like a ball he rolled from one palm to another. Long after Pauline's rage had subsided and the children had gone to sleep, he slipped into the old chicken coop he'd converted into a workshop and lay down on the new sawdust—cedar and mahogany and pine commingled—which only a day earlier he'd laid down like a bed of moss on the dirt. The limbs of a cherry tree brushed across the roof, and in the distance an owl hooted. Much closer, the night insects chirped away, unconcerned with the other life forms quieting themselves and bedding down for the night. The sky, clear and cloudless, glittered like a sequined dress. He couldn't see anything beyond the circle illuminated by the oil lamp, but he wasn't concerned with the imagined or real thing that lay out there beyond the converted chicken coop. An old sewing machine, whose tabletop had been devoured by termites, stood before the worktable. He envisioned the scrolled metal legs, with Singer stamped across the back support, as part of something else, living a new life far removed from its former one. He hadn't yet determined what it would become. The base of a dining table? The sides of a bench? Sometimes, he still liked to think of himself as an engineer, but in truth he was a former math whiz who once taught high school math and chemistry while he saved for university, and who now worked as a carpenter and knick-knack maker who turned other people's garbage into something of value.

He took the table apart, sawing and breaking the weakened wood, dousing it in gasoline, which he hoped would kill any remaining termites or at least stun them until morning when he could burn the piles of wood. He sanded the rust and paint from the scrolled metal, ran his fingers over the smooth surface he had revealed, then wiped it clean and painted it anew, brushing with quick strokes though he knew it was work best done in daylight when he could see the crevices he had missed, the bubbles of paint he failed to smooth completely. But he worked steadily through the night, moving his hands like a robot calibrated only to move a brush back and forth.

That night, while he worked with the scent of sawdust and paint tickling his nose, he also broke down and rebuilt himself. He took the man Pauline had seemingly discarded, stripped bare his soul, tore apart every bit of his life, the one fact he couldn't dispute—he hadn't discouraged the girl from coming to his workshop—and began rebuilding a man who would indeed be valued. A man who had control over his own life.

While the paint dried, he sketched out the top of the table, trying to decide on a round or square top or a plank of wood that retained the uneven circumference of the tree trunk with its natural grooves and pockets intact. In the end, he chose the circular top with its natural characteristics erased.

By morning, when slashes of sunlight began appearing, when the dew drops still hung on the leaves, when Pauline emerged from the house and looked around the verandah and down the hill for a glimpse of him, he had a plan to save his soul and his family, to remake himself as a carpenter planes and sands and remakes wood, a plan that even the devil couldn't mock.

He would become a priest, remake souls instead of other people's discarded things, make up for his one great sin with a life of pious devotion. And make up for the one life he had irreparably wrecked—Plum's.

He lay down on the sawdust, his nose against the scent he liked, and slept. By the time he woke, the sun was way overhead, the house above the workshop quiet. He brushed the sawdust from his body, cleaned up, bathed away the scent of sawdust and paint, and left for the Baptist Church in Mt. Carey. He took the narrow, rutted, and marl-filled road that emptied out onto the main road and continued along until he reached the slight hill upon which the Baptist Church stood. He waited for the pastor to come, his surety and confidence in his decision to swap his current life for the priesthood building as he waited in the shadow of a palm tree on the rocks that overlooked the stony graveyard. Somewhere below the church lay the bones of one or another of his relatives he hadn't known and whose offspring he wouldn't ever know. He wasn't concerned with progeny, though. Instead, he was concerned with something else he had come to understand: what it meant to have agency, to have the capacity to exert power and control over his life. Despite the scandal threatening to disrupt his life, he felt he had agency, the power to choose another way of living. If he couldn't teach or be an engineer or make do with the life he had built in Anchovy, he would become a priest. Engineering and the priesthood were one and the same, he thought; engineers built foundations for buildings, and priests, likewise, helped congregants build foundations in Christ.

The pastor, the Reverend Alexander Turner, who was also on his way out, didn't bother with pity or judgment. Instead, he laid his hand on Lenworth's head and prayed. In the end, Lenworth's rationalization about engineering and the priesthood being one and the same didn't matter. The pastor, who had his own checkered past, endorsed the plan wholeheartedly, recommended a seminary in Maryland where he had once taught, and fished from a drawer the paperwork to get him started.

"Got this for another young man who changed his mind," the pastor said. "You will make better use of it."

And so Lenworth started on a journey toward a career he never imagined, an escape hatch that took him out of Jamaica to the Maryland suburbs, away from the life he had pulled together in Anchovy and the problem with a student that threatened to mushroom into a permanent stain on his character and life. And so he defied the devil making a mockery of his good intentions, the devil's attempts to muck up the life he had pulled together in Anchovy.

7

Outside, the rain pounded, the droplets tat-tat-tatting against the window and sprinkling through the open bottom half. The sound of the rain blocked out the muted sounds of life rising from the neighborhood streets. Slivers of light slipped in through cracks in the blinds, making shadows on the wall.

Plum moved down the stairs on bare feet, her shoes in hand and a small bag slung over her shoulder. Alan was already outside, double-parked on the tight street, the headlights forming halos in the rain. It was too early to matter how he had parked and where. Plum sprinted, raindrops tickling her skin, her feet tramping through water pooled on the uneven sidewalk and the mud around an oak.

"Morning. Bad day for this." Plum smiled tentatively at Alan, reaching back at the same time to drop her bag on the back seat.

"Never a bad day. It's just rain."

"Too early in the morning for that spiritual talk."

"Still cranky, I see. But I promise. It's not raining there."

There was St. Michael's, a water town on Maryland's Eastern Shore that Alan had picked for the crabs and the water—mostly for the water because Plum liked seaside and riverside towns and he had come to like them too. She could sit by the water for hours, staring out at the flat body, watching birds dip and rise with a beakful of marine life, contemplating the segments of a waterman's life, or by a lazy river listening to the trickle of water over rocks.

They left the city behind. The sky lightened and the rain eased, and before long, the sun filtered through the clouds. Plum closed her eyes, shutting out the uninspiring highway, the abandoned or seemingly abandoned farms that butted up against the Interstate, and the little pockets of modern life visible from the highway.

"Tired," Plum said, abandoning all pretense that she would speak.

Plum hadn't wanted this trip, but Alan, urged on by Plum's parents, had pushed it on her. He pushed the trip for his own personal reasons, and her parents for a less selfish one: Plum was depressed, had been since her return from Jamaica, and they thought that Alan could pull her somehow from that depressive state. She had let him into her life slowly, allowing him to meet her parents and allowing her parents to think that theirs was a serious, concrete relationship. In truth, Plum and Alan were still tangled in a cat and mouse game, Alan continuing to chase his elusive love and Plum shying away from a commitment of any kind.

Plum had come to know this stretch of I-95 well, and she measured how far they had gone by the bumps on the road, the starts and stops for tolls, the shifting sounds of the tires against grates or concrete bridges or asphalt.

Well on the way, deep in the southern part of New Jersey, Alan reached a hand across the gear shaft to Plum's knee. He glanced at her, and back at the road. "What happen? What you so down about?"

"Nothing. Just a part of everyday life."

"It has to be something more specific. Tell me."

"Nothing you can do anything about."

"Maybe I can't fix it. But talking about it might help."

"Not this time."

"I can't take the silence." Alan, who wasn't necessarily talkative, talked on about random things—the violations he wrote up as a public health inspector, how glad he was to be done with inspecting pools now that the summer was over, how badly he wanted another job in public health that didn't involve trekking across the five boroughs, closing a restaurant for multiple violations only to see it reopened in record time with the same staff and a new name.

Plum gave up the pretense of sleeping. "What other type of job would you do?"

"Education. Implementing programs. Studying the impact of some new initiative. Anything that doesn't involve writing violations."

"Go for it," Plum said. "You were always good at analysis anyway."

"I'm looking."

Plum shifted her eyes back to the passenger window, the cars on the opposite side of the road, her mind drifting in the lull back toward her second great disappointment: finding Lenworth's mother but learning nothing about his whereabouts.

"Did I tell you my parents are moving to Fort Lauderdale? Leaving me the house."

"Ah. Big house. At least you won't have a mortgage."

"Yeah. Want to fix it up. Redo the bathrooms and get rid of the carpet. Fixing it up real nice for when you decide to marry me." There was a playfulness about Alan, but a serious note in his voice as well.

"Who says I will?"

"You will."

"Why you so sure?"

"Two reasons. One, despite how you act, you love me. And the second thing, you're here, and always with me. That tells me something."

Plum had no argument for the latter. She was indeed always with him and dependent on his loyalty. "Not ready yet."

"What will make you ready?"

"Just not ready. I'll tell you when." Then, "How will I know that you will not leave?"

"The same way you know I will not deliberately crash this car. Trust."

"That is hard for me."

"I know. And I wish you would trust me enough to tell me why."

"It was a long time ago. A schoolgirl thing."

"And this is an adult thing. Different circumstances. Grown-up people. Grown-up business."

"Yes." But in the parallel, running conversation in her head, Plum added, *and no*, because Alan was roughly the same age as Lenworth had been when he took off and left. What she had with Lenworth had been grown-up business as well.

"I will never force you."

"I know. Just not yet." Once again, she skirted the real reason: She had unfinished business, a daughter she hoped was just a phone call or two away.

That Sunday evening Plum stayed at home, blending sweet potatoes to make a pudding, keeping her fingers busy so as not to think. At seven, the kitchen clean, the pudding in the oven, the mixing bowls and blender put away in their rightful places, Plum went back upstairs to her room at the back of the house. She stood with her back to the door and dialed.

"Sunday Contact."

The voice was what Plum had been waiting for. Still the deep baritone caught her off guard. "Good evening." Her mouth felt as dry as sand, but she pushed the words out, reminded the host of her previous call, thanked him and the listeners who had called with the tidbits of information that had led to Lenworth's mother. "I found his mother. No luck there. She hasn't seen him for just about the same time he disappeared from my life."

"Okay, give me his name again."

"Lenworth Barrett." For the second time, Plum listed the details she knew: Lenworth was born and raised in Woodhall, Clarendon. Lived for a time in Greenwood, Trelawny. Went to William Knibb High School and Moneague Teachers' College. Has an eight-year-old girl.

As he did on Plum's previous call, the host repeated the details Plum had given. And to her, he said, "Tough, eh. Every little detail you can give the listeners will get you closer to finding your daughter. Give us a number where listeners can reach you."

Then she waited.

The morning after, Plum stood at the window, waiting for the phone to ring. She was sure that someone else would call. Within minutes after her call the previous night, calls had started coming in, some with promising details and others with farfetched ideas of where Lenworth could have gone.

Outside, her father was hunched over a ragged garden that was largely weeds and anemic herbs, plucking bell peppers or lackluster cherry tomatoes from two feeble plants. He shouldn't have been home at all. She willed him to stay there in the garden at the back of the brownstone, hidden, out of view of Plum leaving to catch the train to downtown Brooklyn for the afternoon shift. She left earlier than normal and missed the call and message that would change her life forever.

Later, much later, when her parents had already gone to bed, Plum returned, and caught the message that stated simply, "I know a Lenworth Ramsey who lived in Anchovy with a little girl who is about eight years old. Round here, he went by the name Lenworth

Ramsey, but every piece of mail that used to come to him at the post office said Lenworth Barrett."

She jotted the details down, her words on the page like a first grader's nearly illegible scribble. Then she took another sheet and rewrote the details: Lenworth Ramsey, Anchovy.

Plum thought first of Lenworth's mother, and called the telephone number where his mother said messages could be left. And waited again for another response.

A day later, Plum stood with her back to the door, listening to the ringing phone, waiting for someone on the other end to pick up and connect the pre-arranged phone call between Plum and Lenworth's mother. Again, she waited, hung up and called again and again, until at last, she heard the line opening up and a voice saying, "Hello. Good evening."

"Good evening. This is Plum Valentine."

"Yes, yes. She right here. Hold on."

His mother, voice raspy, almost breathless, was anxious to get out what she knew. "Glad you could call. You know my mind run on you the other day."

Plum felt a lightening of her spirit. Her body slackened, hope again bubbling like a spring emerging from the earth.

"Ramsey." His mother continued, her voice quickening as she laid out the possibilities. "His grandmother's name was Ramsey. That his father's mother. And from he turn seventeen he wanted to change his name from Barrett, drop his father name and pick up his granny own. Hate his father and couldn't wait to get rid of his father's name. He even get the deed poll paper and all. He loved his grandmother bad, bad. But not him father at all."

"You really think it could be him?"

"Could be him, yes. His grandmother had people out that way. I don't know where exactly. Could be Hanover or Westmoreland or even Mobay. Not so sure. Just know it was over on that side."

Still, even with the uncertainty, his family's tenuous connection to the western part of the island, his mother had given Plum something on which she could hang her hope: another possible name, another identity. Perhaps she had been searching all the while for a man living under a different name. Those were the details she passed on to the private investigator and again waited for what she thought was inevitable.

8

The scent of jasmine hung in the air, commingling with the scent of fried plantains and the previous night's roast. Plum held an express mail envelope from Jamaica, inside of which was a familiar brown envelope with her typewritten name. She slid her finger beneath the flap, hopeful for a concrete clue.

Inside was a map to a house on a hill in Anchovy. The months and years of searching came down to a sheet of paper from the private investigator with a crudely drawn map pointing the way from the main road, left of the abandoned train tracks, past the secondary school, down a rutted road, a quick left turn and the house upon the hill.

Two days later, Plum was on a plane to Jamaica, pressed up against the window, then rushing again through customs with a single wheeled bag. Outside, the heat embraced her. At another time she would have stood for a moment to let the sun warm her body that was still chilled from the forced indoor air. But she moved quickly to the van and off-site car rental office, then away from the oversized villas sprouting out of the hillside, the hotels overlooking the sea and the tourists so at home in her country in a way that she had never felt in theirs. And then she checked herself, for she was as

American as some of the tourists were but still not as comfortable in her own country as the tourists were in any place they visited.

At Reading, she turned left toward Anchovy. How close she had been on her last trip here. This stretch of road—winding, and dark from trees that towered overhead and filled the gully to the right— wasn't familiar to Plum. She drove slowly, carefully, blowing the horn just before rounding each curve of the road, holding up impatient drivers more familiar with the road. There was no place really to stop and let them pass. On one side was the gully and on the other a wall of damp rocks with ferns and weeds growing from the crevices. Plum pressed on, counting her breaths, her hands tight on the steering wheel.

The road flattened out and houses, small and not as flamboyant as the buildings on the coast, emerged on the left and right. The road, still narrow, wound around corners, until at last it opened up to a commercial stretch. She let the vehicles pass and as she waited bought a drink from a roadside vendor. Then she was on the way again, looking out for the point where the railroad crossed the main, the school, and a road on the left.

Again, Plum practiced her breathing. "I am your mother," she said again and again. "I've been looking for you for a long time now." She didn't know what she would say to him.

The yard was overrun with weeds. The grove of banana and plantain trees and cocoa plants at the bottom of the hill was choked with weeds as well. Plum knew immediately that she wouldn't find him there, but she climbed the hill anyway, hopeful, feeling her way with a stick through the knee-high brush, climbing until she reached the steep stone steps that led up to the wrap-around verandah. To the right of the house was an old chicken coop that someone had built too close to a cherry tree. Perhaps the tree had come after and had grown up and around the chicken coop. It didn't matter. Up the steps. She glanced once to the left and once to the right, her eyes glancing over the chicken coop, catching a glint of metal from within it.

On the verandah, she tested the boards then stepped gingerly, avoiding the slats of wood that looked soft, like pieces that would crumble under her weight. She could see nothing through the windows, and the locks, though they jiggled and felt weak, didn't budge. Plum wasn't certain what the empty house could tell her, but she circled it, walking again through the brush to the back of the house, where someone had once had an outdoor kitchen. The blackened zinc sheets and stones remained, a testament to another life. Beneath the house, in the dark crawl space, she found a forgotten doll, its hair matted and face grungy and missing one of its legs. She caressed it as if it were indeed a child forgotten beneath the house, then cleaned it at the pipe that jutted from the bottom of the large water tank and left it in the sun to dry.

Eight years of active searching had come to this: an abandoned house, an outdoor stove and a doll (signs of a former life, but not necessarily *his* and *hers*), no trace of where Lenworth and her daughter had gone, no trace even of the girl's name. There was no telling how long the house had been empty. Weeks? Months? Years? She wouldn't cry. Instead, Plum forced her disappointment deep within, and buried again the words she had practiced for her little girl.

There was no use in waiting, but Plum waited anyway on the verandah, her arms on the railing, her eyes trained on the hill and the roof of the house in the valley below, her body like that of a woman expecting her family or visitors to appear any minute at the bottom of the hill. Clouds shifted in and out. Smoke rose from an outdoor fire near the house below with the rusted zinc roof. Goats let loose in the morning bleated as they made their way back home. Only when the sun was nearly down did she leave, weaving her way back down the hill in the shadows of the large breadfruit and star apple trees, and back down the long hill past Reading, through the city of Montego Bay and on to a mid-size hotel in Ironshore. She took with her the one-legged doll and an unconvincing conviction that her search would end right there at the house in Anchovy. She had come up empty too many times, and each time she walked away empty-handed she relived that first night, waking to find her baby gone, coming home to a house that was no longer hers, feeling again like a castaway abandoned at the first sign of trouble.

That night would have been her last. What saved her? Perhaps divine intervention. Perhaps the dirty, one-footed doll. She bathed it, wiped the skin clean with cotton balls doused in facial toner and detangled the hair, snipping stubborn knots with tiny manicure scissors, then braiding what remained. A mother without anyone to mother, without even an inkling of who her lost child had become. She left the hotel room for the beach, the vast body of water slapping up against the shore, with a plan to walk out to sea and not return. In the lobby, the hotel manager pulled her wrist and body toward him, dancing her into the night's party on the patio overlooking the beach. The music, which from upstairs had only been a soft pulse, thrummed. He danced her into a circle of tourists, all dancing too fast for the beat, seemingly unaware of the rhythm. Her body betrayed her mind. It moved to the music. Her feet, her arms, her head, her hips, her lips fell in with the changing reggae beats, and she remained in the circle, a dark-skinned woman among the lighter-skinned tourists, teaching them how to feel the rhythm and move with the rhythm instead of against it.

As if they sensed her thoughts and knew her plans, no one left her alone for long. The party host danced her into a corner and across the room, into a circle of tourists who, from the set of their faces, had miscalculated the timing of their exit from the room. And when Plum eventually escaped the music and the movement, the guests staying in the room next to hers fell in as her escorts (or she theirs), walking as a unified group back to their respective rooms. By the time Plum escaped the seemingly endless party, it was too late to sleep, impossible even to quiet the thrum of the music in her head. She had little time left to pack, little time to think about her earlier plan to head out to sea. As if he knew, the concierge called and the staff came to take her bags and send her on her way for the early morning flight.

At the airport, an older woman who was flying for the first time latched onto Plum, telling her about the grandchildren born abroad whom she hadn't yet met, how lonely it was being a grandmother from a distance, limited to sharing second-hand stories with her friends. Plum wanted to share her own pain of being a mother without anyone to mother.

At the check-in counter, Plum changed her mind and her ticket, pushed her return back by two days, re-rented a car and drove back through the city, up the long hill back toward Anchovy.

First, she stopped at the primary school and asked the principal about a Barrett or Ramsey girl.

"What her first name?"

But when Plum couldn't give that, the principal became suspicious and said simply, "I can't give out any information like that."

And back to the houses around the one on the hill.

"Canada," one neighbor, an elderly woman with a hunched back, said.

"No sah," her husband replied. "All of the Ramsey dem in England."

"Gwennie tell me Canada."

"Gwennie no know nutten. When she ever get anything right?"

"Dearie, ask Rose. The wife and Rose were friends. Third house past Nurse. The one with the big mango tree in the yard and the blue verandah."

And on to Rose's house with its blue verandah and red steps.

"Friends? She never tell me nutten. Is after them gone I hear that they pack up and leave. Friends?" Rose sucked her teeth and shook her head. "Never see no friend like that."

With each conversation—*sweetest little girl and the baby boy too; never did hear where the wife come from*—Plum's despair grew, pushing her back to where she had been immediately after Lenworth disappeared. She couldn't help but think he knew she was coming, had perhaps heard her voice on the radio or heard from someone else that she was searching for him, and had in return gone underground like a species of marine life living deep within the sea.

⟋

Inside the airport itself, Plum couldn't see the sea, but she felt it calling her. Yet, she couldn't answer the call, and when she could indeed see the sea from the small plane window, it was too late, much too late to go.

Looking out the window, she imagined a stick figure adrift in a boat. A castaway. The teenager who had been tricked into going to Jamaica in the first place by her own mother. The teenager who found trouble on the island and later found that her parents were unwilling to welcome home an unwed daughter turned-mother. Not a true castaway. Not just yet. By the time she returned to the rented cottage to find her Mr. Barrett, Lenworth, gone, she was in her mind a true castaway, twice-abandoned by her mother and once by her lover.

Plum left that castaway, that abandoned girl, behind in Jamaica—a stick figure in a boat on the vast sea below, rowing without oars, her crying drowned by the plane roaring above. A speck in the distance disappearing to nothing.

9

A transformed Plum came back to Brooklyn, back to the neat lines in immigration that snaked toward stern and focused immigration agents. The female customs agent who greeted Plum spoke through her teeth, verifying Plum's departure and her return, questioning the purpose of her visit, which Plum couldn't, even if she wanted to, truly reveal. "Visiting family," she said, even though she hadn't seen a single relative or person she knew and the empty house and doll were the closest she came to seeing family.

Nothing to declare. No rum. No ackee. No breadfruit. No fried or escoveitched fish. No illicit scotch bonnet peppers or bush teas. Only a one-legged doll that was of no interest to anyone but Plum.

Outside, organized chaos. People as busy as ants in a disturbed anthill, pulling up and easing away from the curb, hefting suitcases, exchanging kisses and hugs, and shuffling passengers in crowded cars. Plum stood alone, sucking in the exhaust, acclimating to the blaring horns and the rapid and constant movement that defined New York. She wanted to be somewhere else, or if not to slow time and live each moment deliberately. Then she stepped off the curb into a slowing taxi, regretting immediately that she had chosen to step away from the curb and into that specific car driven by a

Nigerian—inquisitive and chatty—who looked up and back at her through the rearview mirror each time he spoke. "Coming back from the islands?"

"Jamaica."

"Yeah, mon." He laughed and looked up at her again, checking whether his accent made her laugh as well. "I love everything Jamaican. The women," he looked up again, giggling like a school boy, "reggae, ackee and saltfish, jerk chicken, curried goat. Everything. Everything."

Plum turned away instead, toward the window and the blurred lives on the other side of the highway, the family cars zipping by the taxi, carrying families. That was what she wanted—a replacement for the loneliness (though she felt alone rather than lonely). A child to take the place of the one she never got to raise. A husband to take *his* place. A new Plum to replace the castaway, the stick figure left adrift in a boat.

And so she detoured to Alan's place on East Thirty-Third Street, #237, to the rowhouse his parents had passed on to him when they moved to Florida, and which he was slowly converting from three distinct apartments to a single-family house. He had repainted the front door a bright green, and it stood out among the drab brown front doors of the neighboring houses. Dust hung in the air, escaping from under the weight of their feet and her luggage on the tarpaulin, floating up from the thick plastic wrapped around the living room couches and tables.

"You've done a lot," she said.

"My father was a good a teacher. But you know it's not all my work, right? Hired a company to do the heavy work."

But what Plum remembered was Alan complaining about his weekends during his teen years given over to his father, who thought he was grooming his son to take over the family business. Alan had learned much that his father taught, except for the love of it.

"Three bedrooms upstairs and a bathroom finished. Just the kitchen and basement left."

"All for you alone?"

"For now, yes."

Plum knew what he meant. Through the haze of dust, they walked to the unfinished kitchen. She fingered the tiled countertop, stopped to gauge the depth of the sink, the roominess of the space, the natural light filtering in. "Oh. You built a deck. Much better than the window alone."

"It beats walking down to the basement to get out to the back-yard."

"Convenient, yes."

Upstairs to the three finished rooms, light yellow on the walls of one, peach on another, ecru on the walls of the third. She opened the closets, walked from window to wall as if measuring the width of the rooms. On to the bathroom to look at the reclaimed claw-foot tub and glassed-in shower, the black-and-white subway tiles, and back to the yellow room. "I can see our baby in here," Plum said, looking at him, her gaze unwavering, her lips open slightly as if to pull her words back at the first sign of rejection.

In the end, she chose him, instead of he her, and he was content to let it be, to let what he thought was inevitable fall into place. "Me too." His grin swallowed the rest of his words.

Plum didn't tell Alan about the missing baby girl or Lenworth. In her mind, Alan was a stand-in for the missing two, the baby girl especially. But she didn't want Alan to think that she was motivated by anything more than love, and she wanted a clean slate, not one tainted by the past.

⟋

In the days following Plum's return, the private investigator went again to Anchovy to confirm Plum's news. He, too, toured the empty house. And he inquired of the neighbors, the postmistress, the cooperative bank, the local schools. He too came away with nothing concrete.

"No man, is Canada him gone."

"He have people in England. There him gone."

"Him gone a foreign."

"Me hear say him get work on a ship. Me no know where the wife and the pickney dem gone."

"The wife? Pauline. One day him come back wid har and say a him wife. She never talk much so I don't know where she come from or where her people are."

He couldn't determine if the residents in Anchovy were telling the truth or how one man could disappear so many times without a trace.

"Part of me thinks they're covering for him," Plum told him. Unlikely as it was that the entire community had conspired to cover for Lenworth, the thought lingered. "And the other part thinks he heard I was looking for him. This whole business about him going to Canada or England or getting a job on a ship is just a lie. And he's there on the island somewhere."

"Could be."

"No more bad news," Plum told him. "Only so much I can take."

She moved forward with her plan: A quick wedding—a brief ceremony in a public garden and a low-key reception in a church hall—followed a year later by a birth. A year of forgetting the lost child, the one-legged doll and how close she had come to finding the child who had been taken away. Forgetting until the moment the babies—twin girls—eased their way into the world. Vivian and Nia. Even then, the minute they were born, they looked exactly as she remembered her first born. Plum wouldn't, and couldn't, let them out of sight, not for a minute or two. The old fear returned. There was no forgetting. The stick figure in the boat was still with her, still afraid of the past repeating.

PART 3

Belonging

1

Opal didn't know it yet, but at fourteen she was living her mother's life—at least partially—looking for a way to matter and to be loved or lovable. For she had once been lovable and so precious her father named her after a gem with an iridescent rainbow of colors. The way he told it, he alone was responsible for her name, he alone who thought her precious. She believed.

Yet, here they were, again at a crossroads, a boarding school in Jamaica like an immovable mountain between Opal, Lenworth, and Pauline.

"I'm telling you, high school in Jamaica is the best thing for her." Pauline had a way of punctuating her words with her hands or whatever object she held. She moved her spoon now, raising it up and down like a drummer without a drum.

Lenworth, with his head bent and palms like a tent in front of his face, said no. "You're not sending my daughter away like somebody dead-lef'."

"So you going to leave her to run around like a vagabond?"

"Vagabond?" He looked up, face wrinkled, one corner of his mouth lifted scornfully.

"Maybe not vagabond." Pauline pulled her word back. "But you know what I mean. She can't just do as she please. You have to set some rules."

Lenworth looked at Opal, and quickly looked away, his words dissolving like honey in tea. His daughter, he thought, and corrected himself. *Her* daughter. He stressed *her*, for Opal had morphed into a life-size version of Plum, a permanent reminder of the woman he should have loved to the very end.

"Tell her where you go after school."

"The library." Opal spoke in a whisper, the pain of not being believed evident in her voice.

Lenworth knew it to be true, for he had followed Opal from school at least once to find out for himself exactly where she went and why. He didn't tell Pauline, though.

"Your homework is never done." Pauline, incredulous still, raised her palms then dropped them back on the table in exasperation. "You spend all evening in your room doing homework. So what do you do at the library?"

"I write movies and plays."

That, too, Lenworth also knew to be true. He had found and read through Opal's stack of marble notebooks, filled with one-act plays and half-written movies. Once he found the notebooks, he went back time after time to learn about the world his daughter created, stepping away each time thinking that his daughter hated her life and escaped into her own altered reality to get away from the present.

Opal's movie that week was about the Tainos, a group long extinct from Jamaica, decimated by hard labor and the diseases brought to the island by Christopher Columbus and the cohort of explorers, diseases for which their bodies had built no immunity. In her notes, Opal had written that she wanted to return the Tainos to Jamaica. In one corner she had described the small house in Anchovy, the long ride down Long Hill toward the coast, the walled compound at the foot of Long Hill and the sea directly behind the wall. She imagined the sea butting up against the land for the concrete wall and the thick rows of trees that had grown up around the wall blocked outsiders from seeing what went on within the walled compound. Opal wanted to set her movie in an inlet behind the walled compound, with the city of Montego Bay to the right and to the left the jagged coastline stretching toward Negril. The script was still in its infancy, with Opal unable to move beyond the thought of it, unable to determine who would win her war: the Tainos returning to an island that wasn't necessarily or specifically their ancestral land or the descendants of African slaves who had been brought to the island hundreds of years earlier. She hadn't figured either how to write herself into it. Her movies had one basic storyline—Opal the savior, needed, accepted, lauded.

"Discipline," Pauline was saying. She had turned to Lenworth, and she punctuated her words with a slap of her fist against her palm. "She needs to learn how to be disciplined, how to get her priorities straight. And the only place I can think of is a boarding school in Jamaica. That private school we're paying for isn't doing a thing."

"Yes," Opal said. "I want to go."

"No." Lenworth spoke more forcefully than he intended. He softened his voice and repeated, "No."

"Why not?" Pauline dipped a tea bag once, twice, then squeezed it against the spoon. "You think she too good to go to a school in Jamaica?"

"I told you already. You're not packing up my daughter and sending her anywhere."

"But, what if I want to go?" Opal's voice was small, like that of a girl not used to speaking her mind, and afraid of her words disappointing the listener.

Lenworth looked up at Opal and again pulled his eyes away. Again that plea in her eyes, that desperate look, so like her mother's. And again, he closed his eyes, tented his fingers in front of his forehead. He pictured Plum, the misery of her teenage years at the boarding school, how she longed to be back at home. Yes, Plum's situation was different; she had been tricked into going to Jamaica. But he wouldn't think of Pauline sending Opal away, wouldn't think of Opal going that far and discovering the truth he had been hiding all this time. "No," he said again, more forcefully this time. "You're not sending my daughter away." Only he did not address Opal's question.

Lenworth knew there was something more in Opal's plea, a longing for something else. Lenworth could compartmentalize Opal's life in two segments: before America and after.

Before America, Opal was a tomboy, partial to flicking marbles in the dirt, needling her way into a cricket game, fashioning cars and trucks from boxes and bits of wood, tramping through the bush with the neighborhood boys to explore a murky pond or cave. She played with a doll just long enough to pull its legs from its body to investigate the hollow space inside and remove more easily the thin pine needles and scraps of sawdust she had fed through the doll's tiny mouth like noodles. Then, she had no interest in fashioning doll's clothes, or curling or braiding its hair. Back then, when he pictured her as a teen, he pictured her as an athlete, more at home competing in a game than confined in a classroom or any domestic setting.

But, as it turned out, he moved the family long before Opal's life unfolded fully. Nearly seven years had passed since Lenworth, Pauline, Opal, Craig and the newborn baby left Jamaica for Greenbelt, Maryland. They came at the end of August when the grass was still green, the trees full and fragrant, and the humid, sun-filled days suggested nothing of the chill that came two months later. Neither the promise of a new beginning nor the novelty of an immigrant's life warmed Lenworth and Pauline's frosty relationship.

But Opal, who was too young to understand her father's transgressions, too young to question his repentance and who had no reason not to believe in his dream or his transformation to a repentant seminarian, embraced the small apartment—two bedrooms, a den that was barely big enough for a twin bed, and a balcony, the only outdoor space that belonged to them—to which her father had ferried his family.

The apartment was nothing like the house in Anchovy, with its small, adjoining rooms and expansive yard. The trees in the complex, ornamental instead of fruit trees, weren't meant for children to climb. And, indeed, if there were no apples or mangoes or star apples or almonds to pick, what was the use in shimmying up a tree trunk and stepping out onto a branch twelve feet away from the ground? Still, the balcony was more spacious than the den, the quadrant of a room in which Opal could barely turn around without hitting her knees or elbows on something. It was the space, or lack of it, that tempered her boyishness.

In Greenbelt, there was nothing to explore—no caves, or murky ponds, or abandoned wells—just a few children staring back at her from their own balconies and sometimes from the too-green grass between the buildings. She turned inward instead of outward, and, along with learning how to be an American—the required words and phrases and attitudes, remembering to say "on vacation" instead of "on holiday" for holiday was a specific day not a week- or month-long event—she learned how to be a girl, to like gold hoops in her ears, bangles that jangled when she moved, shoes with a bit of a heel, polka dotted tights, and boots that ended midway up her calf. She became a little more like her stepmother, finding use for the mirror, befriending the girl who stared back at her. She morphed into someone else: a girl who cared that her colors matched, who preferred dresses to pants, fashion magazines to comic books, every shade of nail polish and shiny lip gloss.

Lenworth looked at her as if she had been reborn, a newborn shedding her birthday wrinkles and mottled skin, growing each day into her own. Seeing how she became a life-sized wax doll or commemorative figurine of Plum that haunted him. Seeing how he had managed to make every woman and girl in his life seem inconsequential and small.

And then he looked away. He didn't exactly pretend that Opal didn't exist at all. But it was close. He did it subtly, turning down her third grade photos. In them, she had smiled instead of staring back at the camera stubbornly, defiantly refusing to smile. He removed Opal's photos from the wall and replaced them with photos of the boys caught in the midst of a mischievous antic, surprise or amusement oozing from their faces.

Opal didn't notice it then, not at ten or eleven years old, not until much later, after he had finished with the seminary and his training as an Episcopal priest, not until they moved to Brooklyn, not until the ladies from the altar guild came to help the new priest and his family settle in and decorate, not until one woman said, "So where are pictures of Opal? You must have some pictures of your daughter. Such a pretty smile too. And those eyes . . ."

That Opal, with skin the color of a coffee bean, didn't resemble him was clear. That she didn't look like Pauline was clear. To look at the family—Lenworth's milky-brown skin, heavy eyelids, and thick, bushy brows running across his forehead; Pauline and her sons, who, like her, had light brown skin; and Opal, a darker-skinned other with unusual topaz eyes and eyebrows so thick, so wide the outer edge dipped low and down toward the outer corner of her eyelid—it was hard to tell Opal physically belonged to them. And she knew it because people stared at her eyes, at her complexion, at her family's eyes and complexion, the strangers' awkward glances calculating and minds deciphering the ancestral line that could have made it so, and concluding without being told and without concrete evidence that one of the two adults—her father or stepmother—wasn't genetically hers.

That he called her his daughter was all that mattered to the churchwomen. They didn't question her true parentage. She belonged in the photos and on the wall. Which is how Opal came to realize that her own school photos had been turned away or down, and one, still in the frame, had been put away in his desk drawer. Which is how she came to believe that he no longer saw her but saw someone else staring back at him, someone he preferred not to see.

Yet, she wanted to be his. His daughter. His offspring. His family. His ballerina at the front of the stage, on her toes, lifting her arms as gracefully as a butterfly fluttering its wings, leaping like an acrobat suspended in air. But as far as Opal knew, he never came to the recitals, or if he did, he sat in the back, invisible to her on the stage, or snuck out early before the other parents excitedly mobbed the stage, throwing roses at their girls, regardless of whether they danced or simply stood shyly on the stage staring back at the audience.

She wanted to be wanted and seen.

Lenworth knew that, but he couldn't and wouldn't grant her wish, couldn't face the life-size reminder of the gravity of his mistake. And he couldn't send her away as she also wanted. Instead, he left Opal waiting to *belong* to him again.

2

At last, Plum had become the daughter her parents wanted her to be—responsible, settled, successful in her own way, a model her parents could even hold up to wayward cousins and neighbors' children. She had gone on to become a specialist in blood banking, and worked now in a university lab alongside a team of researchers studying cancers of the blood. Plum had done better than her parents ever imagined and her success had earned her a belated gift: a family trip at her parents' expense to Disney World.

The congress of six—Plum's parents, Nia and Vivian, Plum and Alan—sat now in the resort's lounge area, three of the four adults cooling coffee, Plum sipping tea and the six-year-old girls, who were too anxious to eat or drink, bouncing from chair to chair. Plum and the girls wore Minnie Mouse ears, and the girls had matching tutus. To see Plum then, relaxed, teasing her daughters, it was hard to imagine that she had fought vociferously against the trip, against her parents' gift, against the premise of princesses and unrelenting beauty and magic and fairy dust that turned evil into good. Underneath it all, Plum was against pushing on the girls the idea of a happily ever after and setting them up for the ultimate heartbreak.

Plum would have preferred a Caribbean vacation, a week on ei-

ther her island or Alan's—Barbados—or even another place altogether that was wholly new to them. She would have preferred a
few days on a rustic family farm, a hike up a riverside to the place
where the water emerged from the ground. Ultimately, Plum wanted her girls to learn early on that life sometimes disappointed. And
she wanted the girls to have the tools to deal with their disappointments, whether the loss of a playground game or an early love or
failure to achieve a dream.

But now Plum smiled and pretended that she hadn't objected at
all, pretended that the magic of Alice's Wonderland or Cinderella's
Castle was true to their lives. To soften it, they planned the trip
around a fiftieth anniversary celebration in nearby Kissimmee for
Alan's grandparents.

In truth what Plum's objection hid was the stark reality that her
life revolved around three distinct buckets: the twin girls, Alan, and
her work. She had come back from her last trip to Jamaica, the disappointment of Anchovy, with a keen focus on mattering, on not
being a person so easily discarded and left behind. Plum hadn't let
up at all. She became the perfect wife, mother, daughter, and employee, anticipating everyone's needs and meeting them, and setting aside her own.

Outside the peach walls, the heat was like a thermal blanket
they couldn't remove. Plum scrunched her face against the sun and
sought a bit of shade. But the girls would have none of it. They ran
to the car, spreading their enthusiasm like pixie dust on the adults,
an enthusiasm that didn't let up throughout the entire afternoon in
the park.

Later, when the girls were sufficiently tired and morphing into alternate versions of themselves, fiends really, Alan and Plum slipped

out of the rented townhouse for the anniversary party in a beach-front mansion.

"I have a surprise," he said.

"I'm too tired for surprises." Plum flipped the passenger mirror and looked at the made-up alternate version of herself.

"You'll love this one."

"What is it?"

"I got us a hotel room. It will be just you and me without the girls."

"No, no, no, no, no. No. Cancel it."

"You need it. We need it."

"Cancel it," she said again.

"One night, Plum. You think the girls can't live without you for one night? You think your parents will run off with them?"

One, two. One, two. Plum concentrated on breathing, stemming the panic rising in her. "You'll never understand."

"They're not babies anymore. You have to let them grow."

Words mixed up and tumbled around her mind. Plum was quiet for much too long, picturing the sleeping girls in one room and her parents in another, also asleep. The moment lengthened and Plum missed yet another opportunity to tell Alan about how she lost the other baby and why even now after six years she hadn't left the girls alone for even a single night.

"The girls will be all right." Alan stopped the car, and held her chin. "You decide. We're going in or going back to the house?"

"Let's go in. We've come this far."

Plum's legs trembled, and outside the car, she reached for Alan's arm to steady her gait. The din of laughter and voices carried through the beachfront mansion. In one corner was a caricature artist, and in another was a jazz pianist whose music rose and fell like waves in the background, a splash of sound and a shush repeating. The long room dripped with red and gold highlights.

Plum stood on an upper landing, looking down on the vibrant

party, at the beaded cocktail dresses shimmering under the light, organza and silk fluttering without a breeze, and at the costumed mime artists serving hors d'oeuvres and teasing the guests. Everywhere there was something red: neck ties, roses, napkins, drapes. The party was perfect, more extravagant than she would have imagined.

Alan came up beside her, resting his arms on the banister and leaning forward. "Imagine us," he whispered.

Plum smiled. "When I think of myself, the picture in my head is me at twenty. So I can't even picture myself that old."

"I know." He paused. "Let's dance."

Plum caught his hand and moved down the stairs, slowly, cautiously, allowing her body to move to the beat. She hadn't danced in public in years, not since her wedding nearly eight years earlier.

"Relax," Alan whispered in her ear. "The girls are all right."

"I should call," she said.

"No. They're all right. After today, they're fast asleep."

"Yes," Plum said. Silently she repeated his words, "The girls are all right. Nia and Vivian are all right." She closed her eyes and willed it to be true and to remain true. She imagined them in the morning running back to her, throwing their arms and legs around her, branding her as theirs and she doing the same. There was a way to truly live without *her*. Plum simply had to embrace what she had, Alan and Nia and Vivian, and believe that the way her life had turned out was exactly the way it was meant to be. It would have to be sufficient.

3

Pauline approached arguments like a construction toy set, returning to attach new pieces to the foundation, building up and out with a single goal in mind, which meant that Pauline and Lenworth were arguing about Opal again. Pauline had returned to the idea of the boarding school, this time holding up two recent immigrant girls from their church, St. Mark's Episcopal Church, as an example. One of the girls had just been accepted to an Ivy League university. Lenworth picked the new pieces off, one by one, shutting down her arguments, sometimes with reason, sometimes with silence.

"Ivy League. And they just got here. But that's what I mean about discipline."

Lenworth chose silence this time. He sat at the head of the dining table like a king at court. Around him, the rest of the family moved. Pauline brought hot serving dishes. Opal brought the plates, and the boys set out the cutlery and glasses.

With everything in place, the family sat like monks at a retreat, platters and bowls moving around the table in an unchoreographed but practiced dance that ended always with Pauline standing with the bowl of untouched vegetables, walking to each member of the family and distributing the salad or steamed vegetables among the plates. As always the boys traded the vegetables they tolerated for the ones they simply wouldn't swallow. Pauline hovered then with a spoonful of blood red beets, the juice dripping onto the rice on Opal's plate, staining it. The boys held their hands above their plates, protesting uselessly. Pauline, undeterred, scooped the slices onto Lenworth's plate and moved round the table robotically.

Nobody traded the beets.

And then the full silence descended, not so much a comfortable one, just familiar to each of them. Lenworth and Pauline's argument hung among them, incomplete, and the children sat waiting for the next piece of it to fall into place.

Lenworth sat with his eyes closed as he chewed, concentrating on chewing or just blocking his family out. Pauline, who insisted on this daily routine of eating together as a unit, looked up occasionally to correct a bad habit, to glare at whomever slurped loudly. The boys, warned over and over about misbehaving at the table, simply sat in near-total silence for the duration of the meal. Opal chewed, waiting for the moment when she could push her chair back, wash the dishes, and retreat to her room.

Much later, the five left for a bowling alley, the family, together, but barely so. They were like three distinct groups, three points of a triangle connected by a thin thread: on one side was Opal; on another, the boys played with toy cars; and on the third, Pauline and Lenworth stood near each other but definitely apart.

In the lobby, he was simply a father in blue jeans and a button-down shirt on an outing with his children and wife. Opal picked at her fingers, scraping peeling polish from her fingernails. In another corner, a woman looked at them, hand over her mouth to hide her whispering to her partner. Then "You from Trelawny?" a hesitant question from the stranger, her face scrunched up and head tilted. "No." Lenworth spoke quickly. "You must be mistaking me for someone else."

"You look just like someone I went to school with. Same complexion and all."

"Wrong coast. I'm from the south coast. I must have a twin out there." He laughed, a bubbly uncomfortable laugh.

"I must know you from somewhere else then. But, man, I look at you and all I could think of was my classmate. Can't remember his name. But I can picture him even now. Couldn't figure out what happened to him. He sat right beside me in class. Middle of the school year and he just never came back. Desk sat there in the middle of the classroom empty for the rest of the year. We imagined all sorts of things about what happened to him."

"Maybe he just moved away."

"Maybe. But, man, you surely have someone out there who look just like you."

The woman stepped back. Across the room, the woman looked on, shaking her head, muttering to her partner presumably about the similarities between the person she remembered and the stranger nearby. Lenworth stepped back in place, back to the triangle, shifting slightly to make an aisle for other patrons to pass through.

He could have said yes, though technically he wasn't from Trelawny. He had lived in the parish for a little while, and he could simply have said so. But he saw Pauline looking on, the question in her eyes. And he saw his future, he and Pauline continuing to live like strangers, one suspicious of the other, and he, cautious, living with the fear of recognition and the life he had built tumbling down around him like a house of sticks.

PART 4

Tea by the Sea

1

Brooklyn, East Thirty-Third Street. The air was a little bit cooler and smelled of rain. Plum polished windows, both the inner and outer sides of the glass, with a crumpled newspaper and a mixture of vinegar, lime, and water. She whistled, thinking at the same time of the uselessness of her chore: polishing the exterior windows when rain had set up to fall. But she didn't stop, simply moved her arms like a wound up doll powerless to stop itself. Behind Plum were her girls—Nia and Vivian, seven-year-old twins—one doing cartwheels, the other watching, both girls lingering really and waiting for Plum to finish and turn to them. They were clingy girls. Or perhaps it was the other way: Plum was an overprotective mother, preferring to have her girls with her, underfoot, within reach. Except for work, she didn't leave them. All these years, she hadn't been able to shake the fear that her girls wouldn't be there when she returned.

But they were there—Nia, the acrobatic one, contorting her body through the air, and Vivian, a quiet observer with a book on her lap, stealing glances at Nia. Nia took risks. Vivian weighed consequences. Together, the girls balanced each other, and often, when Plum imagined them older, teenagers, she saw Nia treating life like a tightrope and Vivian holding the net beneath her sister.

Even if Alan had been home at that very moment, the girls would still have been nearby waiting for her to finish and turn to them.

Nia stumbled and crashed and Plum turned to see her sprawled on the hardwood between the coffee table and the couch, water from a cup pooling, magazines from the rack scattered on the ground like shattered glass and the storage bench flipped over on its side.

"You all right? Where did you hit? Did you hit your head?"

Nia, giggling instead of talking, looked at her sister and the pool of water spreading fast toward the rug. Vivian laughed too, their laughter loud, uncontrollable. Plum moved her daughter's shoulders and arms, watching for a wince, waiting for a shiver of pain, but again got only uncontrollable giggles.

"Enough of the cartwheels."

"She was trying to flip onto the bench and back down," Vivian said.

"Enough." Plum hadn't heard their discussion at all, hadn't heard the usual, "watch me."

Plum shook her head, moved toward the spreading pool, newspaper in hand and layered it on top of the water sheet by sheet.

And drew her breath. It was a hiccup, really. She looked again, closer this time, back bent, water dripping from one half of the newsprint. She ripped the sheet in half, dropped the wet half to the floor, then moved toward the window, sheet in hand, for a closer look in the natural light.

Unmistakable.

Lenworth.

She hadn't forgotten the face, the half-smile, the thick brows, the thin nose. Below the photo, a caption with his name and his title: Priest.

Unmistakably him.

Outside, the rain that had set up came with force, pummeling the plants that had withstood summer, and flooding the gutters and the nearly empty roads. The wind whipped the rain around, sprinkling raindrops against the windows like pebbles on glass. East Thirty-Third Street was otherwise quiet, with everyone, it seemed, hunkered down, waiting out the mid-afternoon downpour in place.

Plum waited out the rain just within view of her laughing, cavorting girls. She held the newspaper up, using the pages as a shield from the girls' gaze. At least for the moment, Nia had given up the cartwheels and handstands and she sat with Vivian playing jacks. Behind the newspaper, Plum's calcified grief, all seventeen years of it, broke apart, and tears almost as fierce as the rain dribbled down her cheeks, settling uncomfortably in the corners of her mouth.

The girls, absorbed by their game of jacks, didn't pay attention to the sniffles coming from behind the newspaper. Plum could have moved to a quieter room—the windowless bathroom, perhaps—to cry unchecked, without worrying about the girls eventually gazing and questioning the reason for her tears. Instead, she chose to remain behind the newspaper, to cry without sound and let the tears roll down her face. Surely, if she had moved in search of seclusion, one or both of the girls would have followed her, wandering through every room until they found her again and transported their game within her line of sight.

Plum wiped her eyes on her sleeve and looked again at the man in the center of the photo, surrounded by a group of community leaders. Other than the hairline that had receded, he was exactly as she remembered him. Thick lips, a deep pink like a painted hibiscus bloom. Thick, bushy brows came close to meeting in the center of his face, their fullness like a miniature ledge shielding eyes that seemed to capture everything. A thin nose. He was a little thicker, of course, but not significantly so. That didn't matter. What mattered was that the man who had disappeared like a deep-water creature into the depths of the ocean had resurfaced in Brooklyn, skimming the water for a long breath of air. He was within reach, a catch she could finally haul in. But how long before he dipped his head and swam again out of reach?

Nia called her mother to stand in as referee for the girls' own inconsistent and slippery rules.

"Coming." Plum wiped her eyes on her sleeve, roughly, quickly, and forced herself to smile as if smiling was another one of those things she had to practice how to do convincingly. She counted her breaths, one, two, one, two, then faced the girls, her actions suggesting that all that mattered were the oversized neon ball and jacks scattered before them on the floor.

Behind Plum, the newspaper, tented at first, flopped down. Lenworth's face kissed the cushion. Six steps away, Plum struggled to understand the rules the girls had established, tried to simplify their game and play it the way she had learned years earlier, struggled even more to quash the anger and the anxiety simmering at the pit of her chest and rising up like bile at the back of her throat. Seventeen years later she was still angry, and surprised that her on-and-off search had come to this: his photo in a newspaper, the name of the church he led in bold letters below his image, the church's address at her fingertips, a face-to-face confrontation a short bus ride or walk away. That he'd become a priest was a shock, a considerable alteration of the course he'd set for himself, tutoring and teaching to finance his studies to become an engineer. Surely, God was mocking her. That he'd migrated to Brooklyn, settled in Brooklyn, was also a shock. And yet, where better to live than the city of her birth, a city of anonymous millions, a place she wouldn't expect him to hide, the very place she had told him over and over that she had come to despise and to which she hadn't wanted to return.

But after he disappeared she had indeed returned. Where else could she go but home?

On the floor, in that moment, she was simply Mother, balancing her girls' competitive nature with her duty to teach fairness ("Remember what I said about rules. Rules make the game fair and make it the same for everybody.") and the art of losing gracefully ("No, no. You don't cry because you lose a game."), while simultaneously instilling in them the idea that people and life weren't always fair and they wouldn't always win. "Somebody has to win and somebody has to lose." Trite, but true. "What matters is that you did your very best."

By necessity, Plum parceled her thoughts and anger, shelved them for a later time, and suggested Monopoly to the girls, another game with rules they all understood. It dissolved into chaos.

Snakes and Ladders imploded as well, when Vivian, whose token slipped too often down the ladder and too close to the starting point, accidentally kicked the board and dislodged the tokens.

At last, Alan, rain-soaked, returned with afternoon treats—pastries and chocolate-dipped ice cream bars. The girls abandoned Plum, at least temporarily. Plum slinked away from the girls, away from mothering, to a dark place where she could simply be a woman who needed to cry. Upstairs in the bathroom, with the mat up against the door to keep out the sliver of light, Plum broke up the remaining block of grief, letting the weight of seventeen years of not knowing dribble away.

Then she stopped, for he was indeed within reach, no longer a character in her dream of a man returning with what he had taken away, but reelable, if only she could close him into a place from which he could not escape.

❧

Later, much later, Plum woke on the floor in the narrow space between her bed and closet, with her face pressed into the carpet and a one-legged doll in the crook of her arm. How could she have slept so deeply in the mid-afternoon? She turned, relieving the left arm that had served as a pillow. Between her fingers, she held the priest's photo, which she'd cut from the newspaper and folded so only his face showed. The full newspaper, minus the page with the article on the priest (an article that she still had not yet read), lay by her side, alongside an old cookie tin in which she kept three memen-toes: an older photo of Lenworth, the one-legged doll and her own hospital discharge papers. She looked at the photos again, returned the old one to the cookie tin and placed the newspaper page on the floor with the doll's head like a paperweight to hold it down. Mostly though, she wanted to hide the smile, his smile, which projected to the photographer and the world a peacefulness he did not deserve.

Yet, Plum unfolded the paper, covered his face again with the doll, and read the words around it. The article didn't say anything at all about her daughter, who Plum could find only through him. It was too late in the day to go in search of him, too late to leave the house without an explanation. Surely, services were over and the church closed up for the afternoon. The meeting could wait one more day, for he couldn't escape now. Not this time.

Plum moved only slightly, but the floorboards creaked under her weight, just enough to bring Nia and Vivian tumbling into the room as if pushed forward by a river's current. Vivian reached for the old doll, while Nia backed away from it, a little afraid of the matted tufts of hair, the splotchy and discolored skin, and blue eyes that didn't blink in concert. The doll clearly wasn't one of theirs. Nia circled the doll and lay down in the crook of her mother's left arm. Vivian followed, settling herself in the opposite arm. Plum held them as if she, or they, had gone away for a prolonged time, pressing the shape of her children into her body and the girls reciprocating. She was Mother again, setting aside the other pressing thought—no longer *where* to find him—but *when* and *how* to do so without completely upending the life she had built, or moving too fast and prompting him to go underground again.

⌒

Nights, Plum had a habit of lying with the girls in the middle of the two beds the girls preferred to keep side by side rather than bunked, and waiting until the rhythm of their breaths had evened out. It was the simplest thing, really, the rhythm of breathing, but it was what she watched each night as they slept and again in the morning when she slipped back into their room to wake them, noting the rise and fall of their chests, the flutter of an eyelid, the twitch of a mouth, listening for a bit of a dream escaping as a word or groan.

That night, she lay as she usually did, flat on her back, an arm around each girl, her eyes on the glowing plastic stars scattered across the ceiling. She fought against dreaming about the elusive reunion or the fallout it would bring and extricated herself from the middle of the beds earlier than she normally would. Across the hall, Alan had fallen asleep, and, except for his snores, the house was quiet. The house was hers. The darkness and the quiet pushed her back where she did not want to go, toward a daydream of the reunion.

On her way down the stairs, she stopped mid-stride, unbalanced, and looked back at the empty bedroom, the guest room that rarely housed guests. The bed, perfectly made, and the knickknacks around the room were a little different from the rest of the house. There was no headboard, just an oversized antique tin poster that she had found at a flea market and mounted on the wall in place of a headboard. At the foot of the bed was another found item, an old trunk she'd sanded and painted a vibrant red. She and Alan had argued about the purpose of the room; he said it made no sense to have an empty room kept ready for guests who never came, and pushing for her to convert it to a bedroom for Nia or Vivian. In return, Plum pointed to the girls' preference for each other's company.

No, she would not dream. She stepped forward and headed down the stairs toward the kitchen. She cleaned, scrubbing the kitchen sink and floor as if rubbing out evidence of a crime, brushing crumbs from the dining and living room rugs, erasing fingerprints from metal and shellacked wood and glass. When there was nothing left to clean, when she had packed away all the toys and fluffed the pillows and swept up all the crumbs, she stood outside on the tiny balcony off the kitchen, barefoot, a knot in her chest, looking out at nothing. Careless, Alan would say. But she stayed there anyway, in the dark, fully conscious that the night had eyes she couldn't see.

Late as it was, after midnight, she made an international call to Mrs. Murray, the former landlady who had once been her savior, who had known her way back then when Plum said *we* and meant *her and him*, when theirs was a basic story: boy meets girl and falls in love. When love and together and forever were the same.

Through the crackling line, Plum said, "He's a priest."

"Priest?" Mrs Murray's voice was gravelly. "What you telling me? You sure?"

"Yes. I saw his picture in a newspaper."

"I would never have imagined that. Where is he?"

"Here. In Brooklyn."

"So close, eh?"

"Real close. Can't let him get away this time."

"I'm praying for you. No mother should have to go through what you have been through."

In the dark, Plum weighed her options, how to walk away from him with exactly what she wanted. She closed her eyes—another careless move in the dead of a Brooklyn night—and pictured one scene unfolding: her standing up in the middle of the following Sunday's sermon, walking to the front of the church and waiting just below the pulpit for him to acknowledge or to ignore her presence, stutter and stumble through his words or just walk away. It seemed a likely option, a scenario from which he couldn't readily escape. She would wait the week for the inevitable confrontation.

Back upstairs, Alan no longer snored but wrestled with his dream, punching at the air and shouting, "Watch me and you." Some nights he acted out his dreams, punching, kicking, lunging at some unseen being. Three or four times a year, when she slept too deeply to catch him or didn't respond quickly enough, he tumbled from the bed to the floor. She was never sure what was worse, her insomnia or this violent and restless sleep.

Now, she rubbed his back, calmed him in his sleep. Curling her legs, she pressed her body against his back and wrapped an arm around him, trying to change his dreams. She lay like that as if this, too, were forever, as if finding the priest wouldn't split their life in two.

Early in the morning, when the sun hadn't yet imprinted color onto everything, when the moon was a fading white in the lightening sky, when dew sparkled on the leaves and grass, Plum thought of another person who should know of her find. His mother, whom she had met only once, briefly, at a time when every dark-skinned girl with deep red lips made her turn her head and stare and wonder.

She called the private investigator and asked him to relay to Lenworth's mother the whereabouts of her son. But even then, she didn't tell Alan, just left that one secret between them. Telling him now, after all these years, would make him question the one thing he asked for: her trust. And stoke her greatest fear: abandonment, her becoming again the castaway, the stick figure left adrift in a boat.

2

Slivers of light slipped in through cracks in the blinds, making shadows on the wall. The rectory was otherwise quiet. That was the way Lenworth preferred it; in its dark state, it showed itself for what it was—someone else's home with stories that were not his buried in the walls. He left the darkened office, felt his way through the living room and up the stairs to bed.

Just as he was ready to turn off the bedside lamp, lie flat on his back and put away the burdens that his parishioners and his family brought to him, the telephone rang. Lenworth looked at the handset to make out the dim black writing illuminated by the green screen. As he suspected, it was indeed a call for him. A parishioner, Evelyn Eastmond, was near death, and her sister thought the time had come for him to give her last rites.

"You have to go now?" Pauline, her voice muffled beneath the sheet, was ready for a fight. "There must be a chaplain at the hospital they can call."

"This is my job, Pauline. This is it. Going when they need me. Praying over the dying." He didn't say there was no chaplain, no hospital, just a woman dying at home rather than at a hospice, and who, weeks earlier, had asked that he be called when the time came.

He kept those details to himself, fully conscious that what he didn't say mattered as much as what he said.

"Yes, but now? You have a family too."

"It's my job, Pauline. You know that. This is what priests do."

"I keep telling you, you need an assistant for times like this. Your family needs you too."

"It's not every day that a member of the church dies. It's not every day that I have to go out at midnight. When was the last time I had an emergency like this? Tell me."

"It might not actually be every day. But you're hardly here."

"Not now."

"If not now, when?"

"Not now." A final, decisive answer that meant he didn't want to have the argument then, that meant he knew that she was arguing about something else entirely. He closed the bedroom door as if to shut the argument within, and descended the stairs, stopping just briefly to pick up a prayer book and adjust his clothing.

Outside, he looked around, hurried to the car, and locked the doors. Inside, he turned off the music and once the car was in motion, opened the windows to let the breeze cool the top of his head. He liked to drive in silence, with nothing but his thoughts, the wind whistling through the open window, the road noise fading quickly into the background. Were it not for Evelyn's imminent death he would have driven toward the Belt Parkway and Long Island and taken a long aimless drive. He would have gone to a beach, staying to watch the sun color the morning sky and the waters. He considered the optics—a priest in a car late at night on a deserted beach—and dismissed the thought.

He would never have thought that he'd welcome this aspect of his job, being on call at all hours. Yet it offered him an escape from his daughter, Opal, and his wife—his daughter especially—not because they were of the gender that he didn't always understand, but simply because they reminded him of the one thing he didn't have.

He never named it, the thing that was lost to him, nor would he admit, ever, that he welcomed opportunities to escape Pauline and Opal.

Loss wasn't something he dealt with well, even though as a priest he should. He had learned, of course, to rationalize some events, to talk about spiritual gains instead of physical losses. Death, the finality of it, was the easiest of any kind of loss for him. There was one rational explanation: a heart had stopped beating. Regardless of what lead up to that final moment—a street fight, an errant gunshot, an aggressive tumor—he could always point to the heart. The other losses—divorce and the breakdown of a lifelong friendship, regardless of who was at fault—were more difficult situations, for they demanded an explanation for why love could fritter away or shrivel up. For himself, he had stopped trying to rationalize the greatest loss of his life. He knew exactly who was at fault and why.

Now, he prepared himself to wait, whether long or short, for Evelyn to take her last breath. As he did in moments like these, he made a list of the things he had lost or left behind: dewdrops on his bare feet; morning fog in a hillside's pockets; the early morning *maa*-ing of an anxious goat; the soft, almost gel-like flesh around a star apple seed slipping around his mouth; walking barefoot on the grass; bursting the young buds on a leaf of life plant and listening for the soft pop; an empty Jamaican beach in the morning, with nothing in front of him but the unending sea with the sun glinting off its waves.

Then he was in front of Evelyn's house in Canarsie, watching the curtain flutter. As he neared the door, it opened, and he stepped inside to face a death that wouldn't wait. Evelyn's anxious relatives pulled him forward into a dark room that already smelled of decay.

The old woman had shriveled, but before her illness, she reminded him of his mother. They had the same high and prominent cheekbones, lips that looked like they'd been blotted with raspberry paint, the build of once lithe and elite marathoners who had gone into old age just a shade heavier from their peak performance days. That, too, was another thing he kept from Pauline. Not coming to Evelyn would have felt like he had abandoned his mother on her deathbed as he had in fact abandoned her in life. He didn't know whether she lived or had died in the years since he'd last left her standing in the yard with her hands akimbo watching him as he walked past the line of orange, tangerine and grapefruit trees in the yard and past the flowering poinciana, to the narrow road, with a crocheted blanket in a bag for the baby that was soon to make its way into the world and for whom he hadn't yet a name. He never returned as he had promised with the newborn baby girl. His mother didn't know either about the boys who came later, and who were now asking questions about his family, who belonged to whom and where exactly they belonged. The boys knew Pauline's family, for she had made sure to return to Jamaica time and time again. But he had offered the boys and Opal no actual glimpse of his family, just random stories that they couldn't confirm.

Evelyn's family clustered around the bed. He held one of her hands and began a prayer so softly none of the others heard. Her hand felt weightless, and he couldn't shake the sense that he was attending to his mother, ushering his mother's soul along. Was his mother indeed on her deathbed nearly two thousand miles away waiting for him to come home? Seventeen years of days and months and hours building up one on top of the other, one fateful decision like a sandbar after a hurricane separating his early life from the second half.

He led the family in song, Evelyn's favorite hymn. Singing wasn't part of the ritual, but he had heard a dying person's sense of hearing was the last to go. And he wanted her to have a cacophony of voices surrounding her. It was what his own mother would want, and since he couldn't shake the feeling that his mother was lying in a bed in Woodhall, Clarendon, counting down her last breaths, waiting for the son she hadn't seen to come, he sang along with the family, saying nothing when the one song became a medley of choruses, and the night turned into an impromptu wake. So caught up were they in song that they missed what they had been waiting for, her eyes fluttering slightly, her last breath, her last heartbeat, her body going cold.

And then his feeling lifted. He expected to, but didn't feel a pang of loss, didn't feel a gaping emptiness as if someone close to him had passed. So by the time he left Evelyn's house, he no longer expected to hear the details of his mother's passing, but rather anticipated that a message would come to him that she was waiting for his return. How and when the message would come he didn't know, and he wasn't sure he liked this ability to divine something before it occurred.

Back on Albemarle Terrace, the rectory was still quiet, the children sleeping deeply, and except for a nightlight in the hall, it was still pitch black inside. Opal, with the exception of her face and her toes, was wrapped completely in the sheets, and snoring lightly. In the next room, the boys were completely turned around. Craig, asleep on the top bunk, had slipped toward the edge as if he had begun to climb down and fallen asleep again before his toes touched the ladder rungs. He righted the boys' bodies and their sheets and tiptoed out, avoiding the toys spread out on the floor like land mines, and across the master bedroom, not wanting to wake Pauline. She slept lightly, like a hen guarding her eggs against mongooses or rats. As he expected, she woke, glanced at the clock, and turned away to the opposite wall. She sniffled once but said nothing, and he tumbled in beside her, back-to-back like a defiant child refusing to speak or acknowledge the other.

He didn't get the deep and satisfying sleep he wanted, but drifted instead into a restless state, between active thoughts and dreams, unable in the end to distinguish between dream and thought. He thought of his mother's cakes and the icing, thick, sweet, hard and with little silver balls mixed into it. She always baked her cakes and puddings on a coal stove, with fire on top and fire below the pan, the heat enveloping the pan as any modern stove would, but the coal and the smoke flavoring the food as no gas stove could. He dreamt of her attending the coal stove, squatting on her haunches, her back to him, while he made circles in the dirt with an old bicycle wheel he had attached to a stick. He woke, for he did indeed remember that toy, and the cart he eventually built with a second wheel and discarded crate. The dream had been so vivid that he felt he had touched the knobby stick, felt the wheel wobble as it rolled over small stones and the uneven ground. And when he drifted off again, he had the same dream of his mother in front of the stove. In the second dream, the fire flared up and caught her skirt. He rushed to her side, grabbed a bucket of water and doused her with it. She patted his head and said, "My boy."

He interpreted the dream as the second sign that his mother was indeed still alive and what he had felt when he attended to Evelyn was his guilty conscience reminding him of how long he had stayed away. It wasn't his mother, he was sure. He turned over, pulled the sheet and the pillow over his head to block out the morning light, and slept.

The house was mostly quiet when he woke, sunlight streaming in through the open blinds, a radio somewhere in the house belting out gospel music. The children were gone, and Pauline as well, off to a meeting or a store or volunteer hours somewhere. He had dreamt of his mother again, and even as he lay there, refitting the pieces of the dream like puzzle pieces, he felt that she was there, watching him as she had in childhood, sitting by his bed as he slept in a fevered state, watching for the seizures that sometimes came upon him when his temperature spiked. Pieces of the dream began flitting away and he reached for the bits he remembered: he had moved into another house, a basement apartment that was already furnished. As he walked through it, he found that the apartment adjoined another, but had no dividing walls, just an invisible line he shouldn't cross. Pauline's name, along with another he couldn't recall, was clearly marked on the house's main front door, silently declaring that he didn't belong up there. His mother was there, though, helping him move his things from the main part of the house to a closet in the basement. He tried but couldn't picture the emotion reflected on his mother's face. He played it over and over, a silent movie for which he had lost the plot.

Even with the bits of the plotless dream spread out before him, the pieces refusing to fit together in any meaningful way, he felt her presence still and chalked it up to the fact that he couldn't interpret the dream, couldn't make sense of how these disjointed pieces of his life had made their way together in a dream. He got up, padded through the house to turn the radio off, stripped off his pajamas and stepped into the shower, believing that his mother wouldn't follow him in there and the water would wash away the niggling feeling he couldn't shake.

His mother was there again when he returned to the room, moving—as the elderly would, slowly, without the sprightliness of the young—from the bed to the bedroom door. He blinked and shook his head, closed and rubbed his eyes, and followed the figure out of the room. Still naked, he went into the kitchen, thinking that satisfying his hunger would take care of the thoughts that haunted him.

Lenworth didn't know it then—and wouldn't know the details for another week, not until all the things that once mattered no longer did, not until after his carefully controlled life had ruptured, not until he had been exposed and the stories about him spilled and scattered like thick mud, drying hard and fast in some crevices, loosening up and moving again in others—but his mother, Girl-ie, had indeed taken her last breath quietly in her sleep. She died an unremarkable death, with no one keeping watch, without song, without a last prayer, holding onto a little piece of paper pinpointing the exact location of her long-lost son. Some two thousand miles away from Brooklyn, his sister woke at 2 a.m. in their childhood home for no specific reason, moved around the house checking windows and doors to ease her uneasiness, and found their mother lying on the floor, lifeless. She held a mirror above her mother's nose to confirm what she suspected, and when she saw no vapor, no fog on the glass, she dropped the mirror and wailed.

3

The darkness of the underground subway station crept up toward Plum, and the dank smell reached up and wrapped itself around her like a loose scarf. Halfway down the stairs, she stopped.

"Aieee." Another hurried commuter jolted by Plum's sudden stop, muttered, sucked her teeth, and made an exaggerated move to bypass Plum. "You can't just stop so."

More angry words floated around Plum and away from her. The city, too busy to stop, didn't stop. But Plum stood there momentarily like a boulder in the midst of a moving stream with water flowing around it rather than over it. Had it not been for a man with two boxes, the second so high it touched his chin, she would have remained there longer, contemplating how to continue her forward movement down the stairs, through the turnstile, onto the narrow platform, onto a train overflowing with artificial light, out again and into the basement lab. Sunlight didn't reach the lab, and she could spend the day there in the lab and the break room without seeing any hint of natural light.

Plum stepped backward up the stairs, away from the man with the boxes, until she was again directly in sunlight and squinting to block it. Like she did after the early morning phone call to Jamaica,

Plum rehashed her reasons for wanting to wait a week to confront Lenworth, for craving the sight of Lenworth cornered and unable to escape, the relief of seeing her daughter, at last. And she worried about losing them, about him escaping again as he had from the house in Anchovy just months before she found his whereabouts. Now, she found she was wrong about the agony of waiting seven whole days, for thinking seven days would seem like nothing, a blip in time, when lined up against seventeen years (6,205 days, give or take a few for leap years) without a word from him.

No, she would not wait. Plum was expected at work at ten, but she rearranged her workday, then sprinted down Nostrand Avenue to Church Avenue and hopped in a route taxi. She was pressed in between two heavy women, uncomfortable and anxious in that position, and also overwhelmed by the commingled scent of artificial coconut and vanilla that wafted from a bottle dangling from the rearview mirror, and the rose-scented perfume one of the women wore. The car moved haltingly, as the driver maneuvered around other stopped vehicles and pedestrians stepping out into the street to hail a passing taxi or to cross against the light.

Plum hopped out of the car across from Bobby's Department Store, and walked back toward the church, where she stood as if she were on a shop piazza waiting for the shopkeeper inside to open up. Plum looked at her watch. 9:10. She had no idea how the church ran its business, whether it had an office and administrative staff who came daily to see to business affairs, whether priests came into the office as any other employee would, whether Lenworth would come that Monday morning.

Plum walked the length of the building, looking for another entrance. Stained glass covered the length of the building, one pane with a throng of enraptured listeners looking toward a group of shepherds. With the vines creeping along the brick walls and shrubs packed in close beneath the windows, the building seemed cloistered.

St. Paul's main doors—which were like those in a fairytale, with three arches overhead and black ironwork extending from the hinges like orderly vines inching pointlessly across the wood—were closed. In the topmost part of the arch were stained glass with candles. "I am the light, the truth and the way," Plum thought, pulling a memory from her teen years in Jamaica, another Anglican church.

She couldn't imagine him here, a priest responsible for this enormous building and two hundred, maybe three hundred parishioners. A room of students, yes. She could picture him in a classroom, and she could picture him before a group of Sunday School students. But how she really saw him was as the engineer he had wanted to become, with his name or a personally identifying symbol etched into whatever building or bridge he had engineered. Back then, when he talked of his adult life, he talked of greatness, leaving behind a lasting reminder of what he had overcome and who he had become. Once, on a beach, he had pointed in the direction of a three-hundred-year-old fort, partially intact, battered by the wind and the sea and countless tropical storms and hurricanes, underlined how despite the spitefulness of nature, the fort had remained, a lasting reminder of another time. That was what he wanted. Yet, here he was a priest, building the intangible among his parishioners. The priesthood, as noble as it was, didn't seem sufficient to express the legacy he had wanted to leave.

Until then, Plum hadn't given much thought to how his life had changed by his one selfish act, how raising a child alone would alter the plan he had had for his life. Empathy was not what he deserved, so she shelved the thought of his dream of greatness frittering away. What mattered? Lenworth was here, within reach, probably behind the red doors, the black matte handle that didn't budge. She went down the street again, toward the back of the church and the adjoining church hall, which had another set of red doors—except these doors were steel and not as ornate as the arched doors at the main entrance.

"Can I help you?" A voice from behind, a baritone.

Not his. She knew instinctively for his voice was etched in her memory and his last words, "*We* have a daughter," tattooed in her mind.

Plum turned slowly. "The priest, is he in?"

"Not today." He waved his hand, a slight brush, as if to swat something away. "Other business came up. Can I help?"

"No, I need the priest. Confession." Plum also waved as if a confession were a light matter easily dismissed. Her heart pounded, the truth bubbling to emerge. But she held it tight, afraid of giving herself away too soon, giving him room to run again.

"The secretary, when she comes in . . . she can make an appointment for you. Give me your name and number. I'll pass it on to her and tell her to call you."

Plum wouldn't leave her name. "I'll come another time." She turned away before he had another chance to question her motive or her presence, to remember her eyes or her nose or her lips or her birthmark—a small patch of depigmented skin where her jaw met her right ear.

Away from the church, Plum cried with her hands covering her face, releasing the anxiety that had started building Sunday afternoon. Then, the crying spell over, she called the lab and rearranged her schedule again. This time, she made it all the way down the subway steps and into a train rattling toward downtown Brooklyn and Manhattan, and walked into the lab, shook out and put on her lab coat as if everything in her life was as it had always been.

The lab itself was quiet. Plum sensed that something had gone wrong, perhaps a grave mistake in typing blood or an experimental treatment involving a patient gone awry. Likely it was something simpler: another episode of Lorna and Marlene clashing about the division of work or Marlene again correcting something Lorna had done. Plum was used to it now, the petty quarrels of the technicians about extended lunch breaks and the division of labor. Plum stayed above it all. She didn't want the friendships or the alliances, just the anonymity of the work.

Plum picked up a waiting specimen and pulled out her stool, ready to begin the process of typing the blood. The collection date—September 11—and time—10:35 a.m.—routine details Plum looked at every day, stopped her this time. There were five more days to her daughter's birthday.

Every year on that date she celebrated the same way, sitting in the dark and counting down the minutes as she had done some seventeen years earlier. She likened it to climbing up stream, up waterfall after waterfall, following a river to the place where it emerged from the earth, either as a gush or a trickle, smooth and jagged stones pressing against her soles, and the water, when it flowed steadily down an incline, pushing her back with a thunderous splash. She imagined instead pushing her body against the flow of water, grabbing with her fingers onto crevices in the rocks, searching with her toes for a foothold, slipping and falling back with each move. Every year, on this specific night that was the pain she felt, water pounding her body, her feet slipping and crashing against the rocks. All night she climbed, alone, teary-eyed, tired. In the morning, she always had an excuse—a cold, a migraine, a sore throat—that explained away her pulling the covers over her head until the girls' chatter and Alan's fumbling through the morning routine quieted and fell away completely.

But not this year. She would meet the anniversary differently, wait and confront him, make him relive what she had lived these past seventeen years, the agony of not knowing growing like a palpable mass in her heart.

4

Even awake, Lenworth found that his mother was present again, along with his sister this time, their images projected on his brain like a movie in 3D, both so vivid, so real he removed his glasses and tried to rub the vision from his eyes. Not that he could. He rubbed and yet they returned, their images still bitingly vivid: his mother more wrinkled, more worn than he remembered, and his sister, a plumper version of the young woman he remembered, also worn.

After all these years, why had they come to haunt him now? Of course, he had failed them too, walked out on them, repeated the pattern of his country's migrant men who sailed to Panama in the early 1900s to labor on a canal. When work on the canal dried up, they went to Cuba or Costa Rica to cut cane and harvest bananas. Still later, they went to England, the mother country that preferred not to mother the colonized migrants who washed up on its shores, and to America that invited but seemed to resent the very farm workers it requested, and to many a country in between. Some returned with the symbols of wealth they had sought. Some came back broken, some disappointed. Some, like his father, didn't return at all. Instead, his father invited them—Lenworth, his sister,

his mother, his brother—into his life only through occasional pack-
ages that came to them via someone returning home, and letters
and photos of an unrecognizable man bundled up against the cold.
With scarf and hood framing his face, he could be anyone. Cer-
tainly he wasn't the father Lenworth barely remembered. Maybe his
father didn't have the papers that would allow his easy movement
from one country to another. Maybe he preferred his new life and
wanted no reminder of the old. Maybe his father, like his son, had
committed a misdeed he couldn't explain. Without intending to,
Lenworth had turned out exactly like his country's migrant men
and like his father. In truth, Lenworth was like a migrant worker
or runaway who left women in limbo—three of them to be exact.
Only Lenworth's departure hadn't been noble at all. And he had
promised nothing.

Why now, he asked again. But he could only imagine the worst,
an impending death or death itself, a restless spirit hovering and
haunting because it could not rest without being appeased. Those
were the kinds of beliefs he had set aside. A man like him, educated,
an escapee from a small and poor country town, couldn't believe
in his ancestors' version of the spirit world, couldn't believe in *dup-
pies*—the restless ghost or spirit of the dead, or the ancestral spirit
who remained in limbo appearing at will or when called upon to
help the family still living. He couldn't believe at all what his mother would believe, that the problems that had befallen him his entire
life were the result of obeah, some evil spell set upon him, which he
could reverse by having a more powerful obeahman counteract the
effects of the spell. He couldn't, and he wouldn't, believe.

Yet he knew there had to be a reason his mother and sister played
so prominently in his thoughts now. And because he couldn't believe in his ancestors' spirit world, he thought their presence could
only mean one thing: His past was catching up to him. But he didn't
know how to prepare.

For the moment, Lenworth had a funeral to plan and a family to console. He went about the business of planning the funeral as if that was all that mattered. He was again at his parishioner's house, around the dining table this time, listening as her sister recounted the dead woman's last meaningful conversation, her life in a small, mountain town and the countless children she helped through school. How, with a disabled and then dead husband, nothing but a primary school education, two children to feed and clothe and educate, she sent off her children one by one, to homes of a teacher and a nurse, so each could have an opportunity she could never provide.

Lenworth heard his mother's story, or something so similar to it, and he almost cried. His mother had done the same, sent him off to another family, only he had looked at it not as his mother attempting to ensure he had opportunities she didn't have, but a throwback to another time when those who had no agency, slaves and their immediate descendants, were sent like property from one master to another. This squandered opportunity, his misreading his mother's and his benefactors' intentions, had led to Plum, his seventeen-year absence from his family, this haunting, this sense of doom that sat upon his chest like a heart ticking slowly toward an explosion.

Lenworth sat upright, a hand to his chest, for he recalled that a sense of impending doom was a cardiac symptom. He shifted in his chair, not wanting to alarm, not wanting to wait, anxious for the moment when he could slip away, make his way to his doctor's office and ask to be seen, or directly to the emergency room. He made a point of looking at his watch.

"She never complained," Evelyn's sister was saying. Then, "You have to go. I know we keeping you too long."

Relieved, Lenworth said, "I have another funeral to attend to."

"Carmen, bring the paper with the hymns and scriptures."

He blew deep breaths, made a point of thinking about his

breathing, realizing, as he sucked in the air, that despite what he taught his parishioners about being ready to meet their maker, he wasn't ready to die.

In the doctor's office, the smell of antiseptic stung his nose. "This is probably nothing, but I feel like something horrible is going to happen. And, no, I'm not depressed. But I've heard that people having heart attacks sometimes feel a sense of doom. So since I can't shake it off, I wanted to check it out."

"Of course, just a precaution."

The doctor went about his business as if he suspected something more. "Chest pain?"

"No."

"Indigestion?"

"No."

"Heartburn?"

"No."

"Any coughing? Dizziness?"

"No."

"Deep breath. Again. We'll run an EKG and maybe set you up for a stress test."

Alone, he felt foolish but assured. Lying with his arms stretched out beside him, leads taped to his body, he assured himself that his panic was only a momentary lapse. Lying there, he made note of the color of the walls, a shade of beige. The color reminded him of sand, and he thought of crabs that were that color. Long ago, on a beach in Montego Bay, he had watched the crabs, their nearly translucent skin and black bulging eyes, how they crawled sideways across the sand then scampered back to their holes in the ground to shield themselves from any suspected threat. At the shoreline, he found yet another species of crabs—tiny hermit crabs—pulling their bodies up and into their shells. So completely did the crabs hide themselves that he didn't know until after he had picked up the shell that a living being was within.

Underneath it all, his thoughts of crabs, their physical presence—spotted or striated shells, translucent bodies—what he really contemplated was the ability to escape quickly and easily from perceived or real threats. Which is exactly how he had lived his entire adult life, like a crab, not so much retreating but escaping fully and completely, assuming a new identity when necessary, protecting himself to the very end.

The doctor returned. "Do what you tell your parishioners: put everything in God's hands."

He knew he should. But he couldn't.

Home again, the little drummer boy still tapped a staccato rhythm in his chest, and that feeling of doom still rode alongside the drummer boy's rhythm. Inside the rectory, Lenworth found chaos: the two boys with plastic swords jousting, dancing round the furniture and over the back of the sofa, and the television playing out the fight they were mimicking and exaggerating; in the kitchen, a kettle on the verge of whistling and Pauline inches from Opal's face demanding to know where she had gone and why.

"You think you're a grown woman, right? Coming and going as you please?" Pauline's voice an octave higher, piercing and cracking under the emotion. "Where were you all evening?"

"At the library."

"Don't lie to me, you know."

"Why do you think I'm lying?"

"Don't come to me with that attitude." And to him. "You need to talk to this girl. She can't come and go as she please. Not in my house."

They had had this argument before, in this very location with Pauline moving between kitchen and dining room, and Opal rooted in place but looking for a way to escape. He glanced at Opal. Her watering eyes held a pleading, desperate look, so like her mother's. He remembered the two of them—he and her mother—on a shop piazza right after a fight. At that moment, he had wanted to get away to let things calm. But Plum had looked at him, her eyes saying, "don't leave me," her lips quivering, her body leaning toward him, one hand outstretched. Back then, he had stayed.

Now, he didn't let his eyes linger on the girl who looked just like her mother, didn't allow himself to see the plea in her eyes. He said nothing, just waved his hand as if swatting away something inconsequential. "We've been through this before," he said to Pauline, and turned back toward his office at the front of the house leaving the two of them to sort it out.

5

Plum kissed Alan goodbye, a long, lingering kiss at which Nia and Vivian stared. Plum wondered as well about the kiss, how closely it was linked to the plan at the back of her mind, the one that paralyzed her because it was simultaneously probable and improbable. The very plan and the reason for it that she hadn't told Alan about. And she couldn't tell him then, not without peeling back the layers of secrets—the reasons behind the multiple trips to Jamaica before they married, the reason she shut down every September 16, the reason she had held him at bay for so long before agreeing to marry him—that she had allowed to compound and conflate that age-old issue of trust.

Trust, Alan thought, was the last thing to go before a marriage truly disintegrated. Respect was first and friendship second. He figured that by the time the trust was gone, the marriage itself was over; love alone, no matter how deep, was never enough to hold it all together. For them, the respect and friendship were still there. They had either bypassed the first two or upset Alan's long-held belief.

Then he was gone and Plum was alone with the girls, who lingered in the kitchen waiting for breakfast, and the rush to get dressed and off to school. Plum weighed the consequences—the loss of her marriage or giving up on meeting her daughter—and chose the one she wouldn't live without. And when she thought back on that kiss, she imagined the possibility that it could have been their last.

Yet, the plan returned, floating, tempting like the scent of forbidden food. So she buried the thought under a crevice in her mind, pictured an image of the brain—the tissue that folded in on itself—pictured her hand lifting a fold and shoving the thought under the fold away from the places in the brain whose sole purposes were remembering, planning, or thinking through consequences. What she thought about though was the first part of the plan: it was her eldest daughter's birthday, and she would confront Lenworth on that day. But the second part of the thought she didn't let linger in her mind. Four days of burying the second part and still that Friday she wouldn't think it, wouldn't let it hatch and grow wings as a plan should.

Instead, Plum filled her mind with everyday tasks, the endless duties that defined a mother's life. She cracked and whipped eggs, buttered toast, sweetened hot chocolate and warmed strawberry milk. She wiped one snot-filled nose, swapped brown leggings for a polka-dotted pair with a tiny hole, brushed the fuzzy hairline of two heads of hair, dabbed a heavy, orange-scented oil to hold wayward curls in place and searched for a second pair of polka-dotted leggings to stop Vivian's belated tantrum. She checked two backpacks, swapped a peeled orange for apple slices, wiped the sticky place in front of the fridge where Alan had spilled orange juice and wiped but not wiped carefully enough, searched the toy box for a yo-yo for the girls' sound bag, then searched again for a whistle when she realized that the lesson was the science of sound and not the sound of the letter, set out chicken breasts to thaw for the night's dinner, emptied a full clothes hamper into the washer, realizing too late that what she added was full-strength bleach and not the color-safe kind.

7:44 a.m. Plum walked the girls down the stairs, through the hall past the living room, through the triple-locked front door and metal gate, down a second flight. Dry leaves and oak bark crunched beneath their feet. Nia skipped. Vivian held Plum's hand, questioning her about where squirrels kept their babies (in tree nests), why animals build nests on thin branches (because the animals are light), how many times baby birds and squirrels fall from their nests to the ground (not often). Plum left the girls at the front door of the school, watched them skip away toward their classrooms, turn around and wave. She waved back, turned away from the double doors, the rubberized mats on the playground and walked back home where, listening to the near silence, she began putting her plan in motion. The refrigerator hummed. The grandfather clock ticked. Outside, a garbage truck screeched as the driver braked. A siren screamed its urgent notes. Without the girls laughing, screaming, running, calling "Mommy," shouting "Daddy," tugging at toys, this was silence.

Plum moved as if she had a settled plan, as if she had indeed let the plan hatch and grow wings, and written down a list of things that she checked off one at a time. Again, she concentrated on the tasks as if the outcome of her meeting with Lenworth and everything that followed would depend on how well she accomplished each task. She returned chicken breasts to the freezer, removed a bag of deveined and shelled shrimp, ran cold water over the chunk of frozen seafood, chopped and sautéed onions and garlic and scallion, and stirred the thawed shrimp over the sautéed bulbs. She set a pot to steam rice, re-removed the frozen chicken breasts and set them in a pan of water to thaw, chopped onions and garlic and scallions again, chopped lettuce and tomatoes and cucumbers, grated a bag of carrots, separated the grated carrots into two separate bowls, sprinkled sugar and raisins in one bowl of carrots, tossed the second bowl of carrots with the lettuce and tomatoes and cucumbers. She tossed the half-frozen chicken breasts into a pot with curry powder, the chopped bulbs, salt, pepper and thyme, scanned the refrigerator and the stove and calculated she had enough for at least five days' dinners. Too much, she knew.

Plum stood still for a moment, shoved the thought she didn't want at the front of her mind back in its place, then tidied the living and dining rooms. She fluffed the toss pillows, folded the throws, got on her knees with the small broom and dust pan and swept the crumbs from the area rug, changed and washed the girls' sheets, folded the first batch of unintentionally bleached clothes—all her husband's.

By noon, she was ready for another outing, this time to the supermarket. She bought enough to stock the refrigerator and cupboards full of the girls' favorite things—cookies with lickable fillings, hard red grapes without seeds, Granny Smith apples they'd sprinkle with salt, pizza dough, cookie dough, green plantains Alan would have to fry, coconut drops and gizzadas from the Jamaican bakery, hard dough bread and guava jelly, Ting grapefruit soda.

At home again, she wrote a simple note: *Will be back late. There's dinner in the fridge and pizza dough in case the girls want to make pizza.* He would wonder, she knew, when she found the time to cook shrimp, chicken and rice and about the reason for her late return. But Plum offered no other explanation.

Plum packed a bag for herself: a book of puzzles, cell phone charger, four fruit and nut bars, four bottles of water, a novel she had twice given up on completing, a thin scarf, the old cookie tin with the newspaper clipping, the one-footed doll and the hospital discharge papers. Four-fifteen. Alan would pick up the girls at five. At 5:20, the girls would dash inside, dropping bags and shoes, filling the house again with sound. Plum took her oversized tote, headed away from the subway stop and the school, turned right toward Church Avenue, left on Church past Nostrand Avenue and Flatbush, meandering past the West Indian grocery stores and bakeries, the Chinese takeout shops and the *what-not* stores that sold a hodgepodge of things.

Plum could have taken a taxi but she walked instead, stepping out into traffic as if she had every right to do so, ignoring the blaring horns, the brakes squealing as cars jerked to a halt, the drivers pushing their heads through open windows to yell and shout every obscenity imaginable. Finally, St. Paul's Place and Church Avenue. She stopped and turned right, looking up at the grey stone building, the stained glass windows, the bright red, double wooden doors at the main entrance shut up tight. Even though she had already been there once, Plum circled the church, walking down St. Paul's Place, past the high-rise apartment buildings on either side of the block, back to Church Avenue, and around again. Three times she circled, trying to slow her heart that was pulsing too hard and her breaths that came in shallow spurts. She reminded herself of her ultimate goal, how close she was to standing face to face with him after seventeen years, how close she was to seeing her daughter.

At six-thirty she was again at the entrance to the church hall. She stopped. Sounds, a thumping sound and voices, drifted through open windows. She climbed the stairs and stepped into the musty foyer. Upstairs, she could see the cavernous recreation hall and caught glimpses of boys dribbling a basketball. Youthful voices rose up from the basement rooms. The Friday evening youth fellowship, she guessed.

Plum took another deep breath and climbed the stairs toward the recreation room. She closed her eyes, realizing after that shutting her eyes wouldn't filter out the odor of must and sweat trapped in the room, and peered again inside. "Father Barrett?"

"Excuse me." The boys stopped mid-play.

Plum hadn't expected a polite answer, hadn't expected them to have heard her question at all. She thought she was still playing out the question in her mind, working out what she was going to do now that she had come this far. The question out of her mouth, she couldn't turn back now. "Father Barrett," she said again.

"Let me see." The boy with the ball turned away toward a door in the far left of the building that Plum presumed led to an office and the sanctuary.

Another boy brushed past her down the stairs to the basement. His words floated back up the stairs. "There's a woman upstairs asking to see Father Barrett."

Plum stepped inside the hall, her ballet flats soft on the wooden floor, unfolded a chair and bent to sit. The seat was lower than she thought and her body fell heavily into it, pushing the legs back, throwing up a screech that floated around, lingering and echoing. She paid attention to the sounds, the soft hushed whispers from the basement, the air circulating in the room, laughter bursting unexpectedly from the rooms below, footsteps coming from the darkened corridor to the left, footsteps coming up the stairs toward the hall, transitioning from concrete to wood, then stopping before her.

"May I help you?" The woman who stood before Plum had eyebrows penciled in place, arching unnaturally high above her eyes, a thick layer of foundation and powder and concealer congealed on her skin, breath that smelled like mint.

"I'd like to see Father Barrett, please."

"I'm Mrs. Barrett. Pauline. He isn't here now but perhaps someone else can help?"

"No, no one else." Plum hesitated, then in a bolder voice, said, "It's a personal matter that I must talk to him about."

Without hesitation, Pauline's eyes dropped to Plum's stomach, rolled over the soft folds of flesh that Plum had never bothered to work to retighten after the twins. Plum straightened her back, pushed her stomach out, flattened her hand against the T-shirt, and sat back waiting for the roving eyes to rest again on her face, which was partly shielded by oversized sunglasses.

"It's Friday evening. Priests have families too, you know. Can it wait till Sunday or Monday when he's back in office?"

"I'll wait," Plum said. Even as she said it, she wasn't sure exactly what she meant, how long she would wait for the priest to come.

"All right then. I'll see if I can get him on the phone."

"Tell him my name is Plum." As soon as she spoke, she knew she shouldn't have given her name.

The boys again dribbled the basketball and each time the ball bounced on the floor, the thump reverberated in the oversized room. Noise filled the room, making it seem smaller. She leaned forward, her chin resting on laced fingers, the small watch on her hand ticking away the minutes. By now the girls would be eating dinner, then settling in for the Friday night movie, which quite likely would be something they had already seen a hundred times. Had she been home, she would be curled up with them too, one girl on either side, her thighs and soft stomach the pillow upon which their heads, heavy with sleep, would eventually fall.

The ringtone—church bells—was most appropriate. Plum stepped into the hallway, hovering on the landing above the steps, the double doors in front of her offering a quick escape, and said hello into the small microphone. "I've gone to see the priest," she told him when he asked, omitting that she had gone to see Father Barrett at St. Paul's and not Father Bailey at St. Matthews. "It won't be long."

Plum was not religious. In truth, she had long given up on God, given up on the belief that God heard and answered prayers, that he didn't give her more than she could handle. She went to church at Christmas for the beauty of the carols accompanied by a harp and bells and violins. Yet, unlikely as it was that she would have gone to see a priest, Alan didn't ask why. She was surprised and relieved. In the background, the chattering from the movie played on and no matter what Alan said, the girls wouldn't take the phone.

8:26. The priest had not yet come. "We're going to lock up soon. Can you come back tomorrow?" Mrs. Barrett's voice was sweet, patient. Four giggling girls passed behind her heading to the far corner of the hall, away from the dribbling basketball.

"I'll wait." There it was, the thought Plum hadn't allowed to fully develop: she wouldn't leave until she saw Father Barrett, looked him in the eye, compared the man he was now with the man he had been before, and asked the question she had asked herself over and over all these years. Why? The probability of a prolonged night, locking herself in the church until he came, was the thought she wouldn't think, and she acknowledged at last that that was the reason she had prepared so much food for Alan and the girls. She didn't know when she would leave or whether he would come at all.

She looked around the room at the two adults who remained— Mrs. Barrett and the warden who held the keys—and the six sweaty boys and four girls.

"You can't stay here overnight," the man with the keys said, laughter in his voice. "We're locking up at nine."

"Make me move," Plum wanted to say. But even in her mind it sounded like something her daughters would say on the school playground. Instead, she pulled up a chair, stretched her legs out and slid her bottom down in the chair so her head rested on the chair's back.

"I'll call the police."

"This is a house of God, a place of refuge. You wouldn't want to do that." Plum didn't yet know why she felt emboldened. "It's kind of an emergency. I'll wait until he comes."

"He's been with the children all evening," Pauline said. "Maybe when I get back he can come."

Children. Plum's heartbeat quickened.

"I'll wait," Plum said. Leaving without an answer wasn't an option. Not after seventeen years of waiting and looking and hoping, of shelving disappointment and fear. Not that particular night.

On the far end of the hall, one girl slipped away from the group, into the long narrow hallway, presumably toward the vestry and the church.

"Opal?" Pauline looked around for the girl she called. "Where's she?"

The girls at the table shrugged, nonchalantly, uncaring.

"Steve, Mike, take Opal home for me. And straight home." She wagged a single finger, underscoring her point, mumbled, "That girl . . ." To the group, "Not a minute after nine."

That girl, the one who had slipped inside the church couldn't be Plum's. Pauline would not have left her, would she?

Pauline's shoes, impossibly high heels, clicked on the stairs. The door locked behind her. The warden pulled up a chair and the boys resumed dribbling the basketball on the wood floor. "It can't wait till tomorrow?" the warden asked. "I haven't even had dinner yet."

"I've been here a long time," Plum said. "This would have been over if he had come from the very first call."

"Father is a busy man."

"Of course. That's why I'll wait." What Plum remembered was leaving Anchovy empty-handed, how close she had come to finding Lenworth and her daughter, and coming away with nothing, disappointment like a pox consuming her body. How close she had come to choosing death.

"I have to run around the corner and pick up my order. Want anything?"

"No."

The warden jangled his keys, looked up at the indefatigable teens still dribbling the ball and running and jumping and hooting. The girls waved their goodbyes and left with him. Plum stood up and stretched, arching her back, then bending forward at the waist, letting her fingers extend to the floor.

"Aren't your parents expecting you at home?"

The boys laughed, dribbled the ball again, but gave no answer. The girl still had not returned.

Plum paced a little, walked back to the landing, down the stairs. She stopped in front of the double red doors and contemplated them—the sturdy steel, the system of bolts, the exit sign that would glow in the dark. She walked down into the basement, looked around and turned back, clomping her way back up the stairs, past the teen boys, through the narrow hallway separating the recreation room from the sanctuary—no light, no obvious signs of a hidden priest—and into the pitch-black church.

6

"You shouldn't be in here, you know." The girl stood behind Plum. Her breath came in ragged gasps.

Without turning around, Plum said, "Why are you hiding in here?"

"I didn't want her to drive me home."

Not her, Plum thought; the words the girl used distanced herself from Pauline. *Her*, the girl said, not *mother* or *stepmother*.

"You should go home. Your parents must be worried about you being out so late."

"They know where I am. Why did you come in here?"

"The simple truth: I thought the priest was hiding back here and you came to keep him from me."

The girl laughed, a short burst of sound.

Plum struck a match and lit one votive candle after another, keeping her eyes on the flames sputtering to life behind the red candleholders.

"You have to pay for each one you light," the girl said. "And pray."

"You don't know that I'm not praying."

"Maybe you should kneel and close your eyes."

"Maybe I prefer to pray with my eyes open."

"I know you haven't put any money in the box."

"Prayers shouldn't come with a fee. It's free to pray, you know."

"You still shouldn't be in here."

"What's your name?"

"Opal."

Plum turned away toward the pew and sank into the red cushion lining the bench. She stretched her legs out in front of her, watching each candle flickering lazily.

"You have to put them out before you leave."

To Plum, the girl sounded anxious, a bit worried now that she would get into trouble for leading Plum into the sanctuary.

Plum patted the empty space beside her. "Sit." The girl did exactly as she asked. "Listen to the silence. You can almost feel the quiet inside here. It's almost like you can touch it. This is what a sanctuary is supposed to feel like. Not with the singing and noise church people make on Sunday mornings."

"This isn't that kind of church," Opal said.

"I know." Even in the haze of darkness, Plum felt the intensity of Opal's stare and the girl's anxiety in every twitch of her leg. "I'm not going to burn down your church. I'm just waiting for the priest to come."

The girl, nervous still, shifted her gaze away from Plum and back to the flickering candles. Plum closed her eyes and leaned her neck back against the bench. The church was cool and musty, the air tinged with a hint of incense and decaying flowers Plum couldn't name. It was too dark to see the floral arrangements on the nearby altar, but she imagined several elaborate ones, a range of colors and textures and shapes, heart-shaped anthuriums, spiked birds of paradise that resembled yellow plumed birds in flight, the cone-shaped ginger flower. Even as she pictured the bouquets, she knew she was thinking of a different church altogether, tropical flowers on an altar at a church in Jamaica, herself as a boarding school student longing for home.

The girl beside her breathed deeply. "I think you mean trouble for the priest. My mother thinks women always bring trouble for priests. And, besides, if you were a member of the church, you'd know his office hours."

"What kind of trouble?" Plum asked.

"I don't know. Just trouble. There was a scandal. I don't know exactly what. But the priest is rebuilding the church and it's our duty to help him keep trouble away. You can't just come out of nowhere and mess it up."

"Then you should go on home. Nothing like a teenager staying out all night after youth fellowship to start a scandal at the church. What will your priest think of a young girl who doesn't go home at night?"

"They won't even know I'm missing." Opal stretched out her legs. "Besides, you're wasting your time. She didn't tell him you came to see him. She always suspects the worst when women come to see him, so she wouldn't have told him at all."

Plum turned toward Opal, parsing through each of Opal's words, she, too, searching through the haze of darkness to see Opal's features. Earlier, she had hardly looked at the girl. She remembered a teenager's lithe body, a girl conscious of the way she moved around the boys, so conscious she kept her eyes mostly down. So Plum hadn't noticed the eyes, whether they were like hers or his, hadn't looked at the girl's nose or lips or ears. So focused was she on getting to Lenworth that she hadn't paid attention to the girl at all. Mostly, Plum dismissed the possibility that she was hers because of how readily and quickly Pauline had walked away and left the girl behind.

"How do you know?"

"Know what?"

"That she didn't tell him."

"She never tells him anything. At least not if it involves a woman."

A quickening now, an urgency to her voice. "The priest, is he your father?"

"Yes."

Plum reached to pull Opal to her, but with the slightest shift she thought of what the girl would think of a stranger hugging her in the dark. And she thought, too, of her own failure to recognize her own offspring. Plum always imagined she would have known her daughter instinctively. But she hadn't, and instead had nearly missed this reunion altogether.

Then Plum felt it, a peacefulness, an easing in every quadrant of her body, the release of every pent-up emotion.

Footsteps and angry, urgent voices echoed from the hallway connecting the church and the hall. "What was her name?" someone asked. "Either of you caught her name?"

"Don't remember." A husky teen voice.

"I'm locking up. You boys go on home."

"What about Opal? We can't go home without her."

Opal stood up, turning in Plum's direction as if to ask, "Aren't you coming?"

Instead, Plum tugged on Opal's arm. "Stay."

Opal shrugged off Plum's hand. "No," she whispered. "You shouldn't be in here. We shouldn't be in here. We're going to be in trouble if we get caught."

"It's too late now," Plum said.

The voices came closer and someone jiggled and turned a lock. Plum ducked behind a pew, quickly stretching her body out on the cold, concrete floor. "Get down." Plum's whisper was harsh.

Opal moved, ducking behind the pew, her hair brushing Plum's forehead, tickling her skin. But Plum didn't move.

"Call your parents and go on home." The warden spoke and the footsteps faded away from the church, back down the hallway connecting the church and the recreation room. "They both must have left."

Caught up now in her own cat and mouse game, a one-sided, misguided game of hide-and-seek, Plum simply said, "Don't worry.

Your father will come for you." Even if Pauline hadn't told Lenworth her name, Plum was sure that he would come. If not for Plum, he would come for Opal, come to reclaim what he once claimed as his and his alone.

7

Lenworth reached for his slippers in the dark, and, as he had learned to do over the years, felt around with his foot for whatever toy, book, plate or half-full glass of juice one of the boys had left untended on the floor. Nothing. He sat upright, his feet dangling from the bed, his soles brushing the top of his slippers. Careful, he thought, or Pauline might wake, and if she did, her voice would come at him in the dark like a needle pricking at an already sore spot.

Every year it was the same. His body remembered what he had trained his mind to forget, and every year on the morning of Opal's birthday he woke long before dawn, in the hours before the birds outside his window started up a series of calls. But he never thought fully and deeply about the baby girl, seventeen years old now. Instead, he thought about her mother, Plum, lying in the hospital bed sleeping at last. The birth wasn't easy, and for a while the doctors had thought he would lose both mother and child. But they pushed, one to reclaim and the other to lay her first claim on her space in the world. Resting, Plum was, as he had always thought, beautiful. Her dark skin glowed as if painted with oil, and her lips, a deep red that needed no additional color from lipstick or gloss, shone. In sleep,

she rested her thumb against her lip as if she had fallen asleep sucking on her finger or was waiting for quiet and darkness to suck on it
again. Every year, he thought about turning back the clock, walking
away from the hospital that night for good, walking away from Plum
empty-handed instead of with the baby girl wrapped in a blanket. In
the crook of his arm, the baby had slept peacefully. When she woke,
her eyes glistened with color, and he named her Opal for no other
reason than she looked up at him with eyes that reminded him of a
precious stone. He didn't think signing his own newborn child out
of the hospital without Plum's knowledge was the worst of his mistakes. Up until then, his greatest mistake was falling in love with
Plum, a student he had once been hired to tutor, and who was at that
time not quite an adult. It didn't matter that he was only twenty-four,
a young teacher himself working temporarily as an assistant in the
school's chemistry lab and tutoring on the side.

Looking down at Plum in the hospital bed with her thumb
against her lip, he was certain he wanted her to have a different kind
of future, not the one conscripted to her now that she had had a child
at seventeen, not the life his mother and sister had. He thought of
what had spurred his life for nearly ten years: what it meant to have
agency, to have the capacity to exert power and control over his life.
And he wanted Plum to have the same. What he had thought of in
the days leading up to her being at the hospital seemed like a plan
etched in stone. Walking away with the baby seemed like the only
gift he had left to give Plum. His gift would mean Plum could have
a life, a promising future, a university experience like any other
young adult, a clean slate to start her life again. And he had indeed
followed through on that plan: he left with the baby, not bothering
to stop to scratch out a note to Plum explaining his *gift* to her.

His gift: a future, an unencumbered start to whatever life Plum
chose to live. In essence, power and control over her life.

Only, they hadn't talked at all of what she wished or wanted. He forgot that his gift to Plum meant he was robbing her of the very control he thought he was giving.

Now, like he had done every other September 16, he imagined Plum waking seventeen years earlier to his inadequate gift, bawling perhaps, her surprise melting into despair, her love into hatred, and holding her empty arms out in front for the baby she wouldn't receive, seeing again and again her still-swollen stomach and empty arms, her breasts achingly full of milk that would feed no one.

He closed his eyes to shut out the rest, and whispered the prayer he whispered every morning and night, "Forgive me, Father, for I have sinned." Yet, he had found no way to forgive himself.

Here was Opal's birthday again, come to remind him of what he had taken away, his own inadequate role as a father to Opal, his mistakes piling up one on top the other. Opal, with her mother's eyes and rich dark skin, reminded him day after day of what he had done those seventeen years ago, how he had robbed his own daughter of her mother's touch, how he had robbed Plum of what most mothers craved: cradling the baby to whom she had sung, to whom she had whispered stories for nine whole months. There was no counting the number of times he had to walk away from Opal to hide the unending agony of his mistake, how many times he lied about Plum's fate to keep his own secret, how many times he gave too much to make up for what Opal had lost. And so he had come up with tea by the sea, his gift to Opal and Opal alone, a poor substitute for time with her own mother but something he imagined Plum would have considered or even done.

He would take her to Coney Island that morning. Breakfast—tea, scones or bagels and fruit—by the sea with his daughter was the best that he could do on this birthday morning.

Behind him, Pauline snored lightly. Her breath rustled the sheet, and its every movement was to him a whispered reminder of how he had failed. What Pauline knew, or thought she knew, was nothing compared to what he had actually done. He eased off the bed slowly, checking again for toys or one of his sons rolled up in a blanket on the floor at the foot of the bed, and tiptoed through the dark house to his office, the place where he found refuge from the eyes that looked at him with a combination of longing and awe of the man they all imagined he was. He didn't think himself worthy of the collar and vestments he wore, nor of his family's love, but week after week he tried to do some good, if not to make himself worthy then to erase bit by bit the gargantuan sin that shadowed his life.

Lenworth remained in the dark office, his cupped hands chest high, mimicking the way his congregation knelt before him to receive the sacrament. He waited for God to speak, to send a blessing, inspiration for Sunday's sermon, even a single word. Like every other night when he sat like that waiting for God to speak, he fell into sleep. His hands drifted down to his lap, his head drooped forward, and his jaw hung loose. Asleep, he was exactly how he pictured himself—a marionette controlled by an invisible string, except in his case he was his own puppeteer, incapable or unwilling to right his own wrongs.

He dreamt again of his mother. She stood outside hanging clothes on a line, the breeze pushing the wet clothes back against her body. The sheets, heavy with water, flapped, thwacked, flicked droplets of water through the air. When she turned around at last, she said, "Oh, you come," just as she had done the very last time he saw her in person. Her disappointment in him was as palpable as the leather seat pressed against his thighs. As he did in every dream in which she came to him, he explained himself. As happened in every dream in which she came to him, she didn't hear a single word he said. He spoke but someone or something muted his voice or plugged her ears. He heard her questions and accusations, but his words, his explanations, were held back by an invisible shield of sorts. They continued like that until he sprung up, weary and frustrated, suspended between sleep and wakefulness, fighting to fall back to sleep.

8

One by one, Plum blew the candles out. Opal, her nervousness growing, paced, rubbing her hand along the gold plated banister leading to the altar.

"He should have come by now," Opal said. "What if he doesn't know we're in here? Maybe we should leave the lights on?"

"Yes, good idea."

Plum stood and tiptoed out, using the illumination from her phone's screen as a dim flashlight, and her hands along the wall as a guide. The room flooded with light and she blinked against it. The empty, cavernous hall would tell Lenworth nothing. She undid her scarf and draped it on a chair, which she placed in the center of the room. Back in the hallway, she turned on another light, hoping it would work like a lighthouse and guide him through the vestry to the church itself.

Opal lay on a pew, her back curled and knees to her chest. "You're going to get me into trouble."

"Not at all. You don't know me, but trust me. You're not in any trouble at all."

"You don't know my stepmother."

"What does she do?"

"Cinderella." Her voice was muffled by the cushions. "Can do nothing right."

"Say that again?" Plum asked.

"Never mind." Opal stood, walked away from the pew and started pacing again.

They were again in their separate places—Opal pacing five steps one way and five steps back and Plum sitting in the front pew looking toward the lectern.

"I know you're worried," Plum said. "But trust me when I say don't worry. I'm responsible for you being here and I will take the blame for that."

"It's not that," Opal said. "My father should have come by now. If not for you, then he should have come to look for me." Opal stopped to look in Plum's direction. "What do you want from him?"

"It's a complicated thing."

"Maybe my stepmother was right."

"About what?"

"Women like you."

"What do you mean?" Plum felt her heart quickening.

"Never mind."

"You're protecting him. I understand that."

"Somebody has to."

Plum hadn't pictured her daughter that way, not as a teenager thinking herself her father's savior, setting herself up to be a footnote in her father's biography, noted for saving her father and attempting even in her youth to right her father's wrongs. She thought of her daughter as a version of herself, bold and brave and assertive when necessary. But here was Opal, a nervous girl, afraid of disappointing, desperate it seemed to find her place in her father's life.

"You're too young to be his savior." As Plum spoke, she realized that perhaps she was talking about herself, the young adult protecting Lenworth from her aunt and her parents' wrath, protecting him from her parents even after he had left and she had come back to Brooklyn broken and empty.

There in the church, the minutes ticking away, the clock inching toward midnight, the thought seeped into Plum that perhaps Lenworth would not come, that Opal who thought herself his savior would leave. That she would lose the daughter for whom she had searched all these years. Seeking a way to ease into what she needed to say, Plum asked, "What happened to your mother?"

"She flew away."

A euphemism for death, Plum thought. "What do you mean when you say she flew away? Do you mean she died? Or do you mean she left?"

But Opal didn't answer. Not directly.

"I saw her once," Opal said, and Plum sat up, imagining for a minute a missed chance to reconnect. "Or maybe just someone who looked like how I think my mother would look."

Opal kept her eyes closed as she spoke. Her imagined memory began outside the windows of the car, where the Brooklyn streets moved at first in a blur of colors and sound she hadn't seen in the Maryland suburbs. As the car got closer to Flatbush, it moved much more slowly—stop, stop, stop, go—the colors unblurred and the faces around which the colors were wrapped became more defined. Street noise burst into the car, which, except for the chatter of the boys, had been quiet most of the four-hour drive from Maryland. Her parents didn't speak, hadn't spoken to each other for more than a week. Both boys slept. Opal, awake, saw the city in reverse. She kneeled on the seat with the seatbelt still wrapped around her body and stared through the dusty window at the streets they were leaving behind. There, on the sidewalk, a woman with one foot on the curb and the other on the roadway, stopped midstride. She raised a hand to hail a cab. The arm, partially covered in green, split the woman's face in two but the half of the face that Opal saw looked a little bit like her own. She opened her mouth to say "look," but the car moved and she was thrown back against the front passenger seat, startling and jolting her father and stepmother, who in turn shouted, "sit properly," and "sit down," their voices in unison but their bodies objecting to any kind of unity.

The face Opal thought she saw was long gone from her memory but the imagined reunion she had created from it remained. She told Plum of the faceless mother and her other family, a mother with whom Opal always had unplanned meetings. She looked in always on her mother and a little girl and boy having an impromptu picnic on a slice of paved walkway in front of a brownstone. Why she chose Brooklyn and not Jamaica was not something she could explain. In truth, though, she had little memory of any house other than the one in Anchovy with the crawl space beneath the house and floorboards that dipped beneath her feet. Curiously, she didn't ever picture her imaginary mother living there with her father.

Always, her mother unfolded a pink, child-sized picnic table, the kind that comes with a miniature umbrella and chairs, and the two children—the girl with plaits dangling over her ears and the boy with a truck in his hand—walked tentatively to the picnic set as if surprised no one else had come. In all the years she had imagined her mother and her family, the children never aged. Her mother arranged three folding chairs, and Opal always looked up at the front door and scanned the windows for a rustle of life inside. Always, her mother lifted a picnic basket and gave the children their dinner then placed two empty plates on the adult chairs, poured herself a glass of juice and sat down to watch the children eat.

It was only then that Opal let herself move forward and encroach upon the private meal. They were in the shadow of an enormous oak. Leaves softened the bricks under their feet and sunshine peeked through the branches, dotting the ground with bits of yellow. They would be a curious sight—a woman, a teenage girl, and a young boy and girl picnicking on a Saturday afternoon in the front yard of a brownstone, inches from the wide paved steps and the small porch.

Only after the meal would her mother invite her inside into a living room cluttered with children's toys and books, stacks of magazines on the coffee table, framed photos scattered around the room, and sculptures and pieces of artwork that her mother had accumulated through the years. Her eyes were hungry, seeking an explanation for her mother's long absence from her life, the life her mother had chosen instead of mothering her.

That's where her reunion always ended, with Opal inside the house soaking up her mother's life, her newfound family in limbo, her mother and the ageless children, watching her encroach upon their lives.

In Opal's voice was a wistfulness and longing that hurt Plum. She was grateful for the dark, and she bent her head and wept for her daughter and herself, and for the simple fact that Opal's chattiness and bravado couldn't replace one simple fact: her father had not yet come to find and claim her.

9

A sliver of sunshine peeked in through the blinds, stirring Lenworth fully awake. Seven already. The rooms above were still. He drew his legs toward the chair, pulled himself up, and tottered to the kitchen to put water on to boil, anxious to escape with Opal before Pauline or the boys woke. Opal's bed was neatly made, the pillows at the head of the bed, forming a slight mound beneath the comforter, and the oversized orange bear still in its usual place in the middle of the pillows. He remained at the door, staring back at the stuffed bear's glass eyes, his body stiff, as if waiting for someone to cast a rod and reel him further in. The window was closed, but he walked toward it to convince himself that it was indeed latched from the inside. As he passed the bed he ran his palm on the comforter, confirming what he already suspected: the bed was cold.

Next door, in the boys' bedroom he counted the shapes—two— and kept time with the rhythm of their breaths. He walked the hall again, and descended the stairs slowly and deliberately. He jiggled the locks and checked each room, peering underneath tables and in the closet as if he were again a young father playing hide-and-seek with his young daughter. And as he moved, he thought back to the previous night, Pauline coming in, jangling her keys as usual and calling out as she walked from the front door to the kitchen. He hadn't moved from his desk, pausing only long enough to throw his greeting over his shoulder. He didn't recall Opal's voice, and he wouldn't have thought anything of her not coming back with Pauline that Friday night because she often stayed later and returned home with the boys who lived next door.

He headed up the stairs again, a little quicker this time around, calling Pauline's name the moment his feet landed on the top step. Even before she opened her eyes, he asked, "Where's Opal? She's not here. Where is she?"

"Look at how long you've been awake. Why are you asking me?"

"She's not in her bed. She didn't come back with you last night?"

"I left her there with the boys from next door. They were there at the church. In the gym."

"So she didn't come home at all?" Even as he asked, Lenworth realized his question made him sound like a disconnected parent. How could he not have known his own daughter hadn't come home? He pulled the robe tight around his body. "I'm going next door."

"Dressed like that? In your pajamas and robe?"

"Yes, dressed like this. My daughter is missing and all you care about is what people will think of how I look?" He was already at the bedroom door when he finished speaking, moving so fast he nearly slipped on the rug, and again on the stairs. He heard Pauline struggling with a dress, her slippers flapping on the wood floor.

But he didn't stop running until he was on the neighbors' stoop, two footsteps away from the door, his finger already reaching for the doorbell. He pressed once, twice, three times, stopping when he heard shuffling behind the door. Carl, the father of the boys, opened the door a crack, looked out.

"Sorry, I know it's early. But Opal . . ." Lenworth paused, waiting for Carl to fling open the security gate, then stepped back out of reach of the gate. "It's Opal," he said again, taking a step forward away from the morning light to the dark interior, keeping his voice low. "She's missing. Don't know if she even came home last night and I thought that maybe the boys would know where she is. Pauline said she left Opal with the boys there last night."

"You don't think . . ."

"I don't know what to think." Lenworth was inside the house now, waiting for his eyes to readjust to the dark. Pauline slid in behind him, her breath on his neck, her bare hand brushing his.

"Let me get the boys."

Pauline leaned in to him, laying her fingers on his shoulder. But he stepped away from her ever so slightly, then moved again to lean fully against the back of a sofa. Upstairs, feet padded around on squeaking floors and squeaking steps, and he straightened himself as the boys and their parents came toward him, asking as he stood if the boys—still sleepy, still rubbing their eyes—knew anything about Opal's whereabouts.

"We thought she left with you," the older of the two boys said, leaning slightly to look at Pauline. "One minute she was there and then she was gone. So we thought she left with you. And that woman left too."

"What woman?" Lenworth asked.

"A woman who was there asking for you. She too just disappeared."

"Woman? What woman?" He turned to Pauline. "You didn't tell me about a woman."

Both boys lifted their shoulders up into a shrug, the answer Lenworth hated most of all.

"She said her name was Plum." Pauline opened her mouth at last.

"Plum?" He didn't recognize his own voice, the squeak that escaped his lips. "Plum?"

"She wanted to talk to you but since you were home with the boys I didn't call. I figured whatever it was could wait."

Beyond repeating Plum's name, Lenworth had no words at all. He had no strength in his legs either and he reached behind for something to hold, but his hand simply flapped like an awkward fin. He caught himself, pulled his hand in against his body, nodded and left, struggling, as he walked, to maintain his composure. It was, after all, what was expected of him. Everyone expected a priest to be composed at all times, whether he prayed over the living or dying or counseled a couple not yet ready for marriage. He held himself together only by repeating a question he couldn't answer. Why now? Why now? Why now? He sensed the neighbors and Pauline staring at him walking so fast he was almost trotting, his robe, open now, flapping behind him. He slowed his steps and his breathing and then he asked himself the other pressing question: How did Plum find Opal? Or was it the other way around: how did Opal find Plum?

From his own front door, he heard the urgent and insistent whistle from the kettle, the boys, awake and alone, calling and crying. The sounds spurted outward and even after he turned off the flame and Pauline quieted the boys, the raucous sounds lingered in his mind, rising to a grating, irritating crescendo. He couldn't panic and yet he did, knocking a stack of papers loose. He sensed Pauline's presence. She stood in the doorway with her hands around the boys' shoulders, waiting for him to speak.

"Go," he said, quietly. But the second time he uttered the word it was a sharp bark that seemed to spurt from the depths of his stomach. He bent over the desk and breathed in deeply, closing his eyes as he concentrated on sucking in air. He thought of the secrets that would come tumbling out now: the very first scandal that had chased him from the high school for girls in Brown's Town, Jamaica, his own daughter whom he had taken and kept all these years from Plum, the incident that prompted his escape to the seminary. His past was hurtling forward, rapidly tumbling into his present and shattering his vision of the future.

10

Plum woke with her breath catching in her throat, a feeling like drowning. Her nostrils were clogged, head and eyes heavy, and her body felt as if it had indeed struggled against a strong current all night. She had slept in fits, and now, barely awake, her mind foggy and body achy, she clutched at the space beside her, reaching for the bodies of Nia and Vivian, and came up empty. "No," she whispered at first. Then, more awake, she said it again louder, all the while feeling around her, pressing her hand into the cushion, bumping up against the sloped back of the pew and her tote bag and back down to the soft velvet cushion. Panicked, she swung her legs down, stood up, looked around and made out the stained glass windows, the sunlight up against the thick, colored glass impossibly trying to filter through, and remembered where she was and why. She slowed her breath, closed her eyes and breathed in deeply, sucking on must and the lingering remnants of incense.

Across the aisle, Opal lay on her belly, one arm between her face and the cushion, her legs crossed at the ankles. Plum stepped back.

How close she had come to seeing Lenworth. And yet he hadn't bothered to come at all. She was forgettable. Forgotten again. Not just Plum this time, but Opal as well.

For a moment, Plum panicked, pushed through a feeling of doom in which she pictured Lenworth packing in the night and leaving again once he heard her name. Plum tried to steady her heart, her mind, the pressure of blood pulsing through her arteries, easing the anxiety and fear settling into her body, the calcified heartache, the anger at the man who once had her heart and discarded it. Despair as deep as the feeling that urged on the stick figure in the boat.

Plum walked down the aisle and back, playing through various scenarios in her head, picturing Alan and Nia and Vivian. The girls, who had never spent a night away from Plum, would be waking now. Vivian was usually the first to rise and shake Nia awake. Tights and leotards and tutus and ballet and tap shoes. A flurry of disorder in the girls' room. The girls walking out to something very wrong—the television silent and dark, without animation, without the artificial and tinny voices of their favorite cartoons, an absent mother, a worried and disheveled father, the kitchen silent and odorless, without the scent of cinnamon and nutmeg and vanilla rising from the Saturday morning's staple breakfast—cornmeal porridge—and the house itself worried into an uneasy quiet. Perhaps Alan and the girls weren't home at all but out finishing up their fifth or sixth or seventh hour of searching for her, or at a police station describing her hair and face and body, Alan reluctant to accept that it was too early to file a missing person's report, trying to make the police officer understand that every year on this date Plum spirals downward to a place he had never been able to pull her from, realizing too late that he implied Plum was chronically depressed, and realizing even later that depression and suicide were too often linked. Indeed they were. But Alan didn't know about the stick figure in the boat on the mighty sea, disappearing to nothing. Had he known he probably would have scoured the waters, Brooklyn's seaside towns that were accessible by bus or train—Coney Island, Sheepshead Bay, Brighton Beach—and would have found out from Plum's parents about a night she spent sleeping on a boardwalk bench in Coney Island, her eyes to the dark sea. He wouldn't have hesitated to save her from herself.

But there she was, alive, disappointed but neither suicidal nor depressed, a woman once unforgettable to Lenworth, but now forgettable. She had Opal. Now hers. Plum had her now. And yet, she didn't. Not fully. Not completely. There was, of course, no certainty that Opal would believe Plum's version of events, no certainty that she would walk away from the only parents she had known. And still Plum wanted one more thing: to know the why of it all. Midstride, Plum stopped and looked up to the pulpit as if looking at the man she had come to see.

"What would you tell him?" Opal gave herself away, and walked toward Plum who had remained in front of the altar, looking up at an imaginary person. Plum didn't answer immediately, and Opal sidestepped her, taking the marble stairs two at a time, brushing past the enormous eagle lectern and toward the pulpit. "It would be funny if you interrupted his sermon. Just stand right here." Opal shouted "Hello!" and giggled, then looked again at Plum. "It would surely wake up the congregation. They never listen to him anyway." She shrugged, took another step toward the altar and shouted "hello!" again. Her voice echoed in the near-empty church.

"Shh. Not so loud." Plum stepped back, let her weight rest against the front pew. "Take me to see your father."

"No."

"This is important. There was a reason I wanted to see him last night. The time and the day were important."

"I can't go home now."

"Why?" Concerned, even a bit protective, Plum stepped closer.

"Why don't you go home and come back tomorrow? You can always talk to him after church."

"Why don't you want to go home?"

"Can't you tell?" Opal's emotions shifted again. "He doesn't care about me. Even if he didn't want to see you, he should at least have come to find me." Opal waved her hand, trying to brush aside her earlier words. But her voice was choked. "Maybe he hasn't missed me yet. But by now, he must have come in to say 'happy birthday' and noticed that I'm not there. And if I'm right, all hell is breaking loose."

Plum moved quickly then, closing in on the altar like an animal let loose from a noose. "Happy birthday," she said through sniffles.

"You're crying. Why does my birthday make everyone sad? Even you, a stranger."

"Your father, is he sad on your birthday?"

"Yes. Sometimes I just wish he would forget the date altogether. Just let the day pass without acknowledging it. Maybe that would make it better for him."

"You shouldn't be sad because he's sad."

"I'm not. Besides, I'm too old now to be excited about my birthday. It's just a day like any other."

"Is the thing you're crying about the same reason you came to see my father?"

"Yes." Plum turned away, searching for a way to say the simplest of words, *I am your mother.* Instead she cried, the depth of emotion overtaking her body and surprising Opal, who stood away from Plum.

When Plum's emotions settled, she wiped her eyes and turned back to Opal. "If you could wish for anything for your birthday, what would it be?" Plum's voice was almost normal again, except it quivered and she spoke low as if she wanted no one, not even Opal, to hear at all.

"Tea by the sea."

"How so?"

"When we first moved to Brooklyn, my father used to drive to Coney Island on Saturday mornings and walk along the boardwalk. He goes by himself. Except on my birthday. He takes me. Just the two of us. And afterwards we sat on a bench and drank tea from tiny little teacups. My stepmother's porcelain cups with little flowers on the side. No matter how cold it was or how tired I was, it felt like everything was perfect. I was the perfect daughter. He was the perfect father. It felt like we were in a storybook. And nothing else that came before mattered. We didn't really speak, but it felt just right. It felt like the world was all right." Opal threw up her hands. "I don't know how else to explain it."

"You're doing just fine. I understand."

"That was the only time I drank tea. And I felt like a little girl from a different world. Like a princess drinking from those dainty cups. So I guess that's my birthday wish, to feel like I matter to somebody."

"You matter."

"You're crying again."

"Sorry. I do that sometimes." What Plum held onto was the simplest fact: Lenworth hadn't forgotten one thing. Tea by the sea was Plum's thing, the way she spent her Saturday mornings or holiday mornings when she was home from school: on a nearly empty beach with a thermos of tea, toast or fruit. Sometimes it was just Plum and the fishermen hauling in their catch. Sometimes Lenworth met her there, standing first at a distance and watching as she looked out at the flat and endless sea.

From her enormous tote, Plum removed two bottles of water, a box of apple juice, and two apple turnovers. "It's not tea by the sea," she said apologetically.

"Ah, breakfast. Guess you really came prepared to stay."

A moment's hesitation, then, "My girls like them."

From the pew in front of Plum, "So what is the plan?"

"To see your father, of course."

"Isn't it obvious? He does *not* want to see you."

"No. He doesn't." Plum hesitated. "Take me to him. This is my last chance. It's either you take me to him or I make trouble for him here on Sunday. I'll stand up during his sermon and tell the congregation what he doesn't want them to know. And that's not what you want. I can tell. You still want to protect him."

"Who says I'm protecting him?"

"You're here. You stayed last night. Protecting him from me. Or running away from something."

"He's coming."

"I'm not so sure. He would have come by now."

"He's coming. I guarantee that he's coming soon."

"Why are you now so sure?"

"I just know it."

"I like to have alternatives. If he doesn't come by noon, then I want you to take me to him."

"I'll tell you where he is. But I don't want to go home."

"Ever?"

"Just not now."

"What are you running from?"

Opal's eyes slid away again. Plum looked away too, certain now that she had pushed for too much. She couldn't mother Opal. Not just yet. Not without those four words: I am your mother. Opal gathered her things, her purse, retied her laces and fluffed the cushion beneath her.

"I'll tell you where he is. But you have to promise not to tell him where I am. And I won't tell anyone we were here together all night."

"I can't let you walk away like that. You're not as old as you think."

"Seventeen is old enough."

"Believe me when I tell you that at seventeen, you're not old enough. You're not ready to do it all by yourself. You're not ready for all the disappointments. You're not ready to walk away from everything you know and live on your own." Plum bent her head, trying to catch Opal's eye. But Opal shifted her eyes again away from Plum, and her neck and shoulders followed.

"All right." Hesitation. Disappointment. "Let's just go now." Opal led Plum through the passageway to the hall.

Unlike the church, the morning sounds—sirens and loud voices—bounced through the walls and around the cavernous hall. Red and blue lights, weakened in the daylight, danced against the windows. "Too late," Plum said. "They're here. Not just your father but the whole police force."

"I told you he would come." Almost immediately, Opal's bravado wilted. "What's the worst that could happen to us?"

"I don't know." Yet Plum did. She anticipated kidnapping or trespassing charges, Lenworth leaving in a hurry and taking her daughter with him. Again. "It's not you who's in trouble. It's me."

"Is the thing you want to talk to my father about worth getting arrested over?"

"Yes." Plum, her face pressed up against the glass, said, "The church door. We could leave through the church door."

"Maybe." Opal, breathless, seemed excited now by the game, the one-sided hide-and-seek.

They went back through the church, not quite at a run, not quite at a trot, Opal ahead, thinking and talking too fast and trying to control her jagged breath. And failing.

At the back of the church, standing up against the red wooden doors, keyholes stared back at them. There was no knob to turn, no bolts to undo, just keyholes that needed keys.

"Then back to the first plan. We wait." Really, Plum wanted only to hold on to Opal a little bit longer, to say what she hadn't said earlier. The manner in which Lenworth had come, with police officers and flashing lights, guaranteed her nothing beyond the time she had with Opal there in the church.

"Not here," Opal said. "Choir room. Upstairs. Come."

Plum followed, extending the cat and mouse game, wanting Lenworth to come yet prolonging the search to avoid the police. And so they moved, Plum, who understood the consequences of being caught with a girl who they surely considered a runaway— kidnapping charges or something just as serious—following Opal, up the stairs to the room that was home to musical instruments and robes and books. Both breathless, anxious, waiting, hiding upstairs in the musty choir room.

11

Lenworth's carefully scripted life was falling apart, splitting open without his doing. He likened it to an egg with a life inside, opening on its own time, the chick emerging, its life no longer contained or constrained.

He was of two minds. He could fight for the life he had built, contain the truth before it exploded and news of his family troubles spread amongst the parishioners. Or he could walk away from the life he had built and allow Plum and Opal to be together as they should have always been. Of course, there was the small chance that Opal was not with Plum but elsewhere in the city or out of it, alone and unprepared. But he knew with absolute certainty that Plum, once she had Opal, wouldn't let go of her.

Lenworth chose the former, the life he had built. He imagined the story already spreading from one parishioner to another, beginning with his neighbor, the father of the boys who should have taken Opal home, telling one person after another how Lenworth had run, flown, once he heard Plum's name. And he imagined the variations of the story that would be passed on. Before the end of the day—perhaps even before noon—the entire congregation would know that his teenage daughter hadn't spent the night at home where she belonged. He imagined the gossip—out with a man, a runaway, passed out somewhere. Or perhaps even the truth of what he had done seventeen years earlier.

He was anxious now, angry too, at how Opal had singlehandedly orchestrated his downfall and brought down the shell he had built around his family. The fall, almost biblical in its magnanimity and as epic as anything Shakespeare ever dreamed, was nothing Lenworth could have imagined.

He couldn't panic and yet he did, fumbling and causing another stack of papers to fall as he tried to find the church lawyer's number. He could think of nothing else to do but call the lawyer, to lay his problems upon someone else.

Lenworth didn't know exactly where to begin, how to tell his story so George, the parishioner who also served as St. Paul's attorney—and the two wardens he had brought along with him—would understand that his missing daughter wasn't really missing at all. How could he tell the attorney that he didn't want to involve the police, that Plum deserved this opportunity to have her daughter at last? The three men were dressed for tennis, and Lenworth apologized for interrupting or postponing a game.

George, the attorney, accustomed it seemed to waiting for his clients' stories to evolve from the truth to the very real truth, spread cream cheese on a bagel with quick, deliberate strokes, then measured a teaspoon of honey for his tea.

Lenworth's voice was as quiet as he had ever heard it, a little boy's cry for help. His daughter was missing, and though he should have been working his way back from that urgent and immediate fact, he began his story elsewhere, on the island all four of the men knew, in a little town called Anchovy that the three visitors didn't know, in a little house on a hill that outlived even its builder's expectations. A man with a motherless child, deliberately forgetting for the moment how he had come to be the baby's only parent and the circumstances under which he and Plum had come to be parents at all.

"I think Opal's mother has found us, and has Opal now," Lenworth said at last. "I want to find her but I don't want to involve the police."

The men before Lenworth couldn't see his guilt, the pressure inside him easing even without certain assurance that Plum and Opal were together. As if they hadn't heard how he had come to be Opal's only parent, they asked what right had Plum, absent from Opal's life for seventeen years, to return and take a child she hadn't raised? They wanted justice. But where they saw injustice, Lenworth saw justice—mother and daughter together.

"First, we'll go to the church," George said.

The four of them climbed in George's car for the short ride down Church Avenue to St Paul's place. By the time they arrived at the church, Lenworth in the back seat like an isolated prisoner, the police were there. Yellow tape cordoned off the entire block, and from where the car came to a stop, he could see a tarp on the sidewalk, inches from the steps that led up to the church hall's red steel doors. He opened the car door quickly, uncertain of what he was about to encounter, and touched his neck to confirm he had worn his clerical collar. He took a moment to steady himself and mutter a three-word prayer: *God help us.* Then he rushed forward through the thin crowd of people who had gathered to watch and up to the yellow crime scene tape marking an artificial border around the tarp on the ground. Don't think the worst, he told himself, then took determined steps toward the uniformed police officer guarding the crime scene tape.

"I'm Father Barrett." He touched his collar again and then kept his hand upon his chest. "Is it my daughter, Opal?"

"Sir . . ."

"Is it my daughter?"

"Sir . . ."

"This is my church and if it's my child I have a right to know."
His voice was harsher than he intended. He remembered the reason
he had come and dialed back his anger. "My daughter," he said. "She
didn't come home last night. Is that her?" As if he could discern the
shape or age or gender of the body beneath the tarp, he shifted his
eyes to the slate gray cloth. But he couldn't tell which end was the
head or feet, whether the body was thin or large.

"Captain," the young officer called, then he stepped back to
whisper to an older man, whose beard and hair aged him more than
his face. Seconds later, the young officer turned away and walked
back to the tape. "The deceased is an old woman. Caucasian."

Lenworth exhaled so deeply, his breath fluttered the yellow tape.
"Thank you, Jesus." He bent at the waist as if he could no longer
hold himself up and watched the cold, bitter tea he had swallowed
earlier trickle from his mouth onto the ground. "I'm sorry," he said
after wiping his mouth with a handkerchief.

"It could be a parishioner," the police officer said. "We might
need you to identify the body."

"My daughter," he said. "I have to find my daughter." He took
a step back, ashamed of his inability to hold himself together, and
aware now of the broader possibilities of his daughter's absence.

"This whole area's a crime scene. Nobody's going past here now."

The captain returned, this time to pull him behind the tape away
from the officers who stood around guarding nothing but air. "Delores Walker. Does that name ring a bell, Father?"

"Yes, she's on the altar guild. Comes in Saturday mornings to
prepare the altar. Is that her?"

"Yes."

"Do you know what happened?"

"We have to wait for the medical examiner's report. But it looks
like a heart attack. There's no obvious injury. No gunshot wounds.
No knife wounds. And not a robbery since she had her purse."

"Has anyone been inside the church?"

"It's locked. From the looks of it, she didn't get inside."

Before he could ask, another officer called the captain away, and Lenworth was left on the side of the tape where he wanted to be, but no closer to the red door, no closer to getting someone to focus on his missing child. He patted his pockets, realizing then that he had no keys, no way to get into the church through the front door at the other end of the block and, even if he could get through the police officers standing around, no way either to open the doors to get into the church hall.

"My daughter," he said again.

The officer threw his hands up, his exasperation slipping out along with his heavy breath. "We have a dead woman over here. For missing persons, you have to report her missing at your local station. Nobody's getting inside there for now."

It was unlikely, he thought, that Plum, having found the child for whom she had searched for seventeen years, would remain at the church, within his reach. No way, he thought.

"A prayer, at least," he said to the officer, "for Delores." In the midst of the prayer, he heard a deep male voice say, "Plum Valentine. I'm looking for Plum, is that her?" The man who spoke held the hands of two little girls, both of whom looked up at the man, their father he presumed, as if they hadn't seen him or heard him like this before. The girls looked exactly like Plum. Like Opal. Again, the light brown eyes and skin as dark as hers. Neither girl smiled but he suspected that if they did, he'd see the dimples too. There was no mistaking to whom the girls belonged. He didn't finish the prayer, but turned around and took the man's arm. "The deceased is white," he said, "and elderly. It's not your wife."

"Thank you."

The fact that Plum was missing too, confirmed what Lenworth suspected: Plum and Opal were together.

12

Aware again of how quickly it could end, how quickly she could lose something precious, Plum said, "I want to show you something."

Opal was lying on the floor like a dog in the sun, fingers clasped beneath her head, staring at nothing.

"You asked if what I want to talk to your father about was worth getting arrested over." That Plum wasn't ready now to call him by name said plenty. *He. Your father. Father. The priest. Reverend.* Any one of those monikers would do. Just not his name, which she had not uttered in eight years, not since the day she left Anchovy heavy with disappointment that all she found of her daughter was a naked, dirty doll. No identifiable trace of him. That she would call him *Father* and *Reverend*, despite knowing what kind of a man he had been before he entered the seminary, made her chuckle. But there was no joy in the sound. She wanted to cry, wanted to let out all the emotions that had built up. And she cried, fumbling in her bag as the tears clouded her vision, reaching down, wading through a package of chewing gum and keys, a notebook and a novel, a book of puzzles, more fruit and nut bars, until at last she found the pouch with the palm-sized mirror inside. "Come over here." She held the mirror up at arm's length, watched her daughter watching her, watched herself watching her daughter, two pairs of topaz eyes, unusual in their dark skin.

"Look at me."

And Opal did. Plum looked back at the face she hadn't been able to see in the dark, back at the eyes, so like her own, eyes that stood out against such dark skin, the eyes that at one time or another prompted a stranger to ask if she wore colored contact lens. The high cheekbones. The dimples. Down at the slight build, a dancer's or runner's body, without the defined or bulging muscles. Down even further to Opal's long toes splayed in her sandals. Looking and waiting for Opal to fit the pieces together. Looking and seeing a gradual awakening, the glimmer of tears. Looking and seeing what she hadn't expected—something a bit like disappointment or disbelief. Opal blinked and looked away instead of embracing Plum.

"I am your mother." Plum waited a moment.

"You're dead. He said you died in childbirth."

"I wanted to name you Marissa. It's Spanish, means 'of the sea.' Your birth wasn't easy. I slept after you were born and when I woke up he was gone. And you were gone. Without a word. Without even leaving a note. I couldn't even remember your face. Didn't know where he took you."

"He told us you were dead."

"What else could he say?"

"I don't believe you. He wouldn't just leave like that. That's not the kind of man he is. And if that is true, then how did you find me?"

"I didn't know it was you. I saw his picture in the paper. I wanted him to tell me, on your birthday, why he left, why he took you."

"Kidnapped? You're saying he kidnapped me? He wouldn't do such a thing. *My father* wouldn't do such a thing. He's a priest." Opal dropped her body back into the space beneath the robes, hiding but not quite hidden.

"He wasn't always a priest. He was a different man then."

Opal didn't leave, didn't reject outright the possibility that Plum was right. Yet, Plum couldn't haul her catch in, couldn't own her, couldn't take Opal's hand. Not yet. Opal, so like a clam, washed ashore and exposed, then burrowing back into wet sand for protection against the pounding wave. Plum could lose her forever. Plum couldn't lose her forever. Not again.

She didn't beg. The girl and the moment were hers.

13

George drove them away from the small crowd outside the church and the coroner's van that remained. Most of the police officers left too, cruising slowly through the congested street behind George's car. Lenworth saw the city as he hadn't seen it before. He saw the people—the slim, the fat, the playful teens, the toddlers holding on to the hands of adults walking too fast for their little legs, those who looked like the morning had caught them in the previous night's clothes—rather than the street lights and the brake lights of slowing vehicles. He scanned the faces for Opal's or Plum's, hoping to see the familiar eyes, Plum's easy smile. Would she still have the smile, the slight gap between her upper front teeth?

"Now, this business about the kidnapping," George was saying, "you're not going to say a word about that. As your lawyer and the church's lawyer, I'm telling you not to tell the police anything about how you came to have custody. The most important thing is to find Opal."

"All right." But it wasn't.

Outside the precinct, George turned around, leaning his head against the headrest.

"Now, is there anything going on at home that would make Opal want to run away? Anything?"

"Nothing."

"Has she ever run away before?"

"No."

"Drug use?"

"No."

"Alcohol?"

"No."

"A boyfriend?"

"No."

"I'm not asking you anything the police won't ask."

"I understand."

"They don't always make a missing teen report a priority at first. After all, she's seventeen and teenagers run away all the time. I'm just telling you that so you understand what we may be dealing with inside there."

"Thanks."

The air was warmer now than it had been hours earlier when he stepped outside in his green robe and slippers, and cold again inside the air-conditioned building.

George was more right than wrong, and not satisfyingly so: That she was just another runaway. A teen with a secret life kept hidden from her family—whether a lover or addiction or pregnancy—details she was too afraid to share. A teen with a hunger for freedom or the illicit activities New York City promised. That he would find that she had been out with a boyfriend. That she would turn up in a day when the freedom she craved proved to be something else. That he should wait for her to come crawling back home.

George was more incensed than he at the scenarios the police officer laid out, at how the officer, in a few simple words, had managed to reduce Opal to a statistic: one dark-skinned girl among a large number of white- and dark-skinned teenage runaways. Later he would learn that there are upwards of 1.5 million teenage run-aways a year, a staggering number that shouldn't have surprised a priest accustomed to hearing confessions, more aware than others of the messiness of people's private lives.

It was too late then to reverse the strategy he and George had agreed upon in the car, too late to tell the officer about Plum, to backtrack from the agreed-upon story about a seventeen-year-old runaway and invoke Plum's name, shift the attention somehow from the supposed ordinariness of a teen runaway to the more con-troversial parental interference or parental kidnapping charge. He couldn't without incriminating himself and not without painting another picture altogether of a dysfunctional home, and inadver-tently confirming the police officer's suspicion that Opal ran away to escape something at home.

Except for passing along Opal's photo and descriptions of what she had been wearing—blue jeans, the uniform of American teens, and a T-shirt, the color of which he could not definitively say—there was little more he could do at the precinct. Go home and wait. She will call. Or she will return.

Lenworth stood on the sidewalk outside the rectory like a recalci-trant teen returned home by a friend's parent. The tiniest flicker of movement at the window and he knew Pauline was just inside the door, with questions or an argument waiting to tumble from her lips. The story he'd told, years old now, was simple. Opal's mother had died in childbirth. Surely not her name or how they'd met. That he had taken the baby and left Plum alone in the hospital, childless and without a job or a home, just so she could, in his mind, get on with the life he had caused her to lose, no. That Plum had come to reclaim her daughter, no.

Too late now. Seventeen years of lies had caught up to him, had *arrested* his life as he knew it. And it had arrested his and Pauline's life together, permanently blocked any possibility of their moving forward in a meaningful way. Their life together could only be lived backwards now—she parsing through everything he had said and done, looking for the truth, and he doing the same but mining the details to find out where he could have backtracked to find Plum and righted his wrongs. He had never bothered to look for her, the mother of his first-born child, never enquired of her whereabouts or tried to find out if she had indeed taken advantage of his 'gift' to her and gone on to live a productive life. All these years in Brooklyn he could have opened a phone book, looked for someone named Plum Valentine and if not her then called other Valentines until he found her parents or someone who recognized the name. He could have called her aunt in Jamaica, of course without revealing his true name, to inquire of her whereabouts. But he hadn't. Too ashamed. Too guilty. Too fearful of the outcome: losing everything and gaining nothing.

The curtain twitched again. He glimpsed the boys instead of Pauline, both kneeling on the couch and looking out at him standing like a statue in the driveway contemplating the old rectory, the borrowed house that soon would no longer be theirs. Nothing, he knew, would remain the same after this. Just as quickly as the boys appeared, they disappeared and reappeared at the front door, still in pajamas with cartoon characters on the front and back. Craig lifted his fingers in a listless, tentative wave, and Lenworth waved back, his own greeting just as anemic as his sons'. That the boys were there at the door meant Opal hadn't returned, neither voluntarily nor involuntarily, and Pauline had spent long, anxious moments at the window looking out. He took another step, then two more halting ones, bent to pick up the neighborhood paper he never read, and stopped short of the step up from the sidewalk to answer the question that came at him from both boys, the younger boy's question an echo of Craig's. "Where's Opal?"

"We're still looking for her."

"Did she run away?" Craig, again, the matter-of-fact one.

"No. No. She didn't."

"But Mommy said she ran away. Gone to live like a bum on the street is what she said."

"No, no." He couldn't imagine Pauline saying that, going so far as to characterize Opal as a street child. "Opal's just missing, that's all."

He suspected Pauline was just inside the door, waiting to catch him saying something he shouldn't, something like, "Your mother doesn't know what she's talking about," or revealing a bit of truth that he wouldn't tell her directly. He knew then that he wouldn't go inside, wouldn't stand before her and add another lie to the hill of lies he had told over the years. Since becoming a priest, he hadn't lied, not exactly, not directly. Instead, he shut down the questions he didn't want asked or which he didn't want to answer and built up a wall of sorts around the parts of his life he didn't want to talk about. It meant that Pauline knew much less than a wife should know, and, shut out of his life, hovering outside the walls he had built up around himself, she was lonely, alone.

"You should go on back inside. I just came to get the car and go back out to look for Opal. Go on inside and lock up."

Just inside the door, on the small hall table, were the keys, and he grabbed them, then stepped back and hurried away to the car on the curb before Pauline could step out from wherever she was hiding and come outside. In the rearview mirror he glimpsed her pink slip of a dress floating around her body, her arms flailing as she waved at him to stop. But he angled the wheels and pulled the car out, nudging it carefully forward so as not to reverse, so as not to risk looking back, catching her eye and willfully ignoring her flailing arms. He cut the angle much too close to the car in front of his. The car lurched forward and he pressed the gas pedal, easing out into the street, slowing at the stop sign and moving ahead. Even though the windows were closed and he didn't hear her call, the sound of his name coming from her mouth lingered in his head, loud and frantic. Len-worth. Len-*worth*. For a long while that was all he heard, not the reggae blaring from passing vans on Church Avenue and Flatbush Avenue, not the whoosh of traffic on the Belt Parkway, not the siren of an ambulance bearing down on his car and zipping around him at the very last minute. All he heard was his name, a prolonged and frantic call.

14

To look at Opal cloistered in a musty room, waiting for her father to come find her, and realizing slowly that her father would not come at all. To look at the girl lying flat on her back with her knees brushing up against the choir robes, and see the disappointment tattooed on her face, her eyes brimming with tears. Plum felt Opal's disappointment in every quadrant of her body.

"Let's go," Plum said. "You can have your birthday wish. Tea by the sea."

Opal looked up, her eyes watery, her face crumpled.

"I just ask that you take me to your father in return."

They left the way they had come up the stairs, Opal leading, Plum following, Plum nervous and uncertain that even this plan wouldn't fall apart.

The church hall was quiet, eerie, and immediately outside the church, the street that earlier had been swarmed by police had eased back into a relative calm. How easily they left, as if no one had come to look for them at all, as if their absence didn't matter to anyone either.

Just on the corner, Church Avenue was as busy as ever. Too many buses, cars, pedestrians nudging and pushing to claim their own space. Two policemen appeared, their presence on the street nothing extraordinary. One looked at them and then away, no recognition or awareness that one was a girl reported missing and the other a mother and wife also reported missing. Neither had been missing long enough to cause alarm beyond their immediate families.

Without looking back, Plum reached for Opal's hand, and Opal, too big to be led, old enough to lose herself in a crowd and find her way home, reached forward, twined her fingers through Plum's and skipped forward to match Plum's pace. She didn't let go, didn't protest. For the moment they were neither hunters nor hunted, just mother and daughter strolling in the afternoon, dipping into a Caribbean bakery for patties and coco bread, two cups of red peas soup and water.

Plum waved at a taxi, wanting to quicken the ride through the crowded city. On the sidewalk, just in front of the aquarium, Opal pointed at it and said, "Let's go there." She moved headlong through the crowds, running through the tunnels as if she were still a child.

Plum emerged from the tunnel squinting at the sunlight and waiting for her glasses to darken in the sun. "Why here?"

"I've never been. Been to the boardwalk so many times, but he never took me here. I've always wanted to come."

The sea lion show was beginning, and they wandered in that direction, toward the trainer, a woman in yellow plastic boots, who dipped her hands into a bucket to pull out a fish for each of the obedient and anxious sea lions. A whistle or a clap and the sea lions barked, contorted themselves like gymnasts, danced, balanced a ball on their noses. Obedient. Perfect. All for a reward of fish they didn't have to hunt.

"It's unnatural, is that what he said?" Plum asked.

"Yes. He said something about the animals not jumping through hoops when they're out at sea."

"I can hear him," Plum said. "But it's beautiful. How else would you get to see how the marine animals live?"

Outside the aquarium, the beach was still full, the sand dotted with bodies. Like sprinkles on an ice cream cone. Like scattered marine life waiting for a giant wave to pull them back out to sea.

Plum had imagined moments exactly like this, a simple stroll with her daughter, an easy conversation about the ordinary things. It wasn't tea by the sea, but perfect in its simplicity. Perfect because Opal's face lightened and her anxiety eased.

15

Lenworth drove to Coney Island, the very place he had intended to take Opal that morning, and by the time he arrived, the
boardwalk was crowded with a hodgepodge of bodies—most in
clothes better suited for another, smaller body—and the amusement park had taken on the traits of a never-ending carnival. He
didn't like it like this—raucous and crowded—but preferred it in the
morning when the boardwalk shops were still asleep and the smell
of hotdogs, fried potatoes, fried dough, and grilled meat didn't hang
in the air like clouds too weighted to move. In fact, he preferred
that it remain a relic of another time, with just the façade of historic
buildings and his imagination filling in the costumes reminiscent
of that long-ago time. In the early mornings, the sun highlighting
aged brick walls and old neon signs, the amusement park felt a little
bit like an abandoned town, a historical site recreated for exhibi-
tion only. The boy engineer buried deep within him could sit for
hours and stare at the parachute jump, the Wonder Wheel and the
Cyclone and imagine it being built, one steel post and one wooden
plank at a time. From bare earth to a looping track, he could see
it all going up, sweaty men layering the planks at equal distanc-
es apart, hammering and stomping to test a beam's strength. He

imagined a life that could have been—he as an engineer, building his own landmark, putting a semi-permanent mark on the earth.

Instead, he gave up that dream for the priesthood, a desperate bid at the time to save himself and his family from disgrace.

He left the carnival atmosphere behind and walked past the historic parachute jump, and beyond to the quieter residential side, which the crowds largely avoided. He wasn't sure exactly why he had come here then, whether he truly thought Opal would have come to a place that was his sanctuary. Yes, he had taken her there for birthday breakfasts—tea by the sea—but would she have come on her own? Was he simply stalling, holding off his inevitable demise?

Indeed he was. There he didn't have to pretend that Opal was missing, didn't have to pretend that Plum hadn't come back to claim what was rightfully hers, didn't have to pretend that Opal wasn't a permanent reminder of what he had done.

Just off the ramp at West Twentieth Street, a film crew was setting up lights and moving police cars in random spots along the curb. The scene was set to reflect a hurried arrival, haphazard parking by officers running toward an emergency. And it occurred to him that what he was doing—strolling along the boardwalk just after reporting his daughter missing—was suspicious in itself. If the police asked, how would he account for his day without appearing to be a father nonchalant about his missing daughter? Which random stranger would recall seeing him, a priest in a black shirt and white clerical collar strolling along the boardwalk in the early afternoon? Not a hurried or anxious man, searching frantically for a missing girl. He couldn't make himself look frantic, not when he knew that Opal was with Plum, not when he knew that Plum wouldn't harm Opal, not after so many years of longing and waiting. Still, he returned to the car, two blocks away from the water, on Mermaid Avenue near a Catholic church.

He didn't want to return home and wait, with Pauline lurking in the shadows, her questions coming at him as sharp as a finger jabbing his chest. Who is Plum? What did she want with you? Is Opal with her? Is she Opal's mother? Where was she all this time? What kind of lying, conniving priest are you?

The thought slipped so quickly and quietly into place that he almost missed it. Plum was the one for whom he should be searching, whose life he should be turning inside out, whose secrets he should uproot. Not Opal's. There was a chance he could salvage his life. He slowed the car and turned around, certain there was a library nearby or a community center, someplace where he could search for records or, at the very least, find a telephone directory.

He didn't have to drive for long, for there, near the Catholic Church, was the Coney Island library. In the library, he did what he should have done all these years. He opened a telephone directory and searched for Plum Valentine, a name so unique that he found it and her Flatbush address almost immediately. Why hadn't he thought of looking for her first before involving the church committee? Contained a scandal before it bloomed into something bigger?

He headed back the way he had come, at full speed now, zipping around vehicles, ready to press the horn at the slightest provocation. The wind whipped through the open window, tossing around exhaust fumes, the smell of gasoline, the odor of rotting garbage that came from a passing truck. But he left the windows down, letting the whoosh of wind break the silence in the car and stir up the thoughts in his head.

16

Another house. Another time. Twelve years before he and Plum met in Discovery Bay. Twelve years before he fully understood how what happened then when he was still a teenager would play itself out when he was twenty-four, a young teacher facing a student with a broad smile that revealed her dimples, and an eye color that seemed too light for her dark skin.

Lenworth was still a boy—fourteen years old—with a duffel bag too large for his meager belongings. He stood outside contemplating the crisp white paint, the red shingled roof, pink and white bougainvillea bushes on either side of the walkway leading up to the grand verandah, two large columns supporting the verandah roof, the intricately carved front door. One sweep of his eyes and he took in the grandeur of the house, which would have swallowed the house he'd just left. It was the kind of house he had admired from afar, a big house for a *big man*, a man of means, one who had either spent time abroad and returned to live out the remainder of his days in a house three, four times the size of his childhood home, or the educated one who had prospered on the island despite the country's growing dependence on IMF and World Bank loans and remittances from relatives abroad, and the widely held belief that the country was sliding backward (morally, spiritually, financially) instead of forward. The *big* man, who stood beside Lenworth, waiting to usher him into the house, was a distant relative of his mother. He had indeed gone abroad and prospered and returned, not to the family land in Woodhall, Clarendon, but to this beauty of a house in the shadow of the Greenwood Great House. Lenworth knew nothing about architecture and design, Greek or Roman or colonial influences, Spanish-style homes with arched doorways, or plantation style homes with wooden shutters and sweeping stairways. He knew only that this was the house of someone with the kind of money his mother wouldn't even dream of having.

The distant relative, Warren Joseph, and his wife, Rosie, who also stood with them, were childless, that is if he believed some reports. And if he believed other reports, they were a mean and cantankerous couple whose children wanted nothing to do with them. The boy, who stood with them, not only didn't know what to believe but had no choice in the matter of whether he returned to his mother and sister in their ramshackle house with the dirt yard, or followed the stoosh couple into the crisp white house in Greenwood to live as their child and houseboy, getting schooling in exchange for house and yard work. He went up the stairs. The checkered tile glistened beneath his feet. In the midst of those columns, he realized finally that he was no longer a boy, not a boy waiting here for his mother to come get him, and not yet a man. In limbo. Sent away. Dismissed. Bartered. Now fully responsible for bartering his own education in exchange for a bed and a roof and pseudo parents.

He found he was not alone. There was a girl too—Ava—a relative of Rosie's, who like him one day found herself with a bag packed with her meager belongings and moving to a house whose sheer size mocked the inadequacies of her former life. That they were chosen out of all their siblings and cousins to have this chance at a greater life wasn't lost on either. It wasn't a question of whether they showed promise that merited an opportunity, but sheer luck that they were at the right age—not too young to be separated from their parents and yet, even as teenagers, young enough to still be molded, to recognize and appreciate the opportunity presented to them.

In bed that night, in a bedroom on the lower level of the house—the part of the house built specifically for the domestic helpers or guests the hosts wanted to banish temporarily from the family's more intimate life—he pressed his body against the wall, feeling the coolness of the concrete seep into his body. And eavesdropped on Ava's private moment: she cried as he wished he could. By then, she had been there for two weeks but the grief that filtered through the wall still felt bitter and raw. She cried for them both and prayed.

In the daylight hours, they lived like siblings, brother and sister walking away from home to board a bus to school, returning home in the evening to finish assigned tasks, he to pull weeds or mow the lawn, she to prepare the evening's dinner or meals for the church's hospitality committee under Rosie's watch. At night, away from Warren and Rosie, the teens—confused by hormones and despair and their families' rejection or dismissal and, in his case, his mother's adept bartering skills—lived like lovers, each fumbling with the body's curves and angles, hard and soft flesh, mistaking release for comfort and love.

They didn't think of the possible outcomes and consequences: a baby neither wanted or Warren and Rosie discovering their nocturnal habits. They avoided the first (somehow) but not the second.

⌒

Who were they really, Warren and Rosie, this couple that had given him a new life? This couple with a house boy and house girl—whose parents had bartered their lives: education and a (better) roof over their heads in exchange for light household duties—to serve them and their guests afternoon tea or ice-cold fruit drinks with triangle-shaped sandwiches, and bake the cakes that Rosie passed off as her own at church dinners and after-service events?

They were a product of another time, children of a colonial and postcolonial era, a combination of confused history: dark-skinned descendants of slaves who both wanted and feared independence from the mother country, who had ingrained the concept that anything that originated from Britain was better than anything that originated from Africa, dismissing, for example, with great prejudice the African way of worshipping—the spirited sermon and the congregation's equally spirited response, the swaying and the twirling that resembled a Pocomania session—and accepting without questions the Anglican way, the spiritless songs from a hymnal, quiet acceptance of their Lord and savior into their hearts. British and Jamaican, master and servant, servile and defiant. All these things at once. Confused result of history.

Lenworth was a child of another era—a post-independence baby, who suckled on the heady Jamaican politics of the 1970s. It seeped into him like a plant pulling nutrients from the soil, and he learned that he could and should demand more. And so he did. He dared ask that he and Ava be paid in tangible currency for their labor.

Rosie sucked in air, let it out and sucked again. "I give you a place to stay, pay for your education and feed you, and you asking for more? Ungrateful wretch. You know how many children out there dying for an opportunity like this? How many children out there can't go to school because they have to work and help support their family? What you think would happen to you if I hadn't worked out this arrangement with your mother? You think your mother could afford to pay for all these subjects you taking? You think she can afford to send you to university when you finish school? You not looking at the long term. Just the short term. Just the ready cash you want. Short-sighted and ungrateful. But, you know what, if you don't like it here and you think we're cheating you out of what is yours then leave. Go on back home. Don't think you have to stay."

But he stayed: to finish the school year; to accept, as was promised, fees for a university education and launch, as he dreamed, a
career as an engineer, building grand houses and elaborate bridges
that were simultaneously functional and grandiose. Staying meant
Rosie and Warren began to watch him ever so closely for a defect or
a chink in his façade, a reason to return him to Woodhall. And they
found it. His mistake, he displayed visible anger, clenching his fists,
ready to demand payment for Ava, when a friend of Rosie's came
to borrow Ava (without payment, Lenworth was sure) to help the
neighbor prepare for a party.

"Borrow?" he asked. "Who in this day and age come to borrow
a person?"

Ava was halfway to the car, looking back at him, her eyes pleading for him to stop.

"You take it too literal," Rosie said.

"Too literal? If she borrowing her, she not paying her for the
day's work. Nothing literal about that."

"So you come out here to embarrass me and put yourself in business that's not yours?"

There it was, the chink, the defect: his brazen disregard for how
his words, once uttered, fluttered and filtered. In the end, Ava left,
her eyes pleading with him, the look between them something Ros
ie couldn't decipher, but suspected held an undercurrent of something else. Rosie's suspicion was greater than her knowledge, and it
fed her certainty that there was something between the two teens.

Rosie didn't wait for Ava to return, to catch them in the (suspected) act. His life once bartered could be bartered again. He could
be and was returned because of the small defect in his character,
Rosie's suspicion of something she couldn't quite name. His future,
so bright, was pulled away from him, whipped back behind a magi-
cian's curtain with a single flick of the hand.

There was no easy way for Lenworth to compare the grandiosity
of one house with the simple, functional rooms of another. No way

to gauge beforehand the letdown or the things he'd miss: cold tile beneath his feet in the morning, a shower instead of a splash in a bath pan, soft grass underfoot instead of packed dirt, a bedroom to himself instead of four to a room, a proper kitchen, a stove that lit with the turn of a knob. Or the things that once removed he would come to hate: a makeshift stove that he got going with sticks, paper and kerosene, the smell of clothes hung to dry near a smoky stove, his mother and sister waiting for life to come to them, his mother's learned habit of deifying the wealthy. How easy it was to look down on a mother who grew up under the same circumstances as Warren but hadn't managed to move forward at all. No way really for him to understand then what it meant to have agency—the ability to exert power and control over his situation.

So years later when he met Plum, when he was tutoring high school students to make money because the promise of a university education had been taken back, he understood precisely why Plum felt disposable, easily cast away when she made a teen's mistake. Except when he met Plum, he wasn't confused by a teen's hormones and despair, and he didn't confuse release with love and comfort. With Plum, they were one and the same.

✎

Another house. Another time. Plum's belly delicately pressed against a white T-shirt. Plum had changed from a summer dress with a billowing body to the close T-shirt and returned to sit with him outside. A lizard chased another through the potted ferns. She swatted at mosquitoes. He sat rigidly waiting for her aunt to come, barely waving a hand when he felt the mosquitoes settling in and biting. He had sat there many a time, on the verandah, helping Plum understand Pythagoras's theorem, square root and cube root, the equations that baffled her but thrilled him. There was no thrill now, just a gnawing burn in his stomach and a heart cartwheeling in his chest.

He stood when her aunt arrived, stretched out his hand. But she ignored it, dismissing him for the second time in his life. Plum stood, showing the unmistakable belly, her breasts so much fuller now.

"This is what you come to tell me?" she asked. "Child, how far along are you? Four, five months?" Plum's answer wasn't what she wanted. She flopped in a chair and peppered Plum with questions about what she had told her parents.

He stumbled, drawing a breath, which had the unintended consequence of stifling his words. He wanted to tell her aunt that he loved Plum, that he would indeed take care of the baby and her. But Plum's aunt took that opportunity away just as quickly as she had given him leave to speak.

"You know what, you better leave. Just leave. Go. You can deal with her father when he comes."

For the third time she dismissed him, batted him away as if he were a nuisance fly.

But Plum's father and mother didn't come at all for Plum's graduation, simply cancelled their tickets and Plum's return ticket, leaving her to make her way with him. He couldn't talk of his plans for his new family. As it turned out, his intentions didn't matter in the end.

☙

Yet another house. Yet another time. A month before the baby, his baby, *their* baby was due, he went home to his mother's house in Woodhall to tell her about the grandchild to come. He thought it was a boy. Plum was adamant it was a girl, and she had a name he had forgotten already. He went by bus, up through the hills of Alexandria, up and over the Dry Harbour Mountains, past a funeral procession and pallbearers hefting the casket up a hill too steep for the hearse. At last the bus wound its way downhill into the parish of Clarendon, turned left and on through river town after river town, through Chapelton, which was prepping for market day, and on until he got to the outskirts of Woodhall. He went by taxi down a road too rutted to truly be called a road, the asphalt long washed away by rain. The gullies on either side of the road were lush, a testament of the constant rain that washed away the asphalt or the rivers that had gone underground.

His mother, hanging the morning's wash, looked back as if he had only just left. "Oh, you come?" She pinned the clothes, shooed a chicken, sprinkled the wash water at the root of a tangerine tree and turned away to the kitchen expecting him to follow her there. The kitchen was an outdoor shelter, stick walls and zinc sheeting enclosing a waist-high coal stove. She kneaded flour for dumplings, dropped them in hot coconut oil and waited for them to brown and crisp. He wandered out in the yard, past the chickens that scattered as he moved, the baby chicks that were still a fuzz of yellow, the lazy dogs that didn't bother to bark or question his presence, past the pig pens and on to the star apple and mango trees. He picked what he could—purple-skinned star apples and grapefruit and tangerines—plopping them into a bag for Plum.

When at last they sat down to eat the dumplings and cornmeal porridge, she said, "Read this for me. It come yesterday." *It* was a letter from his father written on blue airmail paper that was both envelope and letter with flaps that sealed the contents in.

Nearly twenty years she had waited for his father to return, to divorce the woman he had married in England so he could get his permanent papers and return for her. His sister, thirty-two years old then, also waited for her man to return, supplementing the support payments he sent with day's work cleaning houses and washing. Nearly all the women he knew were waiting for something or someone to come along.

Would that be Plum too, held down by the baby and waiting, the forward trajectory of her life stalled? Plum wouldn't want to live there in Clarendon, he knew. Not without running water. Not without the sea nearby. Not for a day. And she wouldn't leave the baby there with his mother, to come back to it on weekends and holidays away from campus. No way she, who thought her parents had cast her off like old clothes, would consider it. But reading his father's letter and watching his mother, he could only see Plum, her life stalled, her dream deferred.

He returned the way he had come, by taxi and bus through the lowlands, along roads cut too close to the river bed and which, in the rainy season, were more often impassable than passable, past villages that the country seemed to have forgotten. He had his mother's gift to Plum: a white crocheted blanket rolled up inside a plastic bag. In his mind he had the root of his gift to Plum: a future, whatever she chose, unencumbered, free from the wait for someone or something.

Yet, Plum hadn't been free or unencumbered. He saw it now, how he had miscalculated the equation. How he had mistakenly thought that Plum's parents' disappointment in their daughter was a mirror of Plum's disappointment in herself. How he had mistakenly thought that Plum crying for the loss of her parents was equivalent to her inability to live with being a disappointment to the parents who had put everything into their one and only child, how he had projected his mother's and sister's arrested lives onto Plum. A simple miscalculation. A rookie engineer's mistake: subtracting emotions and passion and color and context, seeing life solely as equations and numbers and angles. Except he hadn't begun training as an engineer and had only built rudimentary things.

All these years, he hadn't allowed himself to imagine the person Plum had become, whether and how she had survived his gift to her. And so now, he had no idea where Plum would have taken Opal. Returning to the place where they last had been seemed like the best place to start.

17

And so to the inevitable, the man for whom Plum had searched for seventeen years, the rectory she believed she should know but couldn't picture. Not that she had ever had any reason to visit the St. Paul's rectory. Not that the rectory had a sign that labeled it as such. This was her mission and she took back control, pulled it back like a baby on a leash wandering too far out of reach.

"Address?" Plum stepped off the curb, waved at a passing taxi, forgoing the bus for the return journey to Flatbush. "We can't put this off any longer. You know that, don't you?"

"Yes."

And so they sat like lovers after a quarrel, Plum pressed up against one door and Opal up against the other, each looking out her window at the city sidewalks, the oak trees growing in a small square of dirt, the food wrappers blowing against the concrete and brushing up against the tree trunks. Plum didn't allow herself to think of Lenworth, to imagine the scene playing out, to imagine even that the police may be there searching the house for clues as to Opal's whereabouts. But what of Alan and the girls? How to return after a day's unplanned absence and selfish silence? How to explain to the girls that she had not run away, hadn't been kidnapped,

wouldn't leave again without first letting them know. How to forgive herself for doing exactly what *he* had done: disappeared without leaving a trail of crumbs so she could be found.

✑

Much closer, from inside the car this time, Plum heard, "this gate."
Opal leaned in from the door, shifting slightly toward Plum. "We're
here."

Here was a narrow, three-story, brick brownstone on a narrow
street—not what Plum would have imagined if she had bothered
to think at all about the rectory. There wasn't a gate at all, just two
steps that led to a short walkway and the front door, a bright red that
stood out against the dark brown brick. Before Opal pressed the bell,
the door opened, and she stood with her finger suspended above the
buzzer looking down at the boys. The taller of the two leaned against
the door, his mouth slightly open as if he expected something less.

"You're in trouble," the other said, before turning and running
away down the hall, screaming "Mommee," as if that was the last
call he would ever utter.

"Daddy left to look for you," the second boy said before he too
ran off in the same direction.

In spite of the boys' call and footsteps padding down the hall,
the house was quiet, like a mausoleum or museum, with photos everywhere. The photos were mostly of the boys, growing from infancy into the young boys they now were. But Opal was absent from
the walls, present only in one family portrait that Plum couldn't see
clearly. Plum looked at the way he lived, the life he had crafted for
himself without her in it, or perhaps more precisely, the life Pauline
had crafted for him.

"So you think you just going to waltz back in here like this?"
Pauline didn't look up from the stove. "All night you out and just

waltz back in like you're a grown woman? You think this is one of
those movies you always trying to write?"

The boys looked at Opal, their eyes round with anxiety.

"So you not going to answer? Hmm?" Pauline looked up then,
acknowledging Opal with a quick glance, sweeping her eyes quickly
to Plum. She hesitated, looked again at Opal and back at Plum, her
eyes widening and eyebrows arching slightly. "Lawd. She's the dead
stamp of you and I didn't even see the resemblance."

"Yes."

"So where you come from now? All this time, where were you?"
Pauline directed her question—an accusation and insinuation that
Plum had run off and left her daughter motherless—at Plum.

"Looking for the daughter he stole from me."

"Stole?"

"Whatever he told you, it wasn't the truth."

"I see that now." Pauline snickered. "He told me you were dead.
Died in childbirth." Pauline tapped the back of a chair. "Is him you
come to see?"

Plum nodded.

"Well he not here. All day he gone, out there looking for you. We
may as well sit."

"I wanted him to tell her himself." Plum pointed at Opal. "I
wanted you to hear from him exactly why he did this."

Pauline leaned in. "I want to know too. I need to . . . well, we
need to hear it from you. All these years, this man lying to me. I
wouldn't trust a word he say now." She looked over at the boys. "Upstairs, you two. Go on now. Now."

Like a detective laying out the evidence, Plum brought out the
mementoes from her bag one at a time. "He worked at my school
then." She tapped the old photo of him standing akimbo on a beach.

Pauline sucked her breath in quickly as if she had heard that
story before. Plum looked up. "Well, my aunt hired him to tutor

me. He didn't exactly teach me at school. But after we met he ended working there in the lab."

Plum pulled out the footless doll, which she had dressed in a premature baby's onesie.

"Betty. Where did you find this?" Opal fingered the matted hair, closed the wayward eyelid that refused to shut when the doll lay flat.

"Anchovy. We finally found the house in Anchovy. By then I'd been searching for seven years and by the time I got there you were gone."

"You really did look for me?"

"Of course." How she had looked.

"I didn't like dolls," Opal said. "Thought there had to be something more inside it, some reason to play with this plastic thing that couldn't do anything on its own. I wanted to play with other children, not this plastic thing that couldn't jump or skip or do anything."

A week-old newspaper clipping. "This is how I knew where to find him. All this time, you were right under my nose. I wouldn't have ever looked for you here."

Another piece of paper, crumpled and creased, soft and yellow with age. Hospital discharge papers for Plum Valentine—the only physical record she had all these years of having given birth to a baby girl on September 16, 1993.

Plum wasn't prepared for this, the quiet retelling of her story that would, to a silent observer, resemble a chat between girlfriends at a dining table. No screaming or anger or fireworks. Just acceptance and quiet. The truth settling like wet concrete into crevices, filling holes in the stories he'd told over the years, adding up to a truth so unbelievable that they believed.

Quiet. Contemplating, all three of them, the man they thought they knew, the holes in the family story, patched up now, the man who had guarded his life so carefully now exposed.

"What now?" Pauline asked.

"We wait." Plum, accustomed to waiting, crossed her arms and settled back in the chair. She could walk away with what she had—her daughter, if Opal wanted to come—yet she wanted to hear his story. Not that his explanation would matter now. Still she wanted to hear it, wanted to measure it up against the grief he had caused, weigh it against the grief she had carried for so long it had fossilized into something hard and immovable, like petrified wood.

"No. We celebrate." Opal pointed to the chicken already roasted, the pot of rice and peas, fried plantains on a platter—the result of her stepmother's habit of cooking when nervous and anxious.

"That's Sunday's dinner," Pauline said, but she moved as she spoke toward the platter. "But of course we should celebrate. It's not every day a mother comes back from the dead."

"Yes, we celebrate." Plum smiled. "I forget I can do that now."

In the bathroom washing up, Plum looked at herself in the mirror, smiling. For so long now she had carried her grief so solidly etched on her face that she had to practice smiling, first a slight lift of her cheeks then an exaggerated lift with full teeth and squinted eyes. "At last," she told herself. "At last."

But why not leave? As soon as the thought came, she dismissed it. Another hour or two and she was convinced she would have what she wanted: an answer, and then her three girls together. She pictured Nia and Vivian, heartbroken, and then wide-eyed and smiling, rushing toward her, their arms and legs wrapping around her own legs and heads pressing into her belly. The girls would have her promise: she would never leave them. She said it to her reflection in the mirror: I will never leave you. And what of Alan? She had no answer yet, but she was sure it would work itself out. After all, everything else was falling into place.

18

Lenworth sensed a shift in the house. Nobody was looking out, anticipating and awaiting his return. The boys, gone now from the window, had moved on to other things, toys and the television, cartoons, no doubt. An entire day away and he returned empty-handed, with nothing—not even a theory he wanted to voice—to explain Opal's disappearance. So he lingered in the twilight, plucking dead leaves from the rose bushes, picking up leaflets that had fluttered into the yard and wrapped around the plants. He watered the garden he tended—his garden, not Pauline's—with the herbs and vegetables tucked away among flowering plants, the cherry tomatoes and red and yellow peppers simply a pop of color like any bloom. Pauline wanted only flowering plants. He wanted a garden like back home that would allow him to step outside and pick what he wanted—a few stalks of callaloo for breakfast, bell peppers and tomatoes for a salad, a sprig of thyme to season meat. In the twilight he did just that, plucked a handful of tomatoes the squirrels hadn't yet found, two cucumbers, a bell pepper, and marched up to the house that no longer awaited his return.

The house was hushed, the television silent and the rooms drenched with yellow light. How unlike Pauline to leave an empty room lit. Had Pauline finally left and taken the boys? She had threatened it and he had managed for some time now to hold her back from moving on alone without him. Or so he told himself. Yet he knew her staying was not his doing, not because of her duty to him. It was stagnation, really, like a lake so polluted, so overgrown with scum and algae that the water didn't ripple. It was, he knew, only a matter of time before she did indeed leave, and this business with Opal and Plum could have been the last offense she intended to suffer.

But there they were—his daughter and her mother, his wife and his sons—all sitting together around the dining table. A cake without candles was in the midst of Pauline's good china. A roasted chicken, rice and a salad surrounded the cake. The boys were underdressed for a formal dinner but with the good behavior to match the occasion. No one spoke. No one ate. No one turned away from him. Even the boys, uncontrollable on most occasions, sat like mute dolls, marionettes waiting for a puppeteer to pull a string. It was too late now for Lenworth to turn away, to slide back toward the door.

"Good evening," he said at last.

Only the boys answered, their words squeezed and constricted. Opal moved first, stepping toward him with her hands stretched out to take the produce he still held in the crook of an arm. She was like a machine, moving and turning away without a word, placing the tomatoes on the kitchen counter and returning to her place at the table, her back to him as if he had already come and gone from the room or was simply a powerless ghost.

He should assert himself, he knew, demand to know where Opal had been, throw Plum out of the house, his house. But he couldn't move, couldn't make his feet take a single step or his lips open to say what he wanted.

"Sit, eat," Pauline said. "It's Opal's birthday dinner. We have a lot to celebrate."

He couldn't decide if Pauline was mocking him or goading him into saying something that would trigger a fight.

"Even her mother has risen from the dead. *That* alone is worth celebrating."

She was indeed mocking him. But he pulled out a chair and sat between the boys, feeling dwarfed, like prey trapped between adult predators teaching their young to hunt. Except in the wild, the trapped animal—deer or antelope or giraffe—would have bolted, made an attempt to get away, put up a fight. Instinctively. But there he sat, a yielding prey, zapping the thrill of the chase, dampening their adrenaline. Or so he hoped.

The boys stared at the three women, anticipating a catastrophe, watching it unfold, powerless to stop it. Lenworth dipped the fork into the rice, acknowledging as he did that he had no appetite for it or the chicken or the plantains. In his dry mouth every bite tasted like a blob of wet paper, tasteless. Though he was the only one chewing, he kept on cutting into the meat, robotically lifting the fork and turning the food around in his mouth. Waiting. Waiting for someone to pounce.

Somewhere in the house, the radio was playing a medley of choruses he'd sung as a boy in Sunday School and morning devotion at both his primary and secondary schools. He caught snippets of the songs and tried to concentrate on them, tried to pull strength from his belief in God the Father as he had taught his congregation to do. In his head, he sang along.

But since he had never managed to escape mentally from situations he didn't like, the song in his head petered out quickly. He had always managed to remain sharply present, to suffer fully every indignity meted out to him, every word of chastisement from family, friend, or foe. Now, he was intensely present, fully aware of everybody—Pauline's exaggerated attempt to make the evening seem like an ordinary one, the boys cowered in silence, Opal cracking her knuckles and steadily gazing at her plate, Plum looking at him and waiting—and fully aware of everything—the garish gold cutlery, the plates with the peeling band of gold around the edges, chicken fat congealing in the gravy, Pauline's lopsided cake hurriedly frosted with store-bought canned frosting. He wanted to turn off the hypersensitivity, but he couldn't. Seventeen years of it and he was tired now of always being aware, always looking back over one shoulder then the other, above and beneath him, always waiting for that moment when it all came to an end. He hadn't anticipated how the crescendo would come, that his daughter would disappear and reappear with her mother, on her birthday no less.

The reunion was like death: inevitable. And, as a priest, he should have been prepared for the inevitable. He should have known that this day would one day come. Not quite like this scene—Opal and Plum and Pauline and his boys sitting together like an extended family, not happy or unhappy, just there, together, aware of the bloodlines and other lines that banded them together, Pauline getting dessert plates and lighting candles left over from the boys' birthday parties, Opal blowing out candles and smiling instead of making a wish.

"I have everything I ever wished for." Opal looked at Plum instead of him, her eyes with a soft and tender look he'd only seen on a woman in love.

19

Like pebbles falling into a waterfall, all of Plum's rehearsed speeches fell away. The normalcy of the moment—mother, father, stepmother, and brothers all sitting down like a blended family for a daughter's birthday meal—unnerved her, burying the words she had planned over the years. A harsh quarrel, a wife throwing a fit or turning her away, even setting dogs loose at her heels—those were the reactions she expected. Yet, she sat again like a trained student at the boarding school that defiantly held on to its colonial ways, her hands in her lap, her knees together, her feet flat on the ground, waiting. A composed student, anxious to please.

Waiting.

Waiting.

Until at last, "Are you dead?" The younger of the two boys, Christopher, emboldened now by cake and frosting and the presence of his father, looked directly at Plum, his eyes unwavering, his lower lip hanging down, and his fingers gripping the edge of the table.

"Christopher." Pauline's voice was stern, yet it had no bearing on the boy.

He held Plum's gaze. "Daddy said Opal's mother was dead."

"No, I'm not dead. See? Feel my pulse." Plum's hand dangled

over the meat, inches above the exposed breastbone and congealed gravy. But Christopher pulled his hands back away from the table, burying them out of sight. "Only your father can explain what he meant by 'dead.'"

"Dead is dead. People don't become undead. Only in cartoons."

"Christopher." Pauline's voice rose higher this time. "Enough."

"But," he said, "Daddy said she was dead. He lied."

What Plum thought in that moment was not how Lenworth and Pauline would deal with the child's outburst—dismissal from the table? A stern talking-to?—but how Lenworth had wiped away her life. She was no more than the scribbles on a chalkboard, removed with a single downward swipe and leaving only tiny particles swirling in the air and landing indiscriminately on everything within reach. Had he looked at her that night in the hospital, still fatigued from labor, drowsy from medication, and seen a dying woman or a woman struggling to live? And she had struggled. And she had lived, pushed and pulled and willed herself to climb from the weakness pulling her under, struggled until she regained the normal rhythm of breathing and came out on top. She had lived to hold the baby she wanted to call Marissa, had lived to look up at him and smile. Triumphant.

Her smile hadn't mattered.

He declared her dead and walked away with her child.

Plum stood up now, struggling to free herself from the chair jammed too close to the table. "Dead?" The chair legs caught in the rumpled rug, and the chair tumbled backward. "Dead." This time Plum gritted her teeth, her lips pulling back and flattening out across her teeth, no longer in the relaxed and slack-jawed 'O' of a question.

The rehearsed speech would come back to her later, long after she had left, and lay thinking through what transpired and what else she could have said, how she could have made her words singe his skin and heart. For the moment, though, all she felt was rage, seventeen years' worth, pushing the word "dead" up her throat, across her tongue and through her clenched teeth.

"You left me there in the hospital for dead. Alone. Not even a note. Just took *my* baby and left. *My baby.* Just walked out like you went to the grocery store, picked up a baby and then walked on home. No thought at all for me, her mother, lying there after hours of labor. Not a thought about me. Just left me there and declared me dead. Dead."

For the first time, Plum looked at him, really looked at him, his eyes downcast, the balding top of his head pointing toward her, his fingers laced beneath his chin as if to hold his head in place. Her eyes on him, he closed his eyes, not just blocking her out, not just blocking out the situation, but dismissing her again.

"You can't even look at me. Look at me. Look." But none of the pairs of eyes wavered. Opal, Pauline and the boys didn't look away from Plum. Lenworth didn't open his eyes to look up at her. "Such a shame. You still can't even see me, the human being you left in that room for dead."

Plum's legs weakened and she reached for the chair, then steadied herself, straightened her back and forgot about needing to sit. Had she had a plan she would know what to do next, how exactly to make him suffer as she had every year since that September day when she woke to find her child missing and the hospital around her so quiet she thought the world had ended.

"That night . . ." She held her breath to prevent herself from crying. "All these years, I've thought of what it would be like to see you suffer. I've thought of killing you with my bare hands. Yes, I did. I've thought . . ."

"Boys," Pauline said, "you're excused. Go on upstairs."

The boys left, reluctantly, looking up at Plum, as if they still, impossibly, thought she was dead, a zombie come to harm their father. She heard them in the hallway, a shuffle now and then, the sounds of children hushing each other, trying to remain quiet but making more noise in the process of it, listening to what they shouldn't hear. Yet she continued laying out her desire to make him suffer, thinking as she did of families on the news, a simple quarrel exploding into something momentous, which, to outsiders with no emotion vested in the argument, was unnecessary violence, another moment to decry the lack of morals in society, the downward spiral of what was once a civilized nation. If only they knew how seventeen years of fossilized grief bred violent thoughts—to her, necessary violence— the desire to knock the smug look from his face, just punching him once in the stomach and watching him double over in pain, punching and punching until her arms tired and the anger and hatred and grief she felt all these years melted and dissipated from her body. And she said exactly that and more. "I could kill you even now."

Attuned to sound—seventeen years of not sleeping deeply, of waiting to spring forth, of never again having something precious stolen while she slept—Plum heard the boys again rustling outside the dining room, their footsteps skittering across the floor. They were more hurried this time, frightened, Plum thought, of what she said. Yet, too incensed by his dismissal of her, his inability to look at her, to say a simple, if inadequate, "I'm sorry," she continued laying out how she wanted him to suffer. "Slowly. Something like solitary confinement and make you watch over and over every miserable day that I have lived. But even that may not be enough, because just like now I can't *make* you watch. So it would have to be something else. Something more painful than that."

It was taxing, the effusion of emotion. Plum stopped again. "So what do you have to say to me? Just tell me why. Let me understand."

Silence. The quiet in the dining room exploded. Plum could hear quite clearly the odd sound of the old-fashioned rotary dial phone carrying from the office at the front of the house across the living and dining rooms, and the boys' hushed request for police to come to the rectory on Albemarle Terrace. It wasn't Plum's place to move, to undo the call the boys had made. It was, after all, up to Pauline and Lenworth to remind the boys that 911 was an emergency line, for true emergencies. And this was one, wasn't it? The boys had their reasons: Plum's anger and threats. And Plum, who had found and confronted her child's abductor, had hers. But there was no record of the parental abduction here in Brooklyn or across the United States. After all, she hadn't imagined he would have been here in Brooklyn, within reach, with the child he had taken from her.

The police came quietly, not with sirens blaring as Plum expected. She knew only because the door squeaked a little as it opened and the alarm sensor beeped. She looked at Pauline and Lenworth, waiting for their next move, waiting for either to go to the door, to pull the boys back, and her chance to move.

At last he moved, waited a few moments before calling out. "Oh, my God. Pauline. Come."

Plum reached the front window in time to see the two boys sprinting into the arms of a police officer, then pointing back to the house, and moving away toward one of six parked cars.

"What now?" Opal asked, her voice a whisper.

"I'm going out there," Lenworth said.

"Oh no you won't," Pauline said, turning away from the window as she spoke. "Not with all those guns pointing at you. Better to call the station and explain."

"Hostage negotiators always call," Opal said. "At least in the movies they do."

"Hostage?" Plum asked.

They were quiet, all four of them. Plum contemplated the turn of events, what exactly prompted the boys to call, what the boys may have said that had led to this. She rearranged her face, her body, thinking that he had somehow arranged this other escape.

"We're not criminals." Lenworth stalked off as he spoke. "We have nothing to hide."

"Who knows what those boys said," Opal said. "You know how

they can make up things. For police to respond like this they must have said something significant."

"This isn't a movie, Opal. This is not some Hollywood movie. Your life is not a movie." Pauline, her hands emphatically punctuating every word, turned away from Opal.

Opal moved back as if each of Pauline's words had indeed struck her physically, each one an individual punch to her torso. She went to the phone, picked it up, listened to the familiar buzz of the dial tone, and placed it back in its cradle. The others stepped forward too and stood around the old rotary phone, the four of them looking down at it as if willing a ring to emerge. When the phone tinkled, the sound as urgent as a kettle's choking whistle, they sucked in a collective breath.

"Hostage?" Lenworth said. "There's no hostage here."

Plum and Pauline looked on at him, trying to decipher the full context of the one-sided conversation.

"No, no. I don't know what the boys said but there's no hostage here. Yes, she's angry but there's no kidnapping and no hostage. It looks like the whole police force is outside there, an overreaction to a little misunderstanding." He paused. "So how can we clear this up?"

Lenworth put the phone back in the cradle. "They want us to come out with our hands up."

"I'm not going out there." Opal held out her hands, her fingers splayed exactly as the police would have wanted. "That's how people end up getting shot."

"This isn't one of your movies." Pauline sucked her teeth. "So who exactly is the hostage here?"

"They didn't say." Exasperated at her, his voice was clipped, almost formal.

"I don't know that they know." Opal again.

"Perhaps they do. When you didn't come home, I reported you as missing. And once the boys called they probably put the stories together." He looked at Plum, his eyes conveying his thought: Plum was the culprit here.

Lenworth returned to the window, shifted the curtain ever so slightly. "So we're criminals now. Hunted like criminals."

"Only one criminal here." Plum looked pointedly at him.

"Blame your sons," Opal said. "And yourself."

So many things Plum wished in that moment—that she'd laid out a plan and involved Alan; that she'd waited to confront Lenworth at the Sunday morning service; that she had gone on home to Nia and Vivian; that she had taken Opal home to them instead of here back to him; that she had been able to let go of the wish to hear him say why. Mostly she wished that she had simply gone on home with her daughter and dared him to come take her away. Of course there was no guarantee that Opal would have gone along with her. Had Plum done that, she would have been the one charged with parental kidnapping. That wasn't what she wanted.

For a minute Plum thought about the stick figure in the boat on the unending sea, rowing without oars, and disappearing to nothing. All these years later, the stick figure was still with her, still afraid of being left, still afraid of her love being pulled away from her without warning. Not his love, but the love of the ones to whom she had given life—Nia, Vivian, and Opal. Even then, so very near the end, she had no idea how it would turn out, who would show allegiance to whom; whether respect and gratitude for a father and his unconditional love would win out over the unknown—a mother who turned up out of nowhere and couldn't even recognize her own face staring back at her; whether Nia and Vivian would accept unconditionally this newfound sister. And what of Alan, who asked an unknown number of times about the significance of the date, September 16?

She turned her back on them all and cried.

20

Lenworth looked at himself inside out. Not in the mirror at every inch of his skin, his bald pate and goatee, the arms with soft undefined muscles. But like a spirit looking down on the body it had left behind and the life the body lived. What he saw was a man who was always running away from something—from Plum, from Opal, from his own indiscretions, from Jamaica, and in a different way, from Pauline. Everything he'd run from had finally caught up to him. But cornered or not, staring like an antelope at the tiger about to pounce, he had one last fight left. He was a quick thinker, had always had to be. And now he thought of a way to come out of this intact, not just alive, but with the foundation of a life he could rebuild elsewhere. He had done it before, not once, but thrice, and would do it again, without Pauline if necessary, with her if she wanted to stick with him through this. He doubted she would do that now. Not again. With Pauline it had never been about love, not the sweeping, swooning kind of love, not infatuation and barely lust. It was an arrangement that grew out of his acknowledgement that Opal needed a mother and he a wife, a stand-in for a child beginning to notice his inadequacies as a parent. And Pauline, the sole unmarried girl among the group of six already-married sisters, fell for him like a bat baffled by the sun, a bee drunk on fermented nectar. When Pauline discovered her mistake, the inadequacies of their relationship and his own indiscretions, she held on. She believed his metamorphosis from sinner to saint, from saved to savior, and, instead of running back home defeated and deflated, she helped him build the public façade. That was then.

Now, huddled in one corner with Plum, Opal in another, the women had united against him. He, who controlled everything, had lost control. That, more than anything, was what disturbed him. That he had no power to stop them, the women in his family, from absconding with their love and respect for him, from ruining the facade Plum's absence and Pauline's presence had helped him build to contain his life. And that was what it was all about, wasn't it? Controlling his own life. Directing his life, operating like a movie director, really, dictating how his story was told and when, shuffling the characters in and out of position, choosing the scenes worthy of illuminating and recording. Giving Plum a chance at a life that his baby (their baby) would have taken away, and in doing so removing any opportunity for Plum to regret having loved him. Giving Opal a mother to replace the one he had taken away. Controlling his life to the very end. Never again being that teenage boy who was returned to his mother, returned to a life and house that couldn't be compared to the mansion in the shadow of the Greenwood Great House, the teenage boy who had his future taken away.

That Opal had chosen her mother over him, that she brought her here into his house, irked him more than Pauline's betrayal. That the boys had betrayed the family, called the police to his home and in doing so catapulted a private family matter onto the local (and probably national) news, irked him too.

Another glance at the women and what he had missed smacked him square in the forehead. His sons hadn't betrayed him. They'd given him a way out. He was the hostage here, the bug caught in a spider's web, struggling to free itself. Like that bug, he had used up most of his energy trying to keep ahead of Plum and ward off his inevitable downfall. But freedom and a chance at a decent life were still possible if he regained control of the only thing he could ever control: how his story was told and when.

But it meant getting outside ahead of the women. It meant being the first to tell the police his story and clear up the misunderstanding that had brought the large police response to the rectory. The boy engineer in him recalculated the equations, weighed the known against the unknown. The police knew Opal had been missing. The police knew Opal's mother was in the house threatening him. But they didn't know how Lenworth came to be the only parent Opal knew.

He moved quickly, giving no warning of his intentions, away from the only woman he had loved too much and let go, away from the one he should have been able to love, away from the daughter with her mother's eyes, whose very presence asked the question he was afraid to answer: why did you leave me? And on toward the front door, his hand on the knob, his fingers on the bolt, opening it slowly and quietly. The door eased toward him, the alarm beeped and he stepped out with his hands up, lowered himself to the ground as the police commanded and waited for them to *rescue* him.

"She let me go." His first words. His last desperate effort to save himself and emerge with his reputation intact. After all, there was some truth there. It was Opal, the rediscovered daughter, who Plum wanted.

"Are there any weapons in the house?"

"No."

"No guns?"

"No."

He should have known the police would storm the house. Yet the speed with which they moved up the short walkway to the front door and inside surprised him. He didn't look at his neighbors who'd stepped out to bear witness to his downfall, or search for faces of his parishioners. But he looked for his sons, his saviors now, realizing that the boys were all he would have left.

21

How quickly it came to an end. One minute Lenworth was there and then he was gone, slipping away again out of reach and without a word. And in his place were police officers handling Plum like a criminal, patting down her body, searching her tote, uttering those words she had never expected to hear directed at her: "You're under arrest." Kidnapping. Holding the family against their will. Terroristic threats. In another corner, Pauline sat like a deflated balloon, her eyes on Plum, then on Opal and at the door through which her husband had left. And back again to Plum, with sad eyes that reflected what Plum had felt seventeen years earlier when she realized she was truly alone.

Opal screamed, "No. It's him you should be arresting, not her. You don't understand." An officer held her back, tried to calm her flailing arms.

"Don't make me handcuff you." Gruffly. To which Plum wanted to say, "No use in struggling, Opal. It will work out better if you just let them take control." But she didn't, couldn't get her brain to open her lips and form words, while also keeping herself from blubbering uncontrollably.

How quickly she was outside in the night—the cool night air a sure sign that summer had come and gone and the fall and winter months were rapidly approaching—out in the midst of the artificial lights trained on the house. Immediately, Plum looked up at the small crowd. It was dark in places, lit in others by a flood of emergency lights. She saw Lenworth though in another car, looking out at her, at what he had orchestrated yet again. Opal stood in the frame of the red door, looking out and struggling with her shoes, pushing her feet down and tying laces without looking down at the knots at all.

The officer started the engine, wasting no time in taking Plum away from the daughter who had slipped from her reach for the second time, away from him. Plum looked behind for a last glimpse of the house and the daughter whose birthday he had spoiled yet again, the man she had once loved. She held on to the hope that at the station they would sort out fact from fiction, the simple, unadorned truth of what Plum had said at the dining table and why, what the boys overheard and misinterpreted.

In the end it came down to a single thing, not love or respect or gratitude. Just the fact of where Opal belonged and to whom. The car started rolling. Plum looked back again, turning only her neck at first, then shifting to look fully behind at Opal dodging the police officer, running onto the sidewalk and into the street, chasing the car. The driver stopped, waited for another officer to move a car barricading the road. Opal was nearly there, had very nearly caught up to the car when it moved again. Undefeated, undaunted, Opal ran toward Plum and away from him, her arms pumping steadily, oblivious of the police officers watching and waiting for her to give up. The truth wouldn't wait. The truth was there, behind the car, running after it, not yet catching up, but moving forward at a measured and steady pace. Plum leaned her head back and waited for what was hers.

Biographical Note

Jamaican-born Donna Hemans is the author of the novel *River Woman*, winner of the 2003–4 Towson University Prize for Literature. *Tea by the Sea*, for which she won the Lignum Vitae Una Marson Award for Adult Literature, is her second novel. Her short fiction has appeared in the *Caribbean Writer*, *Crab Orchard Review*, *Witness*, and the anthology *Stories from Blue Latitudes: Caribbean Women Writers at Home and Abroad*, among others. She received her undergraduate degree from Fordham University and an MFA from American University. She lives in Greenbelt, Maryland.